I0612265

BOOKS BY OLIVIA ASH

Nighthelm Academy

City of the Sleeping Gods

City of Fractured Souls

City of the Enchanted Queen

Demon Queen Saga

Princes of the Underworld

Wars of the Underworld

Mistress of the Underworld

Sentinel Saga

By Dahlia Leigh and Olivia Ash

The Shadow Shifter

The Demon Prince

The Rogue Alchemist

STAY CONNECTED

Olivia Ash occasionally takes over the Wispvine Publishing social media channels on Facebook, Instagram, and Twitter.

Olivia also likes to hang out with Lila Jean in their Facebook group specifically for readers like you to come together and share their lives and interests, especially regarding the hot guys from their reverse harem novels. Please check it out and join in whenever you get the chance! Everyone in there is amazing, and you'll fit right in.

https://www.facebook.com/groups/LilaJeanO-liviaAsh/

Sign up for email alerts of new releases AND exclusive access to bonus content, book recommendations, and more!

https://wispvine.com/newsletter/nighthelm-academy-email-signup/

Enjoying the series? Awesome! Help others discover the Nighthelm Academy by leaving a review at Amazon.

http://mybook.to/Nighthelm1

CITY OF THE SLEEPING GODS

BOOK ONE OF THE NIGHTHELM ACADEMY

OLIVIA ASH

WISPVINE PUBLISHING

BOOK DESCRIPTION

Nighthelm is a city of lies, and Sophia is the greatest lie of them all. Though she has saved the city hundreds of times, the people of Nighthelm don't even know she exists.

Found wandering the Witch Woods as a child, everything about Sophia is a mystery. With no memories and no family, she's raised in secret by the professors of Nighthelm Academy… all of whom know far more about her than they're letting on.

But Sophia does know one thing: she's a contritum, a magical being with a broken soul. Her very existence is illegal, and until she finds the other piece of her soul, her uncontrollable magic will only grow more deadly and untamed.

As Sophia races the clock to find her other half, her magic growing more wild by the minute, she discovers three men who hold a mysterious sway over not just her soul, but also her heart.

The problem? She must lie. No matter what happens, she can't tell them who… or *what*… she is.

Strong and dangerous, powerful and commanding, each of these men make her body react in traitorous ways. Bit by bit, she feels herself becoming whole around them. But for the life of her, she can't figure out which of them has the missing piece to her soul… or how he got it in the first place.

To make matters worse, it becomes clear someone broke her soul on purpose… and she's on a warpath to figure out *why*.

In a world rife with heartbreaking betrayal and intricate spells, the magical creatures of the Witch Woods are closing in on Nighthelm. They all want one thing…

…Sophia.

The monsters of the Witch Woods have discovered what she is, and they want to slit her throat. They'll kill anyone who stands in their way... especially her men.

To save her men and finally heal her broken life, Sophia has only one choice... she will fight. And damn it all, she will *win*.

City of the Sleeping Gods is a full-length reverse harem novel. Get ready for a breathtaking story, steamy romance, mind-blowing magic, one kickass heroine, three gorgeous men, lots of toned muscles, fights to the death, and edge-of-your-seat action.

CONTENTS

Chapter One   1
Chapter Two   11
Chapter Three   17
Chapter Four   28
Chapter Five   37
Chapter Six   46
Chapter Seven   55
Chapter Eight   65
Chapter Nine   71
Chapter Ten   78
Chapter Eleven   86
Chapter Twelve   96
Chapter Thirteen   104
Chapter Fourteen   111
Chapter Fifteen   124
Chapter Sixteen   132
Chapter Seventeen   140
Chapter Eighteen   150
Chapter Nineteen   157
Chapter Twenty   165
Chapter Twenty-One   172
Chapter Twenty-Two   184
Chapter Twenty-Three   190
Chapter Twenty-Four   198
Chapter Twenty-Five   210
Chapter Twenty-Six   219
Chapter Twenty-Seven   227
Chapter Twenty-Eight   240
Chapter Twenty-Nine   246
Chapter Thirty   256

Chapter Thirty-One   261
Chapter Thirty-Two   273
Chapter Thirty-Three   281
Chapter Thirty-Four   286
Chapter Thirty-Five   295
Chapter Thirty-Six   300
Chapter Thirty-Seven   305
Chapter Thirty-Eight   310
Chapter Thirty-Nine   317
Chapter Forty   328

You're Missing Out...   337
About the Author   339

CHAPTER ONE

SOPHIA

*S*ophia crept through the thick, oppressive darkness of Witch Woods with one mission in mind: recon.

She was to see what creatures lurked about in the foreboding forest, to go and do what even the castle's elite guard didn't want to: travel the Witch Woods at night. Her orders: don't engage, merely observe, no matter what she saw—pesky fairies, playful water sprites, angry minotaurs, or even malevolent grimms.

It was the same every time. Train all bloody day, observe all bloody night. Grindel liked his rules.

However, this time, she couldn't just sit idly by.

Not far off the main dirt road that dissected the woods, she crouched behind two, thick twisted oak trees. She peered through the thick foliage of some blackberry bushes. Twenty feet away, in a narrow thicket, a small pack of grimms feasted on stringy, red meat clinging to long bones. Those were not animal bones. They were too long and too thick.

Sophia's skin crawled as she watched them snarl and gnaw on their meal, moving about like toxic fog. Then she spotted a small girl, tears streaking her face, sitting inside the dirt circle they made with their undulating, shadowy bodies, their swirling essence mingling as if one entity. Sophia knew the girl was there in the event they got hungry again, and they would.

Grimms were *always* hungry.

She'd learned that first-hand when she startled a small pack during one of her first patrols of the woods. They had made short work of a burrow of hobs. Twenty, small, twisted and half devoured bodies of the mole –like creature had been scattered about the ground and they were busy trying to dig up another burrow. The sight had left her feeling queasy.

Sophia absently rolled her shoulder, remembering the day a grimm had bit her in the shoulder, almost paralyzing her with the venom they spewed and debated her options. Grimms were evil, pure and simple, with nothing to redeem them. She was sick with disgust, concerned because she'd never seen a pack so close to the high, stone walls of Nighthelm. The vile things usually stuck to the deepest and darkest part of the woods, away from human contact.

There hadn't been a human attack in years. She knew that much because she was usually the one who prevented such tragedies.

Instead of flouncing around in pretty dresses and courting boys her age, she was out here saving the people of Nighthelm from so many monsters that they would never fully understand what she'd done to keep them safe, and at this rate, they would probably never know she even existed. She was a lone soldier in the night with a terrible power that made her a danger to the very people she had spent her life protecting.

Her mentor's voice echoed in her head, telling her to do nothing. To move away. To leave the grimms be. To leave the poor girl to her fate.

Sorry, Grindel, she thought. *Not gonna happen.*

Sophia couldn't let the girl die. Once upon a time, she'd been in that girl's shoes. She remembered being little and alone and frightened with no one to save her. Some nights her dreams would tear her heart and mind apart. Dreams of pain and death. Dreams she couldn't quite grasp when she woke. They were like smoke through her fingers. But she suspected they were more memory than imagination despite what Grindel and Headmistress Mittle told her.

Sophia had a choice to make: defy her orders and probably get a whipping, or let the girl die.

It was an easy choice.

A soft crinkling of broken, dried leaves behind her

drew her attention. The sound was indiscernible to most humans, but Sophia was not like most. She didn't move a muscle as the sizable, softly glowing, green creature stepped out from behind the giant trees and slid in beside her. The *yakshi* was her most trusted companion.

"What took you so long?" she said, as she patted her friend's flank.

He nickered and rubbed his fox-like head against her, careful that he didn't impale her with his antlers. It was his version of an apology.

She put an arm around him and drew him close. She whispered in his twitching ear. "You need to grab the little girl."

He snorted in defiance, and in argument. If he could speak English, she knew he'd be telling her, "No, I will stand by your side and fight."

"I know you can fight, Haris. I know you want to fight beside me, but I can't control my magic and rescue her at the same time." She looked him in the eye. "Do it."

He rolled those oblique yellow eyes of his and blew hot air at her through his nostrils.

She shook her head, rolling her eyes, a hint of a smile toying the edges of her lips. "Don't be a brat."

He snorted again, his sign that he'd accepted what she'd told him to do.

She gritted her teeth, body aching for battle, eager

to move and slice open the monsters. Slowly, she drew her sword from the scabbard strapped to her back. The enchanted inscriptions carved into the blade glowed red at her touch. Through the crimson haze she counted the grimms. She was vastly outnumbered. Ten to one. To kill this many creatures, she would have to tap into the darkest part of herself and the magic she hid inside. There would be pain, and lots of it, but she knew she couldn't leave the little girl to die. She wouldn't. Grindel would punish her for engaging the grimms. Or, at least, threaten to punish her with a lashing or two. The most punishment he'd ever given her was extra circuits on the obstacle course, or once, he made her dig them a new privy. None of those were real deterrents.

She summoned light into her other hand, silent as a ghost, invisible even to the stealthy grimms, and then attacked in a whirl. Forest magic swirled around Haris's lean form like green mist as he burst through the line of grimms, swept up the girl onto his back, and flew out of the pack again to safety. Once he was gone, Sophia let her magic fly from her hand as a distraction. The light magic struck one grimm in the back, making it shriek but doing little damage, just as she took up her sword in both hands and swung at the first grimm in her sight.

The blade sliced through the pulsating smoke. The grimm turned toward her, looming over her like a living, breathing thunder cloud. Its three sets of glowing, violet eyes glared at her with malice. Slowly, it opened its gaping maw to reveal razor sharp teeth and elongated fangs that dripped with stinging venom. The putrid stench of its breath wafted over her and she pulled back, wincing from the burn in her nostrils.

The foul odor brought a memory with it.

She was a little girl, running. Panting with fear.

Sophia swung her sword again, slicing through another of the creatures. Despite the effort of cutting down the creature that was like slicing through tar, her arms never shook from the exertion. She trained for this. This was what she was meant to do.

A memory flashed through her mind again.

Her skin crawled with foreboding and evil as she tried to escape... what, she didn't know.

Pivoting on her right foot, she swung low and then up. The grimm shrieked, its smoke form swirling violently as the steel penetrated flesh beyond the black veil.

Blood. Rivers of it. Splashing over her bare feet.

Two grimms swarmed her, mouths gaping, venom spewing. She ducked under their grasping claws, and came up with another swing of her sword, rewarded with more howls of pain.

Their screams mingled with one that pierced her mind. One from her past. For a brief moment, she hesitated as the past tore into her.

Red blooms on her toes. A screech rips from her young throat.

Something inside her breaks.

Her hesitation cost her. A grimm's razor-like claw slashed through the sleeve of her tunic and scratched her skin. The sting was instant. Wincing, she pulled back to regroup. She briefly looked down at her arm to inspect the wound. Spots of blood stained the linen.

Seeing the blood reminded her of the first time she got cut by a sword, training in the field with Grindel. She'd been slow then, only ten, and a year into her training for a chance to renter society, to overcome her wild and untamed power, so that she was controlled enough to be around other humans. Now she was stronger and pushed against the magic trying to bubble up, keep it down and contained, but she was still not fully in control yet. This was why Haris had to get the little girl out of harm's way—out of her way—to make sure the little girl wouldn't die.

The grimms crowded around her, snarling and snapping at her with their lethal jaws. She looked at each one, calculating her next move. A fierce cramp in her gut caused her to recoil. She took a step back as something inside her shifted and grew. A collective change came over the grimms, as if they sensed the energy vibrating deep inside her body.

Even then, she felt the fracture. The constant shifting and cracking deafened her. The pressure between the two sides swelled, pushing at her body from the inside out. Pain whirled within her chest. Heart felt as if it was on fire. That was where it always started.

Sophia closed her eyes and crouched low in front of the grimms. A blistering ball of fragmented magic swelled in her gut. Whirling, spinning, expanding. She gritted her teeth, tasting blood in her mouth. Hot tears leaked from her eyes. Still clutching the hilt of her sword in one hand, she clawed at her tunic with the other. She was burning. The stench of sizzling flesh filled her nose.

She tried to contain her magic, to push it down, but it was too powerful, too hungry for destruction. A scream tore from her throat as her broken magic overtook her. It ripped through her body, burning away her clothes, and exploded outward, scorching everything in its path within a fifty-foot radius. Trees, bushes, and a few grimms were wiped out of existence.

Weak, and no longer able to hold herself up, Sophia collapsed to the ground, naked, skin slick with sweat, body shaking uncontrollably. Although her vision was spotty, she blinked up at the leader of the grimm pack hovering above her. She pretended she could go again, pushing up slightly with her hands to attack, and tried her best not to show how utterly exhausted she was. But it was useless. She was in no shape to do anything else. Her savage magic did enough damage. To her. To the grimms. To everything around them.

"You," it rasped, its voice grating in her ears, but she was too weak to cover them, "hurt us. You use mountain magic against mountain people."

She shook her head, confused, because the mountain folk comment made no sense—she was just a broken human, but she could see how her vast stores of fractured energy could be mistaken for mountain magic. This was bad, though, since grimms held grudges for life and were relentless in their pursuit of vengeance.

"We curse you." Its body twisted and coiled its smoke form into itself as if in extreme pain. "We will never forget."

Then, with one, loud, blood-curdling growl, the remaining pack of grimms converged as one and disappeared into the surrounding trees, leaving Sophia in the charred remains of the woods she incinerated. In deep pain, with the last of her energy spent, her glowing skin faded to normal and she collapsed. She fought to stay conscious, but she'd never been able to stay awake after an episode.

As she sunk into the darkness, she thought about how she was what the world she protected hated: an "anima contritum," a broken soul, or someone with great magical potential who experienced deep trauma early in life. Long ago, her magic had literally cracked and had become uncontrollable. By law, all anima contritums were to be put to death. Only Grindel, training her in secret, saved her life.

But her life would never be "normal." She would never make friends, never go to school, never go to a ball during the courting season. Girls her age were even courting now, soon to be married off for power or profit in exchange for a life of comfort and status. While that prospect had never struck her as particularly interesting, she had a pang of jealousy that "normal" was a life she would never get to have because of her untamed magic that no one, not even the great and wise Professor Matthew Grindel, seemed to understand.

Thinking about her upcoming eighteenth birthday and the party and presents she would never receive, Sophia finally passed out.

CHAPTER TWO

EDRIC

*A*s was his nightly custom since becoming the youngest commander of the elite castle guard at twenty-four years old, Edric walked along the top of the fortified, white wall of Nighthelm to inspect his squad as they performed their security duties.

But this night, something else brought him here to the wall.

His eyes scanned the Witch Woods surrounding the city as a terrible sensation ripped through him. It took his breath away and he had to put a hand onto the wall to steady himself. It was a combination of worry and hopelessness, anger and fear, something he'd felt every now and then throughout his life. It always seemed to come from the woods, and every time—

Yes, there it was. A burst of light at the center that

lasted for only a moment but destroyed everything in its path. He'd seen the aftermath of this event one time, years ago. A fifty foot radius of scorched earth and burnt trees, and nearby was the tiny body of a wood sprite fried to death. He gritted his teeth, determined to finally find out what this magic was... and why he seemed to be connected to it.

In a city of superstition and magic, he didn't dare tell a soul about his connection. The elite guard had enough to worry about with keeping the king's peace without the presence of the king. Nighthelm had been without a king for over a decade. It was believed the creatures of Ripthorn Mountain, which loomed over the kingdom, killed the royal family and stole the heirs, who had been locked away in the castle since birth to protect them from any and all threats. No one in the city had ever seen them. No one even knew how many heirs there truly were, not their names and ages, or even if they were male or female or both. Some believed the heirs were still alive, but with every year that passed, the kingdom had less and less hope that they would ever be found, and the people's hatred for the creatures of Ripthorn and the Witch Woods grew ever stronger.

No one truly knew about all the things that lurked inside the dark and dangerous forest. Or knew what magic resided there. Rumors spoke of plants that melted human flesh, beautiful sirens in the lake who dragged gullible men to their watery deaths, and of a wizened, old hag who hunted children with an axe and ate them piece by piece. All of it was folly, of course. There were certainly creatures that lived in the darkness that deserved the fear they incited, like grimms, but most were harmless if undisturbed. But tonight, he was going to finally get real answers for himself and for the city he was sworn to protect with his life.

Edric rushed down the stone stairs of the tower and to the gatehouse to gather troops. Two of his soldiers, Graham and Hale, stood at attention and saluted him.

"Commander Axton," Hale said.

"Gather the men to meet me at the stables. We're riding out to the woods."

Hale hesitated, his face turning ashen. "The woods, sir?"

"Yes. Is there a problem, soldier?" Edric asked.

Hale gave a quick shake of his head, then he and Graham rushed off to do as he commanded. Edric knew there was a lot of fear surrounding the woods, but there was no time for it. Not on his watch.

EDRIC

*I*n the stable, the grooms had their horses saddled and ready to go. Edric put on his dark red leather armor as his men suited up. There was a lot of nervous laughter and fleeting looks to one another. The fear was palpable in the stable, but Edric knew his soldiers would ride into hell with him if he asked. And he was.

He stood in front of his men. "For as long as I can remember, the Witch Woods have been a source of dread and wariness. In the academy, they taught us to never go into the forest at night. That we'd be attacked by spiteful wood sprites or eaten alive by grimms."

That sent of wave of panic through the stable. Even the grooms who weren't going out to face demons shook in their boots. Grimms were everyone's worst nightmare. Part of the training at the academy was learning about the horrific smoke wolves that traveled in packs and feasted on human flesh. The alchemists had even taught them about the creatures' anatomy and physiology, so they were all prepared for an encounter. Although, no amount of training could ever prepare someone for a grimm encounter.

Never mess with a grimm. Edric had learned that the hard way. A scar the length of his entire right arm, from index finger to shoulder, was the result of that lesson. A gift from a grimm as payment for Edric's bravado. Still, he wasn't afraid of the beasts. Somewhere inside their vaporous forms was flesh. And flesh could be cut and sliced and slain.

"Those are tales for young boys. Stories to instill fear into our hearts and minds. But we are not little boys anymore." He looked directly at each of them. "We are men. Warriors of Nighthelm." He thumped his fist against his leather chest plate in the customary salute of their home.

Each of his men responded with the same gesture.

He thumped his chest again, harder. The *thunk* echoed through the stable. "We are Warriors of Nighthelm!"

They echoed him, chanting the words like an incantation, growing courage and morale among the troops.

Edric slid his broad sword from the scabbard around his waist. The polished steel glinted in the fire-light. He hefted it into the air. "We are hard flesh, and stout hearts, and steel bones. Nothing can cut us down. We are the defenders of the city and protectors of the people. Nothing can cut us down. We are Warriors of Nighthelm."

"Nothing can cut us down!" The men shouted together, thumping their fists against their chests.

Edric nodded to them, as one by one, they mounted their horses. He was the last one on his horse, leading his squad out of the stable and to the main gate. Their horses snorted and stamped as they waited impatiently to ride out. Edric felt the same. He was eager to ride, to storm into the forest, to find the answers that had eluded him for years. He wouldn't let whoever was responsible get away this time.

When the gate finally opened like the jagged jaws of a great dragon, Edric and his men shot out like streams of righteous fire and flame.

CHAPTER THREE

SOPHIA

*T*he darkness tried to suffocate Sophia, but she struggled against it, eventually blinking open one eye, and then the other. At first, her vision was blurry. She spotted Haris in the shadows of the giant oaks, watching and waiting. Haris paced back and forth, eager to come to her aid. She gave him an indiscernible shake of her head. Grindel couldn't see him. Not in a world of kill first, research later. Sophia didn't want her forest spirit friend to end up a casualty of ignorance.

The stink of burnt grass and weeds filled her nose. She was still on the ground, in the middle of the scorched circle she made, covered in a wool blanket, and surrounded by strong arms. Slowly, she turned her attention to Grindel holding her, his usual scowl even deeper than normal. A sigh escaped her lips, full of relief. She relaxed farther into her mentor.

"Don't look so relieved," he said, nearly growling the words. "If it wasn't for your pending birthday, I'd give you ten lashes for disobeying my orders."

He always threatened punishments like the whip, but he had never delivered. There was always an excuse not to, a *just this time* approach that she appreciated. Even though he was a hard ass, she appreciated that deep down, he at least cared a little.

Clutching the blanket to her body, Sophia sat up, and then tried to stand. Her legs were like melting wax. Grindel reached for her arm to help steady her. Although, she was determined to stand on her own, she accepted the help. He always knew when she truly needed it.

Once standing, she surveyed the damage. The ground was black with soot and ash, leaving no living thing intact. She saw that it made a perfect circle around them, some trees were cut in half and charred to dust. Even the rocks hadn't survived the blast.

"You were instructed to observe only." Grindel kicked at a charred bush, causing it to crumble. Then he whirled on her, his stern, green eyes narrowed. "You deliberately disobeyed, like an insolent child."

She flinched at his tone, although accustomed to it. This wasn't the first time he chastised her for something she had done, and she suspected it wouldn't be the last, but his words hurt a little more than usual. She hated when he used the word "child." She was far from that scared little girl he first took in all those years ago.

He threw up his hands. "This is exactly why I tell you not to engage, just to observe. You don't have enough control. It's been a while since you last had an incident, but we both knew it was inevitable." He shook his head. "You must believe in the training, Sophia. Headmistress Mittle and I are working diligently to find a way for you to finally master your magic, to heal your soul."

Sophia was tired of being frustrated with her training. Grindel and the headmistress of Nighthelm academy—who trained soldiers and sorcerers—talked and acted like they knew what they were doing, but she suspected that wasn't true. The past ten years had been a series of trials and errors, trying to truly understand her and the broken magic bubbling inside her.

"You have been promising me that for years. To fix me." She brushed at the hair that had escaped her braids. The ends were singed a little. "But you haven't helped me. Not really."

"Sophia—"

"You don't know anything more now than you did twelve years ago." Her hands trembled, and it wasn't from the cool night. Frustration and anger at her continued circumstances bubbled to the surface. "You put me through hours of sword training until my arms shook. You made me run through the woods until I retched. You made me stand on one foot on a rock for a day without food or water, and for what?" She spoke the last few words between clenched teeth. Anger swirled inside her belly again. "You don't know if those things are helping. You don't know what it's doing to my *fractured* soul."

He lifted one of his withered, old hands toward her. "Sophia—"

"Bloody nothing," she said. "That's what it's done. Nothing except piss me off."

He stared at her with one white eyebrow raised. "Are you quite finished?"

Her shoulders slumped following a giant exhale. "Yes."

"Good." He pulled his brown cloak tighter around his body. "It's getting cold, and I'd like to get home before nippers come out of their burrows looking for a meal. They make the most horrendous noise when they hunt."

They walked toward the tree line, in silence. Sophia glanced at the spot Haris had been hiding, but he was gone. She sighed, thankful that he had listened to her. Sometimes he wasn't so obedient, instead choosing to be obstinate and insist upon risking his exposure. She was sure he toyed with her on purpose; to give her a heart attack. Then she glanced at her teacher, noticing how old he looked in that moment. His frame was usually thin looking but strong. She'd seen him battle a minotaur once with his long broad sword. But tonight his cheeks appeared sunk in, like the events of the evening had sucked the life out of him. When he turned his head slightly, in a rare swath of moonlight, his face seemed more like a skull. A shiver rushed down her spine, and she looked away.

"Did the girl get back to the city safely?" she asked, hoping the change in subject would eliminate the dread she felt.

"Yes, but with imaginative tales about a giant, glowing dog and a girl with a flaming sword." He shook his head. "I'm not sure how we are going to be able to spin that into something reasonable and not have every city guard coming out here to investigate."

"She's a scared, little girl. No one will believe her."

Grindel mumbled something indecipherable under his breath, then nodded. "Yes, maybe."

She sighed, annoyed with his brusqueness, but she knew she did what was right. At least the girl was safe. She opened her mouth to ask more about the girl, but the sound of horse hooves pounding the nearby dirt path made her pause. Grindel was already on the move to the safety of the shadowy trees. She joined him in the thick darkness of the woods, cloaking themselves in shadow and magic, just as seven riders burst into the black circle.

The horses snorted and stamped the ground, likely agitated by the residue of her magic or wary of the woods themselves. It wasn't often that horses and riders came into the dark forest. The riders were no different. Their gazes shifted from the trees to the burnt grass to the trees again, expressions of awe and fear on their faces. All except one. Edric Axton, commander of the elite castle guard. There was not a single ounce of unease on his face as he rallied his men to focus.

When Edric dismounted and stepped into the orange glow of the lit torch one of the soldiers carried, there was no mistaking the cut of his cheekbones and the hard line of his jaw. Under his leather jerkin was a body of smooth planes and hard muscles. Out of all the soldiers in the city, he stood far above the rest. And it wasn't just his good looks. There was something about him that called to Sophia. Her body always reacted traitorously to his nearness.

She rubbed at her chest, as her heart thudded harder. During her secret visits to the city over the years, she had studied him. One of her favorite things to do was to watch the soldiers work out and practice different disciplines in the training yard near the castle. Because she'd been denied access to the academy, she chose the next best thing: to observe from the shadows of the nearby buildings and copy the moves later when she was alone in the forest.

During those training exercises, Edric had always stood out. He was faster and stronger than even bigger men in his troop. Sophia wasn't surprised when he was promoted to commander. She was deeply attracted to both his handsome features and his bravery, but a few of the village bimbos had been chasing after him and she figured he would marry off to one of them this summer. No point in wanting what she couldn't have.

As Edric walked around the burnt area, toeing the ground with his boot, inspecting the charred remains of a large oak, Sophia wondered why he was there. The city guards rarely came out into the woods at night. In fact, she couldn't remember a time when they had. Something had piqued their interest. Had Edric seen her magical blast from the city wall? She didn't think that was possible, but the commander did seem more observant than most.

His gaze flicked to their hiding spot. She knew he couldn't possibly see them. Something about the way his eyes narrowed as he stared in their direction told her he sensed something. She suspected he had enhanced abilities, especially hearing, as she'd seen him react to something she'd done months ago during one her secret trips to the city.

She had followed Edric from the soldier's barracks to a tavern. Through the window, she watched him drink mead with his fellow soldiers. While others laughed and joked around, he just sat and drank and watched the revelry around him. A very buxom tavern maiden, set more tankards of drink on his table, then plopped herself into his lap and said, "You've been looking at me all night, haven't you handsome boy?"

Sophia hoped that he would push her away, but Sophia knew better. He was a man, after all, and the woman had her enormous breasts in his face. She'd seen Edric with other young women. They literally threw themselves at him. She thought it was pathetic, and tried to deny the pang of jealousy in her heart. She would likely never know the pleasure of a man. It wasn't part of her life's path to have a husband.

Disgusted at the brazenness of the server, Sophia had murmured out loud, "Of course, he's looking at you, silly cow, you've got the biggest udders he's ever seen."

Edric's head had whipped toward the window, and he had laughed so hard, the woman fell off his lap. Sophia had taken off after that, and returned to the cabin in the woods, but the whole time she questioned how he had heard her.

Jostling her from the memory, Grindel placed his hand on her arm to get her attention. When she turned to him, he gestured for them to leave. She nodded, and they quietly fled the area back to the cabin. Sophia had occasionally glanced over her shoulder to make sure Edric wasn't following them.

She knew it was impossible that he'd seen or heard them, and there was something unnerving about his arrival.

At the cabin, while Sophia dressed, Grindel made maca soup. The root was known for its vitality properties. Sophia ate a bowl with a one-day-old barley roll while Grindel drank tea and watched her from his perch by the fire. She was surprised he hadn't chastised her about now needing a new set of clothes, as the ones she had been wearing were burned away to nothing. He'd probably get her more hand-me-downs from the academy.

She supposed it was difficult to keep the cabin, his work, and her secret. He lived a double life. One as a well-respected professor, and the other as a trainer of a broken soul. If he was ever caught, his life would be in danger.

"I have to teach at the academy tomorrow, so there won't be any training." He finished his drink. "You could use a day of sleep anyway. After your episode."

"Yes, sir," she said, as she retreated into herself and finished her soup.

She wondered how much longer her life could go on like this, how much longer the training would continue. What did Grindel and Headmistress Mittle really want for her? There was so much she didn't know about her future, and she hated not knowing.

After quickly washing her soup bowl and spoon,

Sophia retired to her room at the back of the cabin, shutting the door behind her. She was grateful for the privacy of her own bedroom. Especially on nights when she couldn't sleep. Although her body was exhausted, her mind raced.

Instead of lying on her straw mattress, she paced the closet-like space thinking about the grimms and her magical event and Edric Axton, the commander of the city guard. Her thoughts swirled around her head like a tide pool. The images and notions didn't stay still long enough to ponder their significance. She was too edgy to think straight, let alone sleep. .

She popped her head out the window. Haris sat beside the cabin waiting for her, wisps of green twirling around his head, as if his thoughts were as chaotic as her own.

She fastened her black cloak around her neck, and then crawled through the window. She jumped on Haris, and then they took off. Sophia made sure they circled by the scorched meadow to check on the soldiers. She was certain that the pack of grimms wouldn't return, but she had to make sure she and Haris were safe. Make sure *Edric* was safe.

For a few moments, she watched Edric move about, snapping out orders to his men. When his head kept popping up and turning toward her, it was time to go. She couldn't risk being discovered. If he found her, discovered what she was, he would have no choice but to take her before the duchess, to face a trial, and likely, an execution. That was the law.

Something inside her wanted to stay and continue to watch him. She was drawn to him, and she didn't know why. She had so many questions in her mind about her past, her training, her future. Only one thing would help to clear he mind. A long walk.

She rubbed a hand down Haris's flank, urging him to run. She didn't have to tell her friend where to go. He knew their direction. Nighthelm.

CHAPTER FOUR

SOPHIA

*B*ecause her dangerous, broken magic had already been spent, Sophia wasn't worried about walking through the shadowy streets of Nighthelm. She was no longer a danger. Her power would return in a few weeks but, for now, she could safely be around others without incinerating anything or anyone.

Leaving Haris at the base of the wall on the west side where the shadows seemed deeper, Sophia pulled open the iron grate covering the water way that went under the wall. It was used mainly for runoff, but also served as a secret way into the city.

Once through, she crouched at the grate for a few more moments before she busted out. After putting the grate back, Sophia crept along the back lanes under the cover of shadows, and then ventured into the city. Like the multiple times she'd traversed through Nighthelm, she made sure to stay hidden. A young woman dressed like a warrior would draw unwanted attention.

Pressing herself against the back stone wall of a house, Sophia edged around to the front. The lane in front of the row of wealthy homes lay deserted. Music from inside the house drew her attention, and she peered into one of the front windows uncovered by shutters. A young woman, around Sophia's age, played the piano. Family was gathered around her, attentive and listening. Her parents were smiling, pleased with her performance, and her younger sister sat in a chair nearby, fidgeting with the laces of her dress. The scene looked warm and inviting.

A pang of envy speared Sophia's heart. Being part of a family was something she would never have. In fact, she couldn't even remember her parents. She had no idea if she ever had siblings. It was a complete blank in her mind, and Grindel and the Headmistress never spoke to her about it. Years ago, she'd asked about her family a few times, but they never answered her, so she stopped asking.

As she watched the girl's fingers dance across the black and white keys, Sophia imagined that was just one of her many accomplishments. The girl probably painted, did needlework, and was well read on the history of Nighthelm, as all proper, young ladies of courting age were accustomed to. Or what Sophia assumed from the books she'd read on court life in Nighthelm. These things would make the girl an ideal wife for any man. The girl was also pretty with her auburn hair done up into a twist on her head, and fine curls framing her delicate face. It put Sophia's blond, braided hair to shame. Although Sophia styled it for fighting, and not for courting.

Sophia couldn't play an instrument or paint a pretty picture, but she could wield a sword, shoot a gargoyle bat out of the sky with her bow, track game silently through the woods, and best a man twice her size with hand-to-hand combat. But she didn't think any of those skills would attract a man. She'd resigned herself to never court. She would never marry. She was destined to be alone.

Shoving the pointless desires deep down inside her, Sophia continued on her journey through the city.

She approached the merchant section where the houses were stacked together with narrower lanes. She found hiding a little harder here, but Sophia was good at moving as silent as a ghost and melding into the shadows. The black cloak she wore helped as well.

Slinking along the street, she ducked into the darkened doorway of a chemist shop when three, drunken men stumbled out of the nearby tavern. As they passed her, one of the men tripped on a loose cobblestone, nearly falling. His companions grabbed his arms before he could face-plant onto the ground. They drunkenly laughed at the folly, and then continued on their way.

Sophia had put her hand over her mouth to stop a bubble of laughter from erupting. That was one thing about her trips to the city: they were always entertaining. Grindel would definitely give her a few lashes if he ever found out about her forbidden visits. She hated he didn't care if she was lonely. That it was just her and him—sometimes not even him—alone in a rundown cabin in a lonely, dark forest. His only concern was training her for the Headmistress.

With too many people on the streets, too many curious eyes, Sophia had no choice but to go higher. She grabbed a hold of the black timber along the side of the shop, stepped up onto the window sill, and then pulled herself up to the ledge of the overhang of the second story. Her fingertips sought crevices in the masonry, and then she climbed along the side of the wall until she gripped the gutter on the roof, hauling herself up. Once atop the shop, she smiled and stretched out her arms from the exertion. She preferred being on the roofs anyway. She could see everything stretched out across the city to the mountain, and over the wall to the woods and to the world beyond.

But looking out over the expanse of the kingdom made her feel lonely, frustrated, and trapped. She hated her life. Hated the future that was chosen for her by the fate of being born broken, the debts she owed to the Headmistress who held Sophia's life in her hands, who paid for her training in exchange for... what, exactly? Aside from the occasional recon mission, there had never been any favors asked of her, but she knew nothing in life came for free. The debt would come due, and she had a feeling she wouldn't like the price.

Sophia often fantasized about running away. She would travel to a new kingdom, like Ondia, which was by the sea. She read about it in a book. There had even been illustrations of the green city. Colored so by the algae and seaweed from the water. Sophia thought of Ondia as a fascinating place she could get lost in. She could reinvent herself. Be a merchant, or a blacksmith as she knew a bit about forging weapons. No one would fear her. Until she had an incident, of course. Which was inevitable. Then she would be hunted.

No. Running away was not an answer. That would be the coward's way out. And Sophia was no coward.

Besides, she would have to leave Haris behind if she ran. And she would never want to do that. He was too special to her. He was truly her only friend, and she knew that he would fight to the death for her.

A grumbling in her stomach snapped her back to

reality, and she wondered if the vendor near the city center park was still open and had honey cakes. They were her favorite sweet, but she rarely ever had the opportunity to eat them. It wouldn't take much for her to take one without anyone noticing. She would, of course, leave some coins for it, as she was in no way a thief.

She stood then walked to the edge of the roof. There wasn't much of a gap between buildings, so it was a fairly easy jump. Still, she took a few steps back to get a running start. Soon, she leapt from roof to roof, touching only with toes to remain quiet, until she reached the heart of the city, and no more buildings to jump on to. There was only the park. And the oracles that resided there.

Sophia climbed down from the roof and then tucked herself into the shadows that surrounded the circular plaza. The city had been built around the six, massive oak trees, a face carved into the bark of each one. They were said be have been left by the gods as a gift to mankind before they returned to the mountain for the great slumber. Nighthelm had forever been known as the City of the Sleeping Gods, for that reason. The city was said to be the origin of all known magic in the world.

Sophia didn't know the truth of the legend, but she felt power radiating from inside the city walls every time she visited. Sometimes she sensed magic coming from the stone of the walls and buildings themselves.

Wanting to get closer to the oracles without drawing the guards' attentions, she crept from shadow to shadow until she was a few feet away, just outside the fence. In two days, on her eighteenth birthday, she would kneel before the six, great trees with reverence and respect and ask for their wisdom. For most, they stayed silent. If a person had greatness inside them, an oracle spoke. And only one or two of the great trees would vocalize. Never more than that. Once, three oracles spoke, and that was for an important king.

Sophia didn't expect greatness, but she hoped for *something*. Surely, her place in the world carried some sort of significance.

Movement drew her attention. She watched as a young soldier walked past the guards and toward the trees. She recognized him from the academy guard training. His name was Winston, and she knew him to be the son of a general. She'd seen him train once or twice in the yard. He was definitely attractive, with slicked back, brown hair and an aristocratic nose and strong jaw, but he hadn't impressed her with his fighting ability. She could have easily taken him down.

He knelt before the oracles, as was custom when turning eighteen. Sophia drew in closer, hoping to hear the oracles speak to him. Because of who

Winston was, and his family name, she expected at least one of the trees to speak.

"Great oracles, I kneel before you and ask for your favor. Speak to me and tell me my great future." He looked from one tree to the next, frowning.

From what Sophia had read about the ceremony, if the oracles were to speak, they would almost immediately. It appeared none of them had granted Winston any favor.

He jumped to his feet, and spat on the ground in front of one of the great oaks. Sophia sucked in a breath at the insult. Winston muttered something under his breath she couldn't quite hear, but sure it wasn't complimentary, and then he kicked the base of the tree. A piece of bark broke off under his boot. He turned on his heel and then marched out of the grove.

Sophia couldn't believe how insolent he behaved. Disgust filled her over his behavior. Looking at the great tree he insulted, Sophia slipped quietly into the inner circle. Gently, she set her hand on its bark.

"Don't pay him any mind. He's obviously not worthy of your favor. I'm sorry you had to deal with that." She ran her hand up and down, hoping to soothe the wood spirit. "You deserve more respect than that, great one."

The bark under her hand began to glow white. At first, she thought one of the guards had approached with a lit torch, but the luminance wasn't from an outside force. It came from the oracle.

Afraid she'd injured the tree by her broken magic, Sophia snatched back her hand. The glow faded. She looked around to make sure no one had seen her, or the strange phenomenon, and then slipped back into the shadows. It wouldn't do if she broke the most historically significant artifact of her people.

CHAPTER FIVE

SOPHIA

While Grindel taught at the academy within Nighthelm, Sophia ran through her basic sword training in a field, full of tall grass and wild flowers, not far from the cabin while Haris watched from his lazy perch on top of a large boulder. His long, green tail swept back and forth mirroring every deft stroke of her sword. She didn't mind Haris's company as she trained, but sometimes, she wished she could be the one lazing on the rock. She actually couldn't remember a day that she'd taken off to just be a girl and not a warrior.

Although, she didn't have one clue of what that would entail. She couldn't see herself sewing new clothes for herself or baking sweet treats for Grindel. She was barely able to make a decent pot of porridge most mornings. At least, according to Grindel.

Gripping the hilt of her sword tight with two hands, she lunged with the blade. Then she took two steps back and then lunged to the right. She did that move over and over again, alternating between right and left, until her arms shook. There was nothing like a vigorous training session to get the blood pumping. She lowered the sword and wiped at the sweat on her brow. Despite practicing for the past three hours, Sophia still had too much energy to burn off.

She lifted her sword, took a wide stance, and then twirled her blade with her wrist. She stopped, then reversed it, which was a lot harder to do, as it put more pressure on the wrist. Once she'd done that a few times, she twirled the sword in front of her, the tip of the blade tracing the infinity symbol in the air. This was the training Sophia didn't display in front of Grindel. He would accuse her of not taking things seriously, or of showing off. Which was kind of what she was doing. But Haris was her only audience, and likely probably ever would be.

She glanced over at him on the rock. He yawned. Obviously, he wasn't much of an audience. He didn't appreciate her skills.

Balancing the hilt of her sword on the palm of her hand, Sophia flipped it into the air, did a side roll on the ground, then came up, caught the blade, and then lunged as if an attacker was just about to render her in two. She would've gotten to him first. She did it again, this time, balancing the sword on its tip. She executed the same move but slipped during her lunge. She ended up on her back, panting hard.

She stared up at the darkening sky and laughed to herself. It was time for a break.

She got to her feet. "Let's go for a walk. Grindel won't be back for hours."

Haris trilled in answer then jumped off the boulder to nudge her in the side. She slid her sword into the scabbard strapped to her back as they set off.

Together, they walked silently through the croaking woods. Despite all the fear churned up in the city about Witch Woods and the dangers that lurked within, this was Sophia's home. It was all she knew for the past twelve years, and she was fiercely loyal to its charms, however strange they might have been.

There were nymph tracks on the path they took; small imprints of human-like feet spaced very close together. Most nymphs traveled in packs and were harmless, so it was a little odd seeing only one set of tracks. It could have been a nymph that was cast out of the community. They could be ruthless in that way. There were also tracks of other small creatures, like hobs, that were likely out looking for moss and mushrooms for dinner, and the usual, harmless rodents. Nothing that Sophia paid much mind to.

After breaking through a clumping of bushes, Sophia spotted two minotaurs nearby, drinking water from the stream. Thankfully, the creatures didn't look up as Sophia and Haris quietly passed by, careful not to bother them. Minotaurs could be worrisome. When they were angry enough, they could break through stone. But they were far enough away from Nighthelm's walls, Sophia didn't think they'd be a problem. Besides that, she'd never known of a minotaur attack on the city. They were too involved in their own minor squabbles to risk war with humans. Except for that one time with Grindel.

But she thought that had more to do with Grindel getting involved in minotaur politics, and a discussion between clans. He fancied himself to be some great mediator, but in reality, he'd just put his nose in where it didn't belong, and one of the clan chieftains took offense to it and had challenged Grindel to a duel. Thankfully, Grindel was a great swordsman, so the duel didn't last long, and the chieftain had conceded the win. Sophia had enjoyed watching the whole thing. From the shadows, of course. Grindel would've tanned her hide if he'd known she had followed him to the meeting in the first place.

The soft hum of a fairy hive overhead in a nearby tree caught Sophia's attention. She watched for a moment as two tiny, winged creatures came fluttering out of the sparkling yellow honeycomb. They were beautiful with translucent, pearly wings and hair the color of spun gold, but had teeth like daggers and bites like bee stings. Sophia and Haris gave the hive a wide berth. Sophia had been bit before by one of the little buggers and didn't want a repeat performance. Haris snorted in the direction of the hive as they passed. He too had been on the receiving end of the fairies' wraths.

Sophia stopped cold on the path and rubbed at her sternum. In her chest came an intuitive impulse to hide. Seconds later, the thunder of horses echoed through woods. She slipped into a small clump of trees with Haris before a cavalry rushed by on powerful, black stallions.

Upon the horses rode wraith shifters dressed in black and silver uniforms. They were some of the Nighthelm army's best and most fearsome fighters. She'd watched them train over the years and they were unlike anything else she'd ever seen. They could move like the wind and strike like lightning. Her respect for them was endless.

They were likely a patrol from the castle, sent to keep the Witch Woods under control after the grimms episode and her power display he night before, but not even they went out often at night. Their presence intrigued her.

Two patrols in as many nights. She really hoped it wasn't going to become common place. However much Sophia enjoyed her visits to Nighthelm, the woods was her home. And she hadn't really learned how to share graciously.

As the wraith squad passed, her eyes caught a young man a couple of years older than her. Andreas Hylt. He was at the top of his academy class. Their fiercest fighter. She'd seen him train before and it was always exhilarating to watch him move. So much so, her heart picked up a beat as he rode on past. His eyes flitted briefly toward her, even though she knew he couldn't see her as she was cloaked in shadow and magic. Still she felt the power of his gaze. It seemed to pierce right through her.

Sophia wondered what it would be like to fight with them in battle. What it would mean to have a brotherhood watching her back at all times. To have comrades. Friends even. Envy pricked at her and she climbed on Haris's back to follow the cavalry at a safe distance. As always, they moved as silent as ghosts, hidden within the shadows of the great oak trees.

Eventually, the soldiers stopped at Black Tears Lake to water their horses. Sophia urged Haris to stop, and she slid off his back and crouched behind two, thick trees to watch the men as they dismounted and joked about.

One of the men stood on the shore of the lake and peered into the dark water. "I heard there were sirens in the water." He swiveled around and put his hands to his chest. "Big-breasted wenches with voices like angels. I'd love to see one."

"Looking for a new girlfriend, Dayton?" One of the men taunted. "Lilianna already bored of your lazy ass?"

Another of the men, bigger and meaner looking, pushed Dayton. It looked like he was trying to push the man into the water, but he failed, as Dayton danced away, surprisingly light on his feet. "That's the only woman you'd ever get. Some waterlogged creature with talons for fingers and a snake for a tongue." He barked with laughter.

The two started to wrestle, as the other men gathered around and laughed, placing bets on who would win the sparring match. Andreas watched his men for a bit, but his gaze kept scanning the forest, seeming to rest exactly where Sophia and Haris were hiding. He couldn't see her. It was impossible. She was a mere shadow.

However much she longed to stay and watch the sparring match, eager to learn a few new moves, Sophia decided to quit while she was still safe. These were not men to be trifled with. They were elite guards; the best of the best. As with anyone from Nighthelm, they would kill her on sight if they discovered her.

Before she and Haris could leave though, a pack of canids, growling and snapping their large jaws, burst out of the trees–some on four legs, some on two–and attacked the wraith shifters' camp. In an instant, the men shifted—all but Andreas—and engaged the monsters in a fight.

The battle was brutal. Sophia had never seen the men fight in their wraith forms before. They streaked across the ground like black fire, their eyes and mouths blazing red, cloven feet never touching the dirt. One wraith, she thought may have been Dayton, hovered above a canid and swiped his elongated talons across the massive wolf head, cutting to the bone. Blood spewed from the wound, and the monster dropped to the ground, dead.

Another wraith soldier wasn't as lucky, as one large canid, standing erect on its muscular, back legs, clutched him in massive paws, and literally ripped him in half, tossing his ruined body into the lake like sewage.

Andreas stood in the middle of it all, a sword in each hand, cutting down canids as they charged at him. Saliva dripped from wide, powerful muzzles as the monsters tried to bite Andreas in the arms, the legs, anywhere they could. But he was too quick. Too agile. He moved through the horde, hacking and slicing through every fur-covered body, as swift and fluid on two legs as his wraith brothers were in the air.

A wraith soldier dove at one of the canids. His talons struck the monster in the shoulder, rendering a piece of flesh. The canid spun around, whipping one of its legs in the air. It caught the soldier in the side, and he dropped to the ground. Alive, but injured. Letting out a rumbling growl, it charged at the fallen wraith.

Andreas jumped in front of the monster, his sword raised, and hacked at its legs. The blade sliced through a tendon and the animal stumbled, but it didn't fall. It kept coming. Jaws open, blade like teeth bared, it advanced on Andreas as he stood over his fallen brother.

Sophia jumped to her feet. She refused to let anyone else die, even if it meant compromising her position. She unsheathed her sword and then sprung out of the woods and into the fray.

CHAPTER SIX

ANDREAS

*A*ndreas turned as the monster's immense teeth were about to slam around his throat. This was it. This was how he was going to die. Not in battle against a formidable foe, with swords clashing. No. By some filthy stinking creature when his back had been turned. He was disgusted with himself. He'd never let an enemy get the better of him before. Refusing to give in to death's call, Andreas swung his sword one last time with a vigorous battle cry.

From the corner of his eye, a burst of light sailed from the forest and right through the beast, dissolving the monster to ash. His sword cut through air. Amidst the melee, no one but Andreas seemed to notice the blast of magic. Andreas turned toward the forest just as a flash of long, blond hair and pale skin that glowed the same color as the magic she dispensed went by. She lowered her arm and disappeared into the shadows.

He didn't catch her face, and wouldn't be able to recognize her if he ever saw her again. Clearly, this person was deeply magical. Deeply dangerous. Andreas snapped to attention as his soldier instincts kicked in. He made a move to race after the girl to question and detain her. Someone so magical went beyond his understanding. He would have to capture her and bring her to the sorcerers who lived in Nighthelm castle. Maybe he could give her to Ezekiel Wickham. He seemed like a man who needed a hobby. He could study this magical person, whoever she turned out to be.

From the corner of his vision, a brother in arms was locked in battle, losing to one of the great, monstrous beasts. His brothers came first. He would never leave them to their fate if he could do something about it.

Swords raised, Andreas dashed toward the monster that had his wraith brother pinned to the ground. He leapt into the air and then landed on the canid's broad, muscular back. The creature reared up as Andreas sunk his blades into the sides of the massive beast, pushing them in until the hilts met flesh. It bucked and convulsed, but he hung on, refusing to let go of his weapons, twisting them farther into flesh, hoping to meet bone. Finally, after one final, wet, blood-curdling roar, the canid collapsed onto its side. Andreas jumped off before he could be crushed by the dead weight.

He yanked his swords out of the carcass, and pivoted to the side, ready for another attack. Andreas surveyed the scene. All the beasts had been slayed, and his brothers had shifted back to human and were inspecting their wounds. He counted the remaining faces—twelve had survived, two had fallen. Ford and Landon. Both had been fierce fighters and would be greatly missed on the battle field and in the city. Their women would mourn, as was their custom. There were only about a thousand wraith shifter soldiers in Nighthelm as his people did not breed easily. Due to their unstable physical form, not many wraith babies could be carried to term. His own mother had miscarried twice after giving birth to him, dying during the last time. They couldn't afford to lose any more men because of that.

Andreas knew he should be grateful to still be alive. He'd been a breath away from death. But instead, he was on edge. His body thrummed with pent-up energy. He scanned the bordering forest again, but assumed the girl was long gone. In the battle's aftermath, a tense hush settled over the woods. As if it waited for something he couldn't explain.

Deep in his chest, a familiar sensation burned without warning, and he winced. He felt like he was being watched by something powerful, something deadly, and something that had no name. Was the powerful, magical girl still nearby, even if he couldn't see her?

Andreas turned to march toward the surrounding trees and search for the source of his unease, when behind him, Captain Ryder called him over. A wary eye still on the forest, he jogged over to where his captain stood.

"What the hell happened, Hylt?" Captain Ryder barked. "Sutton tells me you should've both been done for. That the canid was on top of you, ready to rip out your throat."

"It was, sir. I really shouldn't be standing here." Andreas's gaze flitted to the surrounding forest again, wondering if he could catch another glimpse of his savior.

"Tell me how that's possible." The captain frowned, the lines on his forehead deepened into rivets.

"It was magic," Andreas said.

Captain Ryder's brow furrowed even deeper.

Andreas gestured to the trees. "I saw a girl come out of the woods and burn that beast to ash with her magic."

"Impossible. A girl with powerful magic?" Captain Ryder's lips lifted into a sneer. He didn't believe women could fight, nor that any could possess magical abilities. It would be rare most definitely, as there were no female sorcerers in Nighthelm. "Besides, nothing else in these woods protect Nighthelm soldiers. We are the most powerful beings in this place."

"The beast had me, sir. I swung my sword as a last resort, and then it was vaporized by a beam of magic."

Captain Ryder narrowed his eyes, and Andreas knew he didn't believe a word. Andreas had a difficult time believing it as well. He wouldn't have if he hadn't seen her with his own eyes. He was not a man of fantasy; he knew what was real and what wasn't.

"You must've been mistaken. You were about to die. There is no shame in that," Captain Ryder said.

Andreas thought about pressing the issue, but decided his efforts were best laid elsewhere. He wouldn't convince his captain of something that was near impossible. So, he just nodded. "I'm sure you're right, Captain."

The captain slapped Andreas on the back. "You saved your brother. Have pride in that."

Andreas nodded again.

"Now, I know we want to mourn our fallen brothers, but that will have to wait." Captain Ryder looked around at the men as they gathered. "Our mission is more important."

Most of his brethren nodded in agreement.

"We have long awaited news on the lost heirs. It's too important to be impatient," Captain Ryder said. "This is why we train, and why we fight. For the monarch's return."

A wave of "a*ye*" went through the ranks.

"The Duchess can't be trusted. She is only a steward of the throne but acts like she was born to sit upon it." Captain Ryder shook his head. "That will not happen while I am still alive."

The men all stamped their feet in agreement. The horses followed suit, until there was a symphony of power spiraling into the sky like a tornado. Andreas was sure that it echoed throughout the woods. He imagined the sound struck fear into all that heard. Would it frighten the girl with the magic? He thought not.

Andreas looked at the moon, taking notice of its position in the night sky, as all wraith shifters were taught in the academy. His eyes narrowed and he frowned. "The messenger from Ripthorn should've been here by now. It's past quarter moon."

Captain Ryder looked up, as did others. Then his gaze met Andreas's, and Andreas saw the despair in the captain's eyes. The man was a loyalist through and through, as were all wraith shifters. They were born to be warriors for the crown.

"Collect our dead and ready the horses. We'll ride back to Nighthelm."

"What about the messenger, Captain?" Dayton asked. "Shouldn't we wait?"

"As Andreas pointed out, he's late. Therefore, he's likely dead. Just as the last." Captain Ryder marched to his horse and then tightened the saddle straps.

Some of the men sighed in frustration, others slapped their hands down on their legs in anger, Andreas didn't know what to do or say. It wasn't the first time they'd come out to the woods to wait for a message from the mountain. They'd been waiting for over ten years. For any word about the heirs of Nighthelm. Not much was known about what exactly happened in the mountain all those years ago. All Andreas and his brothers had was hope. Hope that one day the rest of the royal family would return and the kingdom of Nighthelm would be restored to its former glory.

Andreas thought the royals were long dead, having been killed in the mountain, but nobility and honor were engrained in his people. The royals did the wraiths a great service by allowing them to have a home in Nighthelm when they belonged nowhere else.

Their part of the city was called the Shade, and Andreas knew some in Nighthelm used the term in a derogatory manner. People feared what they didn't understand. Their homes weren't the most spacious or luxurious. Most families lived in small, stone cottages. Those lucky enough to have children, were forced to sleep two or three to a room. Wraith shifters didn't crave riches and the comforts that money bought. They were a people of resilience and tenacity, honor and faith. These were their four tenets that the wraiths lived by, and Andreas had them tattooed on his chest, as did his brothers, to honor those words.

Andreas understood his brothers in arms' dedication to the monarchs. He'd been raised with that dedication as the driving force of everything he did and accomplished. He, however, thought there were more dangerous creatures to worry about than the duchess. She was just some stuffy, old woman clinging desperately to power she didn't deserve or earn.

He'd seen her once during a regiment event the wraith soldiers attended with the elite castle guard. Even from the dais on which she sat regally, inspecting the troops, Andreas saw cold beauty in her silver gown and spiked tiara. She definitely had a noble way about her, but he sensed no real power. She may have possessed magic, but it was nothing more than simple casting and spells for health. He definitely didn't see the danger in her that Captain Ryder and others had.

The real danger existed in the woods. Ever vigilant, ever silent. Waiting for an opportunity to strike.

Andreas looked warily again at the forest, hand tightening around his sword hilt, as he returned to his stallion to prepare him for the ride back to Nighthelm. There were many dangers in the woods. Grimms, fairies, minotaurs, even the sirens that Dayton had joked about. He just hoped that this rogue magic caster wasn't going to be another threat to the city. There was already enough to fear, already enough enemies.

CHAPTER SEVEN

SOPHIA

As darkness settled around the isolated cabin, Sophia sat at the small wooden table that took up much of the tiny kitchen, finishing her bowl of pine nut porridge and staring at the empty seat across from her. Grindel was never late. She'd set out a bowl for him as well, as she did every evening, but it had cooled during the wait. She wondered where he could be and hoped nothing bad had happened to him.

Although, she couldn't imagine what that would be. He taught at the academy, nothing more dangerous than Nighthelm history, and then walked home. He knew the woods better than anyone, he'd taught her how to avoid pesky water sprites and mean-spirited fairies, how to look for signs of minotaurs and centaurs nearby as they were best to avoid. He was quick on his feet and could handle himself with any weapon, including his hands. He had powerful magic and knew how to use it. So, she couldn't think of what could've happened to him along the walk home through the forest.

While she lazily twirled her spoon, her thoughts strayed toward Andreas again and the battle she'd just witnessed. She couldn't get him out of her head. He was the first person other than Grindel and Head-mistress Mittle to ever see her. The first person she *allowed* to see her. Although she was pretty sure he hadn't actually seen her face, just a flash of her form as she darted out of the woods, her magic flying. She wondered if it had been a mistake.

Ever since she'd first snuck into the city years ago, despite Grindel's warning of never going into Nighthelm, Sophia had watched Andreas and his brothers-in-arms train. Fascinated with the wraith shifters and their fierce fighting style, she watched him grow up, from gangly boy to powerful warrior. He was only a few years older than her. It was like she knew him—a childhood friend, even—and she couldn't let him die in the woods, savaged by some mindless beast. Just like the little girl she had saved.

The orders to not engage seemed ridiculous to her. What good were all her exceptional skills, all her years of training, if she couldn't use them to save people?

Frustrated with her loneliness and isolation, Sophia pushed away her empty bowl and sighed. It was never going to get better. She had to learn to accept that. Watching other people live a full, meaningful life was as close as she was going to get to having one of her own.

The door to the cabin opened, and Grindel shuffled in, looking older than he had in the morning. She shot to her feet, relief bringing a small smile to her face. But the shake of his head told her that his late arrival wasn't a good thing. Her smile faded.

"Get your cloak, and come with me."

She did as was instructed and followed him out into the cold night. She shivered once, then drew her cloak tighter around her body, and put up her hood. She wondered if he knew about her encounter with Andreas and the wraith shifters, and if she was about to be punished for her transgression. She wanted to ask but considered the answer might not be what she wanted to hear. Was he ushering her to her doom? It sure felt like it.

Through the darkness of the woods, along one of their well-worn paths, she walked beside Grindel toward Nighthelm. Their destination surprised her, but again, she didn't want to ask. Sometimes not knowing was best. He led her toward the far end of the city wall, closest to the mountain, to what looked like a door crudely carved into the rock. To most, it would've appeared to be no more than a few cracks in the stone.

He stepped inside and beckoned her to follow. Torches were set into the jagged tunnel walls, so she could see where she was stepping, although she didn't need the light. She was as sure-footed in the dark as she was in the light. Her heightened senses served her well in any environment.

Sophia glanced at her teacher. She couldn't keep her tongue any longer. The nerves in her body were too restless. They demanded answers to relieve some of the agony of not knowing her fate.

"Grindel, where are you taking me? You owe me an answer."

He didn't answer, nor did he even look at her. He kept walking, expecting her to follow. And she did, like the obedient solider she was training to be.

Finally, the tunnel opened up into a cavernous hall lit by sconces along the walls. Sophia knew the room was beneath the academy. It was the closest she'd ever been allowed within Nighthelm. She'd always been kept at a distance from the rest of the population, like some diseased creature. That notion had been pounded into her, much like when Grindel smacked her with a stick during some of their training sessions.

She had been to the room a few times before. Usually to see Headmistress Mittle. Indeed, the elderly woman was there, pacing on a raised platform at the back of the hall. Her head came up when Sophia entered and she visibly relaxed. The headmistress seemed genuinely grateful to see her. There was no smile though. Which was not surprising. Sophia had never seen a smile on the noble woman's unflinching, stony face.

Sophia also relaxed, but only a little. While the woman always had nice things to say over the years—words of encouragement even—it was Headmistress Mittle who had originally given Sophia over to Grindel when she was a child for the brutal training she endured on a regular basis. Deep down, some flicker of resentment had always kept her from fully loving the woman who was essentially the closest thing Sophia ever had to a mother. Sophia had no recollection of her own. Obviously, she had parents at one time, but she couldn't remember them.

Headmistress Mittle stepped down from the platform and came towards Sophia, the hem of her heavy, gold and red, embroidered robe dragged on the stone floor behind her. "You look well, child."

"I am, thank you."

"I'm surprised. After your explosive episode the other night in the woods, I expected you to be weak and broken." She looked Sophia over, then gave a side-eye look toward Grindel. Had he mentioned something contradictory to the headmistress? "You don't look broken. You look strong, if not a little pale in your face."

Sophia was surprised she wasn't being thoroughly

admonished. Headmistress Mittle could use words like whips. It stung when hit with them. It made her wonder what Grindel had told the headmistress earlier about her incident.

"You were instructed to do a recon of the woods, and not to engage the grimms." The headmistress paced in front of Sophia. "You deliberately failed to follow orders. Orders exist to not only protect the people of Nighthelm, but to protect you too."

Sophia met the headmistress's gaze. "I couldn't let that little girl die. She was only, like, four or five years old. She would've been torn limb from limb and eaten by that pack. Right in front of me." Sophia's voice rose a little as she pictured what would have happened if she hadn't interfered. "How would her horrible death protect Nighthelm, or me, for that matter?"

Grindel sighed and shook his head, obviously displeased with her outburst. For a moment, Sophia wondered how he would punish her for it. Extra sword training? Cutting wood for the stove?

Headmistress Mittle's face softened a little. "I understand, Sophia. I know it is an impossible choice to make. But you are given orders for a reason. I even have orders to follow. And we must follow them at all costs, however high those costs may seem. There are always other things at play other than what you see in front of you."

Sophia went to open her mouth to argue some

more, but quickly closed it when Grindel pinned her with a hard stare.

The headmistress continued her lecture. "One of our purposes is to make sure the people of Nighthelm feel safe. That little girl, with her frightening tales of the grimms and the mysterious girl with the flaming sword who cut them all to pieces, only make people scared. It does Nighthelm no good to have fear spread across the city."

Sophia was going to say that fear had spread around the city regardless. During her visits, she'd seen a few posters hammered onto walls declaring how dangerous the woods were and that people shouldn't be traveling the woods at night, especially alone. That if they had to travel, to use the east or west bound roads that went around the forest. But she held her tongue, knowing being a wise ass wasn't going to curry her any favors from the headmistress or from Grindel.

Headmistress Mittle set a comforting hand on Sophia's shoulder to assure her everything would be all right, but Sophia didn't feel that comfort. She was disappointed with the headmistress's reprimand of Sophia's actions on that night. Sophia hid her reaction, though, and bit her tongue. Knowing when to pick her battles was something Sophia was quickly learning. Regardless of the consequences, she would do it all over again. She would rescue that girl in a heartbeat.

No matter what order she was given, she would never let an innocent die.

The headmistress squeezed her shoulder, then let her hand drop. As she moved away from Sophia, she played with the thick, emerald ring on her finger, spinning it around and around. "Now you can get back to your training. Get back to what's important."

Sophia sensed it was a dismissal of sorts. But she wasn't ready to go just yet. She had one more question she needed an answer for. The question that had been on the edge of her mind for years. The question for which Grindel would punish her.

"What are you training me for?"

Both the headmistress and Grindel went dead silent. Grindel looked at Headmistress Mittle, who seemed visibly uncomfortable a brief moment before she gathered her composure and faced Sophia, with a slight tilt of her lips. Was that her version of a smile? It didn't instill any amount of warmth in Sophia.

"To heal, of course. We want you to gain control of yourself and your magic so that one day you will be able to reenter Nighthelm society."

For years, Sophia had heard the same song and dance. She planned on changing the music this time.

"You're not exactly training me to be a housewife or a future mother to a brood of children. I'm certain none in this room could picture me doing needlepoint or playing a piano."

Grindel sniffed derisively and shook his head. "You might as well tell her the truth. She'll be insufferable until she knows."

The headmistress pursed her ruby stained lips, then she sighed. She twisted her ring around her finger again. "You've always been told that it was I who found you in the mountain when you were a little girl, but that was a lie." She paced the room, forever twisting the ring over and over. "Another found you. A magical creature of great power who took pity on a poor orphan girl and brought you to me. Your training has been paid for all these years by someone who occasionally asks for favors in exchange for the work we've done to help you once more to become whole."

"Who found me? Who do I serve?"

The headmistress looked at Grindel, he didn't meet her gaze, then she looked back at Sophia. "As soon as your training is complete, you will earn the right to know that information."

Sophia saw Grindel stiffen. It was subtle, just a small lift of his bony shoulders, but she noticed the movement. She'd been around him long enough to know the majority of his tells. And that one said he smelled a lie. Sophia had detected this one on her own, but it was affirming to know she was right. Why was the headmistress lying?

A nameless creature had found her and delivered her to the academy to be trained as a deadly solider for favors in return, all under the guise of goodwill and protecting an orphan. What a bloody crock. It went deeper than that. Nothing was as it seemed. Sophia knew that all too well. She was going to find out the root of it all one way or another.

If they thought she isn't following orders now, they haven't seen anything yet.

Headmistress Mittle gave them permission to leave. As they traversed back down the dark tunnel, Sophia muttered under her breath. "You could've told me a long time ago that I was being trained to be a warrior slave, forever in debt to a stranger with no name."

He clucked his tongue. "Debts must always be paid. That is the way of things. And you owe a great debt for being saved from the mountain."

"I'm pretty sure I've paid that debt and then some."

"You're being overly dramatic, as usual." He shook his head. "You may not enjoy all your missions, but at least you can say you have a purpose in life. For some, that is more than enough to be thankful for."

Sophia nearly snorted in frustration at his meager justification for her brutal life. Indulging the whims of a mystery master wasn't the sort of purpose she wanted.

CHAPTER EIGHT

EZEKIEL

*D*eep in the labyrinth of the hallways in Nighthelm Castle where he studied and sometimes slept slumped over his worktable, Ezekiel, on hands and knees, drew along the stone-tiled floor with enchanted chalk that glowed as he wrote his runes. The blue luminance cast eerie shadows over the stone walls and the portraits of long dead sorcerers and academy professors. For some, those shadows might've instilled fear and wariness, a creeping dread. But for a sorcerer like Ezekiel, it was the residue of his practiced magic. There was nothing to fear.

He'd traveled much of the known world, always seeking adventure and meaning outside the kingdom of Nighthelm. He'd been as far as Ondia, bordering the Serpent Sea to the east, and seen many extraordinary things like dancing lights in the night sky, met many interesting people like a giant that loved to play chess. One night, on the shores of the sea, he'd had an encounter with an undine. She had been beautiful and seductive, but he knew she would've taken him to the bottom of the sea if he had given in to her charms; much like the rumored sirens who lived in Ghost Light Lake in the woods. However much he wanted to give in, he left her where he found her and gone to the tavern nearby instead, to drown himself in ale.

Despite all the beauty and knowledge of the outside world at his fingertips, something always drew him back home. Back to Nighthelm. It was like a piece of his soul was trapped there, shackled by unseen bonds. Shackles he was determined to shatter.

He drew the final rune of the circle then straightened and took a step back to examine his work. It was well constructed and intricate. The lines were thick and clean. Deliberate. This was what all powerful magic needed to work and work well. The circle was perfect. He'd measured the diameter expertly. Every symbol was exactly the same distance from the center. The spell had to be flawless to work the way he needed it to.

He wanted to finally set himself free. To finally be able to leave and never return to this place of so much pain. His nightmares grew progressively worse. Some nights, he was jolted out of sleep, sweaty and gasping for breath. The only thing that would soothe him was to practice battle spells. Thankfully, on nights he didn't crash at the castle, he lived in a large estate in the city proper, willed to him by his parents, away from nosy neighbors with only his servant, Howard, as company. Howard never complained about the explosions in the basement.

Thankfully, Howard never complained about anything, not even when he ended up shackled with a young boy of twelve to raise after Ezekiel's parents were killed. The professors at the academy were also instrumental in Ezekiel's upbringing. Growing up, he spent most days in the academy studying and learning to control and master his magic or in the extensive library reading about history and science. As a man, he still spent most of his days and nights roaming the castle halls. Everyone basically left him to his own devices, as his magical abilities had far surpassed any inside these walls.

Closing his eyes against the onslaught of memories of his family screaming as they were slaughtered by grimms in front of him, and him being helpless to protect them, Ezekiel stuffed them down, deep into his psyche. He needed to lock away his agony and loss if he was going to succeed. He needed a clear head to continue his spell. Nothing could interfere.

With hands raised over the runes, fingers spread wide, he spoke the words and casted his magic. The spell was one he studied for years. Every nuance of it was ingrained in his mind. He had over one hundred pages of notes and practice symbols scattered across his desk. Within seconds, brilliant light burned like a small sun in the middle of his circle. Contained, the magic sizzled and sparked, and in its center Ezekiel saw the blurry outline of a face.

He twisted and turned his hands, manipulating the spell to increase its power, to get a better bead on the face. The jawline was smooth, not rugged. The shape wasn't blocky, but more oval. Ezekiel was reminded of something soft and gentle but with a pointed chin, and high, sharp cheekbones. Feminine.

It was a woman.

Somehow, this woman was not only blocking his magic, but she was the reason he was chained to the city he so desperately wanted to leave behind him. He pressed his magic, pushing past her defenses which were as thick and immovable as the mountain itself, trying to gauge her power and force the spell to complete so that he could discern her identity.

He pushed harder, using his hands to manipulate the energy flowing through the runes. The face in the circle flickered then compressed. He could almost note some features. She was young, maybe even his age, maybe a little older. She didn't carry the air of the any of the elderly ladies of noble families. So, maybe, a commoner. Small, thin nose, nothing hawkish. Her mouth was pressed into a thin line, but there was no mistaking the fullness of those lips. He could almost make out her eyes, the color, the shape. They were the key. The eyes held all, held everything inside a person.

Again, he pushed. Harder. His hands nearly shaking with the effort. Sweat popped out on his forehead and upper lip from the exertion of holding his magic in one place. One slip and it could shatter every fragile thing within fifty feet.

The light brightened, getting hotter. He moved his hand to shield his eyes. Energy in the room pressed against him, running over his skin, until there were goosebumps all over his body. Wincing from the pushback, he knew he'd failed.

The spell imploded.

Energy bombarded him, singing his clothes and hair, and burning away the runes he'd so carefully drawn on the floor for the last month. The scent of electricity filled the room, like the moment after a bolt of lightning had hit the ground. The hairs on his arms stood at attention.

Groaning at the loss of his work, Ezekiel turned and punched the stone wall. Bone cracked, and skin split from the force. He looked down at the cuts on his knuckles. Blood bubbled out of the wounds. Concentrating on it, his skin slowly knitted back together, and the bones clicked back into place. He'd healed himself but hadn't dissolved the anger boiling inside him.

He stared at where the light had been in the center of the circle. Where the face of the woman hovered above the stone ground. Although his spell failed, at least it had given him a vital clue to what he had suspected all along: someone had cursed him. Someone had tied him to the city for reasons beyond his understanding.

Armed with that knowledge, he could do something about it. He was determined to find the woman; more determined than ever to finally be free of this place and his past.

CHAPTER NINE

SOPHIA

On the hard, wooden floor in her room, Sophia crouched as her heart raced and her body shook. She couldn't catch her breath. Something unseen–unknown–attacked her. It was magical in nature, she was certain. Outside her window, Haris whimpered because he knew something was wrong. She couldn't form the words to assure him she would be all right, though she didn't know if that was true. Without air, she couldn't scream, even if she wanted to. Besides that, she didn't want to wake Grindel.

Hand to her chest, she sensed someone poke at her, wielding a branding iron like a weapon. It burned like wildfire, searing her flesh from the inside out. Looking down, she fully expected to see her flesh sizzle and crack, blackened from the fiery assault. But her skin was still her normal pink, not blistering red. Unmarred and unburnt.

But the pain. *Dear Gods, it hurts!*

She looked to her small, open window, wanting to see if there was someone outside, hiding in the trees, wielding commanding magic toward her. But she couldn't move, as if she was forced to the spot on the floor by large, powerful hands, pressing down on her, ripping at her very flesh.

Squeezing her eyes shut, she wrapped her arms around her body, like a shield. She didn't know who was attacking her, or why, but she would be damned if she allowed it to go on much longer. Channeling all her thoughts and all her emotions, she stacked them one on top of each other, constructing a fort, an impregnable stronghold to wait out the attack.

I will not let you in.

Another whip of burning pain slashed across her body, trying to see inside, trying to pry something loose from her mind. Rough finger-like pressure traced along her jawline, molded her nose and lips and cheeks. Whoever attacked her was attempting to unlock her identity. He was trying to *see* her.

Keep out! She shouted in her mind as she balled all her thoughts into one, solid, sphere and launched it like a comet, pushing outward.

Then all the burning pain and invasive poking ceased. Vanished in a second.

Taking in greedy breaths of air, nearly collapsing on the floor on her face, Sophia considered her attacker. It had to be a sorcerer, given the expert command of magic, but she didn't know much about them, and certainly had never faced one before. Not even in Grindel's small library of books did she find any information about sorcerers, except for a paragraph or two in the text about Nighthelm Academy. Unlike the guards and wraith shifters, sorcerers trained in secret, deep in the halls of Nighthelm Castle. She'd never been able to find them in order to observe and learn more about them. Their ways were shrouded in so much mystery, she didn't even know how many there were or how they were trained or even chosen for that matter. The only thing she did know, for sure, was there were no female sorcerers. So, it had definitely been a man attacking her.

During one of her secret nighttime trips to the city, Sophia had witnessed an older man, a sorcerer she could only assume, creating light out of thin air with his hands and putting it into the lamps inside the home. She wondered if affluent families kept sorcerers on staff, as a sign of power and prestige. Maybe even defense. She imagined a sorcerer would be a great soldier to have against an invasion or worse.

She rubbed at her chest, trying to ease the residual pain still clinging to her skin. Concern filled her, as she wondered if one of the city sorcerers had detected her wild magic during the last episode and tried to hunt her down from his fortified room in the castle. She had enough episodes in the past twelve years, that she was sure someone would've taken notice by now.

Standing on quivering legs, defiance and anger made her body shake. Her magic swirled deep in her palms, eager to be unleashed. The sorcerer could keep on hunting. He could try to find her, she dared him to. She was no meek damsel in distress. She was a warrior, and whoever tried to hurt her would find that out quickly enough when she slid her sword through his belly.

Another whimper from Haris had Sophia climbing out the window to soothe him. She patted his head and smoothed a hand over his green fur.

"I'm okay, my friend," she said softly, not wanting to wake Grindel.

He nickered, letting her know his concern for her.

With too much energy and an eagerness to burn it off, Sophia climbed onto the roof of the cabin to watch the sun start its rise into the cobalt blue sky. In three hours, Grindel would wake and she would be expected to start her training for the day. It always started off with a brisk run through the woods. A part of her wondered if she should simply disappear. He taught her well, and even he wouldn't be able to find her. Not with her abilities and skill.

She looked toward the horizon, dreaming of the

castles and cities far away, where she could begin anew. There would be no more porridge making for a grumpy old man who didn't appreciate anything she did. No more early morning sprints across the croaker infested bog, being careful only to step on boulders and not poison-spewing spotted heads. No more shooting arrows into a hanging straw man until her fingers bleed. And no more hiding away in an old, rundown cabin with no family or friends to speak of.

Well, except for her yakshi friend, who even now paced on the ground around the cabin waiting for her to come down and pet him again. He acted like he'd been the one who had been attacked.

The skin-crawling shriek of a shadow falcon as it hunted in the predawn drew Sophia's attention. She watched it swoop down from the highest branch of an oak tree to snatch a nipper from the ground before it scurried into its burrow. The little rodent was too slow, and the falcon too hungry and quick to miss. It was the way of things in the woods. There was the hunter and the prey. Most times Sophia felt like the hunter, but on rare vulnerable occasions she felt like prey. Like now, whoever had cast that magic on her was most definitely trying to hunt her down. It made her wish even harder for a chance to leave Nighthelm and make a life for herself elsewhere.

She could change her name to Annabel and she'd be the orphaned daughter of a grizzled blacksmith and a comely, buxom barmaid. Maybe she even had a sibling, a brother, who had died fighting in the Great War of Six in the west. She'd find a village to settle into and apprentice at the smithy. Before long, she'd be making swords and arrow heads for the soldiers in the nearby castle, and she'd be teaching the young boys in the village how to wield them. Everyone would come to like and respect her. Her skills would become the talk of the village, and eventually, even the soldiers would come to her for combat training. Maybe she'd even be courted by a few of those soldiers and perhaps a young lord. They could all vie for her hand. She'd fall in love, get married, and live happily ever after.

Sophia shook her head, throwing off the flight of fantasy. It would never happen. Only a fanciful story in her head. Yet again, she was trapped by her untamed magic. She couldn't leave until she healed her broken soul. Strangers were in peril when near her. She was too unpredictable in her state. She could injure or kill innocents with her feral power. No matter how far away she traveled from Nighthelm, she was dangerous. It wasn't the city that was the problem, it was her.

Despite being told constantly, she was starting to doubt that healing was actually what Headmistress Mittle wanted for her. The visit to the room under the castle had planted the lack of faith in Mittle in her mind. The woman had lied to her. That had been obvious. Even to Grindel. Sophia suspected it wasn't the first lie either, nor would it be the last. And if she was lying to Sophia, then maybe Grindel was too. Weren't they working together to 'help' her?

Resolute and determined to no longer be a pawn in someone else's game, Sophia decided to defy Grindel and visit the oracles that night to celebrate her eighteenth birthday. That would be the only celebration she would get. She was a resident of Nighthelm, and it was the right of every citizen to kneel before the great trees and ask for their wisdom. If anyone could tell her what she needed to know about her future, it was them.

Grindel and Headmistress Mittle either didn't want to heal her or didn't know how. Her coin was on a little bit of both. Either way, the job was left in her hands. Sophia was more than ready to heal herself.

CHAPTER TEN

SOPHIA

*A*fter making sure Grindel was still in a deep sleep—considering the loud snoring coming from his room—Sophia jumped on Haris and then they sprinted through the forest to the wall. She crept through the tunnel under the stone and then into the city. Everyone was tucked into beds in their respective homes, so she didn't have to worry about coming across anyone. She avoided the guards by sticking to the shadows. Despite their expert training at the academy, the guards weren't schooled to deal with someone like Sophia, who could manipulate the darkness and completely camouflage herself in shadows. As far as she knew, there was no one out like her anywhere else in the world.

She snuck to the center of the city, and the oracles that waited there. Cautious of what happened last time when she visited the oracles, Sophia remembered to wear a pair of black leather gloves with a special rune etched on the inside to help suppress her out of control magic. They had been a sort of gift from Grindel last year. She chided herself for not wearing them before. She'd gone so long without an incident, she'd honestly forgotten all about them. Grindel had reminded her to wear them after her last incident in the woods.

After climbing over the fence, she weaved around the other tall trees and walked to the middle of the sacred circle, and she looked at each face etched into each tree trunk, hoping against hope that her plan didn't backfire. Confident in her entitlement to do so, she kneeled in front of them. Regardless of rank or nobility, every eighteen-year-old in the kingdom had the right to do the same. But she knew if she was caught, she would be punished.

Clasping her hands together in her lap, she bowed her head so low it nearly touched the ground. "I'm not sure what to say here. No one's really told me anything about the ceremony." She sighed, half-doubting that they'd speak to her. If they didn't, she didn't know what she would do. She was tired of being nothing but a broken shell of a person in a world that didn't want her. At least, she had to try. She wasn't a quitter.

She lifted her head and looked at each tree. They

were all ancient oaks, but they all appeared different, each face carved into the wood, distinctive. In an old book she found amongst Grindel's library, she read that each oracle was representative of a great and powerful sorcerer who once lived thousands of years ago, and when they died, each sorcerer's soul had been bound to a certain tree. Sophia wasn't certain if the lore was true or not, and she had been afraid to ask Grindel, as then he'd know she'd been snooping through his things.

"I'm here to ask for your wisdom, great oracles. Now, more than ever, I need some guidance."

She stared at each face, willing their eyes to open. They had to speak to her. This was really her only chance to be whole again.

But am I worthy? Body tense, shoulders throbbing with nerves, her lungs barely filling with air, Sophia swallowed hard and tried her best to steady herself.

"Please," she whispered, her heart aching, "please, speak to me. I don't know what else to do."

Slowly, the eyes of the oracle she had touched opened. Sophia's heart swelled at the sight. Then, one by one, the other oracles looked at her, eyes glowing, their trunks humming with power.

She felt the energy vibrations skimming over her skin. The little hairs on her arms stood straight up in response. It was the moment before a lightning strike when everything was buzzing.

In shock, Sophia gaped at the trees, wondering how they had all awoken. Had she done something to them, just by being here in the garden? Had her magic affected them somehow? Broken them?

When she'd touched the one oracle the night before, had she left residual, harmful magic behind in its roots? Maybe that had infected the others. What if she was destroying them somehow?

It wasn't right that they would all awake for someone like *her*. A nobody. A broken shell. She wasn't important. She was just a common girl, with no noble birth, no royal blood. If it hadn't been for Grindel, she'd be a beggar on the street fighting for her food… or worse, *dead.*

Instead of their leaves turning black with rot and falling, and their branches breaking apart like she feared, they spoke in unison, their deep ethereal voices vibrating over her.

Little bird of sky and stone,
Pleased we are you have finally spoken.
We give you now a single chance
To mend what has been broken.
Is not destroyed, but resides in another,
That which has been torn asunder.
To heal yourself, find the piece,
Will speak to you like thunder.
Before the next harvest moon,

Bring to us of which you've found.
Then a gift you will receive,
Fulfill your true purpose, you are bound.
Not slave, nor trained warrior be,
Your destiny to which you own.
Orphan girl, lost in the mountain,
Need to restore the throne.

With only that cryptic message, the oracles began to go back to sleep. As Sophia gaped, baffled into silence, their glowing eyes slowly began to shut.

When the last tree went completely still, Sophia flinched in surprise. For a moment, she didn't move a muscle as she tried to process what had just happened, maybe she'd been hallucinating, she had been awake for twenty hours and hadn't eaten anything. She considered asking more questions of the oracles, but she heard the running steps of the guards rushing toward her through the park. In another few seconds, she would be surrounded and would have to fight her way out. She really didn't want to injure those guards just doing their jobs.

Although bewildered and wanting to stay to truly absorb the moment, she couldn't let them capture her since she wasn't supposed to exist. If they found out what she was, she would be put to death. No explanation. No trial. Just an execution.

Sophia jumped to her feet, ran across the park

around the other trees, over the fence, then escaped into the shadows. By the time the guards entered the circle, it would be empty. She knew they would frantically search the surroundings, wondering who had woken the oracles but she was already long gone from the area.

Half way through the city, she stopped and pressed herself against the wall of some tavern to catch her breath and to sort out her thoughts. Everything swirled in her head. The oracles' voices, their words. She couldn't believe what had just happened. She very nearly pinched herself to make sure she wasn't in a dream or hallucinating.

For the first time in her life, she felt true renewed purpose. She could be healed. She could be more than a broken soul, more than an illegal creature and a threat to the world around her. She had a true mission —find the missing piece of her soul. The oracles said the piece was in another. Could it really be in another person? Was it in someone she already knew? That didn't seem possible as she only knew two people. And she knew, for certain, her soul didn't reside in either Grindel or Headmistress Mittle. That would've just been a cruel twist of fate.

She wasn't sure what "Will speak to you like thunder" meant either. Maybe when she found the piece, it would tell her somehow. Speak to her? She wasn't sure if they meant it in the literal sense. The prophecy was all so complicated, none of it really made sense, but at least it gave her a way forward, gave her some hope. She would figure it out no matter what she had to do.

The harvest moon was only two months away. It wasn't much time. And what if she failed? Would that mean she would never be healed? That she would remain damaged and broken for the rest of her life? She wouldn't let that happen. There was too much at stake.

And, to top it all off, the oracles only spoke to those who were truly unique in some way—the kings, the nobles, the brilliant minds that would change the world. She was none of these things. So why did all six trees talk to her when the current record achieved by the last king, Duncan Averell, was only three?

She needed to do some research on the oracles. She hoped Grindel had some books on them, if not, it would prove difficult, as she couldn't just waltz into Nighthelm library in the middle of the day and ask for volumes on the history of the oracles. And she didn't think Headmistress Mittle would allow her into the castle to use the extensive library there.

A creeping sensation filled her. Someone was watching her. In her periphery, a door swung shut. She didn't catch a face, only a mere glimpse of a solid form. She didn't even know if the form was male or female. Unnerved, she slipped back into the night.

Haris waited for her just outside the wall. He would be worried that she'd been gone so long.

She would find him, head back to the cottage before Grindel woke, and come up with a plan. The oracles had given her a whole new reason to survive. And she wouldn't let them down. She couldn't. It seemed the entire fate of the Nighthelm rested on her shoulders.

CHAPTER ELEVEN

SOPHIA

*T*he next evening, after a particularly grueling training day, Sophia sat on a rooftop deep in the city of Nighthelm, overlooking a beautiful garden that she'd never been in before. After a long day of sword swinging and running an obstacle course Grindel had set up in the field, she immediately jumped on Haris and came to the city, sneaking in as usual. Her body thrummed with energy. After what the oracles told her, she needed to be around others, even if they didn't know she was there, watching.

Couples paraded along the winding paths through flower beds of windflowers, larkspur, and her favorite, black snapdragons, and around a large, white, stone fountain, water bubbling out of the mouth of a beautiful siren. She shook her head at that, knowing full well that sirens looked more like fish-lipped hags than lovely, full-breasted women. The people of Nighthelm had so much to learn.

Soldiers and their blushing damsels in big, puffy, frilly dresses that dragged on the ground mingled in the large garden, talking and flirting with one another. She almost gagged at the thought of wearing one of those getups. The corseted top alone would be maddening to wear. How could any girl even move, let alone run or jump or perform a round house back kick to an opponent? But she did envy their flirting. She wondered what it would be like to have some big soldier touch her gently with his rough hands or whisper sweet words into her ear. The thought sent a surprising ripple of pleasure down her body.

As she watched more of the mating rituals, Sophia was grateful that she had a week or so before she would be considered dangerous again. She could already feel her power returning with every flex of her hands, so she knew she wouldn't be able to visit the city for much longer. She just hoped it was long enough to figure out the prophecy the oracles bestowed upon her.

She recounted it in her head:

Little bird of sky and stone,
Pleased we are, you have finally spoken.
We give you now a single chance
To mend what has been broken.

That part was obvious. They were giving her an opportunity to fix her magic, and heal her broken soul although she didn't know why they called her a little bird of sky and stone. Sophia wondered if she should tell Grindel and the headmistress what the oracles had told her. Maybe they could help her figure it all out. But it would more likely be that she would be punished severely for seeking out the oracles.

Is not destroyed, but resides in another,
That which has been torn asunder.
To heal yourself, find the piece,
Will speak to you like thunder.

This part was harder to figure out. They were obviously talking about her soul being broken. And that the piece was somewhere out there. It had to mean it was in another person, as inanimate objects didn't hold souls, and she didn't think it would reside in some plant or animal running around in the forest. But how was she going to find the piece? It seemed like an impossible task, especially to someone who was isolated and was never around people.

A girl in the garden giggled annoyingly at something her chosen male companion said, and Sophia rolled her eyes, but it gave Sophia an idea. What better way to talk and touch those around her than by dressing and acting the part. The ritual she witnessed was a perfect cover. She would pretend to look for a husband. She would use the parties and mingling events the city hosted over the summer to search for the missing piece of her soul.

According to the riddle, she would know when she was near a piece of her soul when it spoke to her like thunder, whatever that meant. Maybe she would actually hear something if she touched that person. She didn't think it would be external, like *kablam*, here's your soul mate, but maybe she would feel it inside like a mighty rumble.

She sighed, frustrated. Why did the oracles have to speak in such riddles? Why couldn't they just say, "*Hey Sophia, go find so-and-so, he's got your soul inside him. He's the soldier who lives in the blue house just outside market square.*" She shook her head at her own foolishness. She'd faced the monsters of the Witch Woods alone. Braved countless, dangerous situations and triumphed. She could handle a few randy soldiers and lords while wearing a big, pink, ruffled gown.

How hard could it be to flirt? She'd watched the soldiers enough times off the training field and in the pubs to know what they liked in a woman beyond the big breasts and wide backend. She'd seen how the tavern maids giggled when the men showed off their prowess. There were coy smiles and long looks from under hooded eyes. Soft subtle touches on arms, or legs. It was also in the way a woman walked and held her body that drew a man's eye. There seemed to be a thousand, small nuances, but Sophia figured she was a quick learner. She'd have it down pat by the time she needed to use her new skills.

Begrudgingly, she realized she was going to have to find a few of those frilly dresses she so hated to pull this whole caper off. No one would want to court her looking like a bandit and thief. If it wasn't for her long hair and womanly curves that she kept hidden, the soldiers might mistake her for one of their own, especially if they put a sword in her hand.

For the next few hours, she moved around the area near the pretty garden and studied some of the noble houses to get an idea of what she needed to do to achieve her new goal. She watched two girls about her age sitting on one of the stone benches as they gossiped. She overheard them talking about a reclusive duke who never mingled with the other families much but was infamous for his travels across the land.

"It's too bad Lord Oxford doesn't have any sons," the girl with the big nose and blue dress said, her voice irritatingly whiny. "I'd love to be courted by a lord instead of some of these common soldiers."

The other girl tossed her long black braid off her shoulder and gave the other a disparaging look. "If he did, you know *I'd* be first in line. My father would make sure of that."

"I know. I'm just saying."

"He does have a few nephews and nieces to marry off, I hear. Although, as far as I know, no one has ever even met one. They could be ugly and boorish." The girl laughed. "But who cares, as long as he has money."

The big-nosed girl said, "My mother mentioned he's always traveling, and when he's not, he's holed up in his parlor, smoking his stupid pipe. I don't think he's attended one ball in the past five years."

"Well, at least there are quite a few eligible, young men this year. Tonight's ball should be well attended." The girl with dark hair searched the garden for any of those eligible men, making eye contact with an older gentleman in a top hat.

Jackpot.

That was exactly the circumstance she needed to pull all of this together. A rich lord no one really knew, with no known family to speak of, just some distant nieces and nephews no one had seen or spoken to.

Sophia was about to leave when the big-nosed girl said something of interest. "I'm looking forward to seeing Commander Axton again. He's so dreamy." It looked like she was going to swoon right off the bench.

Sophia didn't blame the girl. Edric Axton was extremely attractive, and she definitely wouldn't mind seeing him up close and personal. Maybe he would be at ball. She wondered if Andreas Hylt, the wraith shifter, attended balls. She wouldn't mind seeing him as well. He intrigued her on many levels. She could try her flirting skills out on them as practice for the real thing.

It took all of five minutes to locate Lord Oxford's estate. There was a gold-plated plaque near the wrought iron gate that said *Oxford Manor*. And it wasn't far from the botanical garden. Once she quickly cased the place, she was able to sneak into the house through a poorly locked servant's entrance at the back of the house. She crept through the downstairs quarters, snagging a ripe, red apple from the kitchen along the way, then up the back staircase to the main rooms. As she tiptoed through the hallways from shadow to shadow, she spotted several of the servants lying about on the expensive couches. One bold lad had his booted feet up on the sofa, drinking tea from the master's fine porcelain.

Obviously, the master wasn't home. Good. That worked to Sophia's advantage. She hoped he was on one of his long excursions to another country and completely unreachable.

As she mounted the curved staircase to the upper level of the estate, Sophia eyed the portraits of the man mounted to the wall. Lord Oxford was an old, portly, grumpy-looking man with barely any hair. He appeared dour in every single painting. Not a whiff of a smile or any light of humor in his blue eyes. Because of this, she wondered what his nieces were supposed to look like. There didn't seem to be any other portraits on the wall, except for Lord Oxford. Hopefully, no one had seen any of his nieces recently, or her mission would be short-lived.

She scoured the vast upper level, looking for rooms the nieces would have likely stayed in. In one small room with flowered wallpaper, she found a large, prettily painted wardrobe along one wall. Inside, several old gowns hung. There were two blue ones with lots of ribbon; something a younger girl would wear. The pink one was very frilly and puffy, and definitely not something Sophia could see herself wearing. Ever. Not even if someone put a knife to her throat. The only decent dress was shoulder-less, with long, bell sleeves, and a scooped bodice. Thankfully, there was no extra scratchy netted fabric underneath the skirt.

She took the dress off the hanger and held it up to herself in the floor-length mirror. The red and black silk fabric complimented her pale skin and blond hair. As she swished the dress back and forth, mimicking dancing, she realized it was going to be damn near impossible to scale a building in it. She had to find another place to get dressed and ready for the ball. Somewhere closer to the community banquet hall the ball was being held at, where she didn't have to climb up walls or shimmy through windows. She would hate to ruin such a pretty frock before she got any use out of it.

While she continued to look in the mirror at the dress, she instead saw her dirty and torn clothes, braided hair, unadorned face, and she questioned whether she could pull this whole thing off. Even with a pretty dress and painted lips and styled hair, she didn't look like a young woman from the city, born into wealthy society. Her arms were too muscular, her legs too thick, she looked like she could wrestle a large sow to the ground. The society girls she'd seen looked like they could barely lift a knife and fork let alone a long broad sword. It was too bad she couldn't engage in a bunch of training exercises with all the soldiers and guards instead to find the piece of her soul. At least then, she would know what she was doing, and would have the upper hand.

The sound of footsteps on the stairs drew her attention. By the varying sounds, she determined that there were two people currently heading her way. She searched the room, spotted a large canvas bag with a drawstring in the corner, scooped it up, shoved the dress into it, a pair of shoes, and a tin of what looked to be lip stain on the dressing table, then slung the bag over her shoulder.

"I swear I heard someone up here," came a male voice from the hallway just outside the bedroom door. It was one of the servants from downstairs.

Sophia silently crept to the bedroom window, carefully pushed the shutters open, and then slipped outside. Grabbing hold of the rain gutter above, she was able to shimmy her way across the wall, and then pull herself up so that she was atop of the house, on the roof, and was able to look out over the garden below again. The two gossipy girls were gone. Sophia imagined they had gone to their respective homes to get ready for the evening's festivities. She too had to find a place to prepare.

There were galas and balls every night throughout the summer. Some at the community hall, some hosted at large family estates. It was prime mating season. And she figured there was no time like the present to join in on the hunt.

CHAPTER TWELVE

SOPHIA

*A*fter finding a place to wash her hair in a stable not far from the hall, Sophia combed it, twirled it with her fingers, and tossed it loosely over her exposed shoulders; a style she'd seen other young women wear. Getting dressed out of sight, but within walking distance of the hall, had proved difficult. She still managed to do it without getting the dress dirty despite the straw and muck.

As she walked along the cobblestone street, toward the grand hall, among several other young women and men, chamber music wafted from the open doors. Violin and harpsichord and piano met in melodic rhythm that made Sophia's heart ache. She loved music and never got an opportunity to enjoy it. When she was younger, Grindel tried to entertain her with a few songs with a guitar accompaniment but they were a pale comparison to the beautiful melodies that swelled out of the hall. She hoped she would get several opportunities to engage with the music and dance across the floor. Not that she knew how to dance all that well.

When she entered the grand banquet hall, with its soaring, painted ceilings and fine furniture, all eyes turned toward her, and Sophia felt extremely uncomfortable. She had to suppress the urge to pat her hair and pull up the bodice on her dress. The lacing had been so tight on the dress that her breasts nearly spilled over the top. At first, she thought maybe the effect was too much, but the appreciative looks she got from some of the young men in attendance was worth the effort. Maybe she knew how to flirt after all.

Young men and women, scattered through the room and huddled together in corners, laughed and chatted over their goblets of wine, all of them adorned in their best. Even the poorer in the city were dressed in their best clothes. The summer balls were the only time each year that the classes mingled. Sometimes, even matches were made across money lines. But not everyone was okay with the event. Even now, the gossiping young women from the garden snickered behind their hands as they looked at one poor girl's plain, green dress and made remarks. Quite loudly, by any standard.

The big-nosed girl, from earlier in the garden, snickered. "Didn't she wear that last year?"

"It doesn't even look washed," the one with the long, dark hair remarked.

"I think she gained a few pounds as well. It's awfully tight."

The girl blushed and retreated to the food table in shame. Disgusted by the other girls' behavior, Sophia joined her at the table.

The girl picked up a small pastry, then set it back down.

"Those look delicious." Sophia plucked the pastry from the silver tray and then popped it into her mouth. She smiled at the girl. Sophia was fully aware that a fine dusting of icing covered her chin.

The girl giggled.

"You should have one," Sophia said.

The girl shook her head, her hand going to the waistline of her dress.

"Your dress is lovely." Sophia smiled at her. "Brings out the beautiful green in your eyes."

The girl blushed. "It's old."

"Doesn't matter. You make it look good." Sophia gave her a wink.

"Thank you." Her gaze drifted to the floor, as if she was embarrassed.

"I'm Sophia by the way."

"I'm Claudine." The girl smiled and did a little, informal curtsy.

"It's nice to meet you." Sophia handed the girl one of the pastries, as she took another for herself.

They both ate them, and then giggled together like old friends. The sensation was an odd one, but not unpleasant. Sophia had never, ever giggled with anyone before. She'd actually never talked to another young woman either.

Claudine gave Sophia a little curtsy. "I must return to my mother, she will wonder where I went, but thank you for your kindness."

"Don't let anyone put you down, especially not those hideous beasts." Sophia nodded toward the gossiping girls. "Drink wine, eat sweets, and dance with every young man here, as is your right. I bet you dance like a fairy in moonlight."

Claudine wrinkled her nose at that and ran off. Sophia realized the girl had probably not ever seen a fairy, dancing or otherwise. She had to be careful with her words or she'd be found out to be a fraud.

When she was gone, Sophia ate a few more pastries. She knew she was being gluttonous, but she never got sweets at the cabin. She couldn't bake, and Grindel never brought home any ingredients for something sugary. It was all meat, not even the good, thick kind, and roots like potatoes and turnips. All day, every day.

As she went to grab just one more, a young man stepped up to her side. She recognized him from the park the other night. The son of a general, Winston something or other; she didn't know his family name. He kicked one of the oracles when they didn't speak to him. Revulsion rose up in her throat when he smiled at her.

"I saw what you did for that poor girl," he said. "It was very kind."

"It's easy to be kind. Maybe more people here should learn that."

"Yes, I agree. There are some here who can be very rude." He gestured to the big-nosed girl and the girl with the long, dark hair, then looked at her and smiled again. "You seem like a nice person. I value that in others."

She eyed him curiously. Maybe she'd seen him on an off night. Everyone had days where they were not at their best. He was attractive, certainly, with slicked back, dark hair and rich, brown eyes. In her boot heels, they were the same height, and he definitely was fit. She'd seen him work out in the training yard before, as he was part of the guard. But there was something just not right about him, and she couldn't quite pin what that was down.

"Thank you," she said.

As a uniformed server walked by, Winston grabbed two goblets of wine off the tray, and handed her one.

She took it and nodded thanks. She took a small sip and grimaced a little. Wine was not her favorite thing to drink. She preferred mead or ale.

"I haven't seen you before. And I would definitely remember," he said.

She fussed with her hair, suddenly self-conscious. "I'm from… out of town."

He eyed her a little too long on the bodice of her dress, which made her a bit uncomfortable. "I'm Winston Kent." He offered his hand, and she took it.

"Sophia." She didn't offer the Oxford family name, as she really didn't want to give this man any more information about herself that was necessary.

He brought her hand to his mouth and pressed his lips to the back, as was custom she noticed. When he let her hand go, she discreetly wiped it against her skirt. The feel of his lips on her skin made her uneasy and she could've sworn that he licked her.

She took a sip from her goblet as an excuse, then turned her head to survey the gala and the crowd. Her gaze landed on Duchess of Westray, who sat in the royal seats on the balcony, looking very much like a queen in her jeweled tiara and heavy, blue brocade gown even though she was only a steward of the castle until the heirs to the throne were found.

With the oracles' words in her mind, Sophia thought about the heirs and her mission to find them. She had no idea how she was going to do that or where to even start. But the oracles were never wrong. She had to trust they would give her the right tools to fulfill the prophecy when the time was right.

She watched the duchess a little longer as she addressed those who came to speak with her. It was annoying how she was a little too comfortable in her role as acting queen. As if she felt Sophia's presence, the duchess turned and met Sophia's gaze. She offered a warm smile and a nod in welcome, before leaning over to whisper something to the servant nearest her.

Sophia turned back toward Winston, who was still talking. About himself, mostly.

"Of course, my father thinks I'll be a general some-day. Follow in the old man's footsteps," he said.

She gave him a little smile and nodded, trying to be polite.

"Of course, the other men in my squad are not pleased with the extra attention I get." He grinned, with an arrogant twist of his mouth. "But it can't be helped as I am being groomed to take command."

At this point, she was not at all interested in Winston or what he had to say. She didn't feel a pull toward him. Nothing roared at her like thunder. Honestly, she was grateful that he didn't seem to hold a piece of her soul because she really didn't like the way his gaze kept drifting toward her chest and the way he boasted about himself was boring her to tears. She wished Claudine would return to the food table, so Sophia could make her excuses to Winston and talk to Claudine instead.

Tuning him out, she continued to scan the people in the hall, taking in how they dressed and acted, like getting lessons on how to interact with people. Luckily, Grindel wasn't one for parties, but he might be forced one night to chaperone. So, she would have to keep an eye out for him and for Headmistress Mittle, though the headmistress never seemed to leave the castle or its adjacent academy.

Taking in a deep breath, Sophia pushed out with all her energy, all her senses, feeling for the piece of her soul. She wondered what it meant for one to speak to her, and if she would recognize it for what it was. Then there was a shift in the room, as if everything went still. All peripheral movement and noise stopped.

Desperate, she looked over the crowd. Somewhere, in this colorful, streaming sea of people, the piece of her soul existed and was reaching out to her with phantom fingers. She had to tamp down the urge to lift her hand and reach out in return.

CHAPTER THIRTEEN

EDRIC

*E*dric couldn't take his eyes off her.

A beautiful girl—with long, blonde hair, soft, pale skin, and a figure that put all others to shame —he'd never seen before stood across the room near the refreshment table, elegant and graceful. He felt drawn to her the moment he stepped into the main banquet hall. It wasn't just her beauty that attracted him but her poise, the way she held herself, the sense of something *other* about her that was utterly entrancing. No other woman could compare.

He couldn't look away, even when the girl on his arm, who'd been throwing herself at him for the last week, giggled.

"Nadia and Alice will be so jealous that I came to the ball with you. I can't wait to see their faces."

Without looking at her, he said, "If you'll excuse

me, Jasmine. I see someone I need to speak with." As she pouted, he untangled himself from her even as she continued to clutch his arm and started across the room toward the mystery girl.

Her gaze locked onto his almost the second he moved, and his heart lurched in his chest. Everyone and everything around him disappeared as Edric walked toward her. It was as if they were the only two people in the whole room. She was so utterly entrancing, he couldn't think beyond her. He didn't want to.

A hand on his shoulder stopped him mid-stride. He whirled around to see the wraith-shifter, Andreas Hylt, dressed in his finest black and silver uniform, dark hair slicked back.

"If this was a different occasion, you would lose that hand," Edric said.

Andreas sniffed. "If this was a different occasion, you'd already be on the ground, yielding to my sword."

"If I remember the last time we sparred, it was *you* who yielded to my sword," Edric said, pointing a finger at Andreas's chest.

Andreas shrugged. "Yeah, but I'm pretty sure I had my dagger pressed against the femoral artery in your leg, when the master at arms commanded us to stop."

Edric nodded and gave a little smile. It wasn't often that the castle guards trained or sparred with the wraiths, as their physicality and combat methods were so diverse. But Harold, the master of arms, thought it would be a great exercise and learning opportunity for the new recruits to see a battle between a human and a wraith. Edric vividly remembered that sparring match they had a few years ago. It was the most evenly matched bout he'd ever had. The wraith shifter was a superior fighter; he had to give him that.

"What are you doing here?" Edric asked.

Andreas arched one eyebrow and made a gesture toward the mystery girl. "Obviously, the same thing you are."

Edric looked around and noticed just about every eligible suitor at the gala was making his way over to where the beauty stood. The other young women in the room were starting to notice and seemed nervous that they wouldn't have anyone left to dance with.

"She is extraordinary," Edric admitted as he glanced back to the girl. She was definitely watching him and a pleasant shiver rushed down his back.

"I won't argue with you there." Andreas also looked her way.

Someone cleared his throat behind them. "Let me guess…"

Surprised, both Edric and Andreas turned to Ezekiel, one of the castle's best sorcerers.

The young man smirked. "The two of you are arguing on who's going to get the girl first."

Andreas narrowed his eyes at the new arrival. "I'm

surprised to see you here, Zeke. You never leave the castle."

He tilted his nose in the air, placing his arms behind his back. "I thought I'd take part in the mating rituals."

"You have a better chance at sleeping with your books than any of these girls," Andreas said, elbowing Edric in the ribs. "Especially if you use the term *mating rituals.*"

Edric laughed.

"Now, Andreas, don't try and be clever. That doesn't suit you. You need a brain to be clever." Ezekiel tapped his finger against his forehead and grinned.

Andreas frowned, clenched his fists, and took a step forward. Edric put a hand out to stop him advancing. "Don't be foolish. This is not the time or place."

Since the three of them were boys, running amok through the academy and the castle, Ezekiel was always able to get under the wraith's skin. Edric figured "being supremely annoying" was just another one of the sorcerer's magical skills.

"I'm here because I needed a distraction from a rather disappointing spell." He rubbed his knuckles against his leg. Edric noticed they were a bit red, obviously healing from something. "And that girl is the most interesting distraction I've ever seen."

It was no surprise to Edric that the three of them were locked in a sort of combat again. They'd been rivals since they could all walk. Zeke didn't wield a sword like he and Andreas did, but his magic carried just as much of a sting. He'd been on the receiving end of a well-aimed spell before. He carried the scar on his torso from where it had burned him, just as Zeke had one on his shoulder where Edric's blade had cut through his leather jerkin. Andreas also carried scars from Edric and Zeke, souvenirs of their childhood games of strength and wit and bravery that took them out to the woods unsupervised, and then from their clashes on the training field.

"Since we're all here," Andreas said, "I propose we set up a friendly little wager."

"Oh, here we go." Zeke shook his head, but his eyes told Edric he was eager for it. He was always up for whatever game Andreas taunted them into. The wraith had always been the one to challenge them to something dangerous and forbidden. He was instrumental in all their secret trips to the Witch Woods to engage in something daring and stupid.

"Go on," Edric said.

"We'll work together to get the girl away from the others, then once we have, we can compete for her hand." Andreas smiled, obviously rather proud of himself for the challenge he came up with.

Edric glanced at Zeke, who shrugged.

A woman spoke from behind them. "Women are not to be bartered or traded off in a contest."

All three men turned on their heels to see the mystery girl, glaring at them, a hand on her beautifully curved hip. Edric was astonished that she was able to sneak over, unheard by any of them. He had enhanced hearing, honed from his years of training and natural skill, but even he hadn't heard a thing. Not one footstep or so much as the rustle of her dress.

She'd moved quickly and silently... which was extremely intriguing. With every passing second, this girl got more interesting.

"How *dare* you consider me as some prize to be fought over and won," she said, her voice clipped with annoyance.

Andreas and Zeke both gaped at her like puppies being scolded. Edric had never seen the two of them speechless before. Especially Zeke. The sorcerer could usually talk his way out of anything, clumsily, but Edric had seen it work a dozen times or more over the years.

Up close, the young woman was even more breathtaking. Her blue eyes flashed like the hottest part of a flame and her delicate jaw line actually clenched. It sent another pleasant shiver down his back. Anger radiated off her, and he had to tamp down the urge to grin in awe at her fierceness.

He'd never met a woman with so much power,

both physically and internally, emanating from within. Not even the duchess exuded this much authority and strength. His gaze took in the cut of her shoulders and leanness of her arms. From the tone of her muscles, she looked like she'd wielded more than a paintbrush or a knitting needle. He knew of some noble women who learned to fence with a light, thin sword called a rapier which pirates from the open seas off of the kingdom of Ondia were rumored to flourish. Maybe she was such a woman.

All he knew at that exact moment was that she was extraordinary, and no matter what it took, she would be his.

In his mind, the contest had already begun. And the prize was the best he'd ever seen in his lifetime. She was a stunning woman, and he felt drawn to her on a deep level, as if the magic of Ripthorn itself compelled him to pursue her.

CHAPTER FOURTEEN

SOPHIA

*A*nnoyed, with her hands on her hips, Sophia surveyed the three men standing before her. As best she could tell, the other part of her soul resided in one of them. It disappointed her, though, that her soul would seek out someone who would think of wooing women as a sport, like these three. She expected better of Edric and Andreas. She thought them to be men of honor. She couldn't have been wrong about them, surely.

Since she'd never seen the third man before, she didn't have a bead on him, but there was something familiar about him. He was certainly attractive, with short sandy blond hair and pleasant, green eyes. There was a playfulness to him she liked, especially in the way he looked at her, like they already shared a secret.

"We meant no disrespect, my lady." The third man

gave her a little bow. "I'm Ezekiel Wickham. A sorcerer of Nighthelm."

She eyed him curiously, taking in his tall, lean frame and sharp manner of dress. A sorcerer. She'd never met one up close and personal. She never thought a sorcerer would be so alluring. He was definitely not like the dodgy, old man she'd seen lighting lamps inside a wealthy estate home. She couldn't see this man working for any stuffy old noble family.

The other two snapped to attention, most likely urged by her interest in Ezekiel, and introduced themselves. She had to press her lips shut, as she couldn't let them know she already knew who they both were.

Edric gave a sharp nod. "I'm Commander Edric Axton of the castle guard."

"And I'm Andreas Hylt, the greatest wraith shifter to ever live." He smiled, heavily putting on the charm.

The other two rolled their eyes at their companion's boast. Sophia nearly did as well, but she held back because he wasn't necessarily wrong. She'd seen him fight. He was fierce and strong and brave.

"May we have your name," Ezekiel said.

"I'm Sophia..." She hesitated for a moment, wondering if she was truly going to go through with her charade. "Oxford."

"A relation to Lord Oxford?" Edric asked.

Sophia nodded. "Yes, he's my uncle."

He smiled. "I never thought Lord Oxford would have such beautiful relations."

"Well, sometimes genetics can be surprising," she said.

All three men chuckled.

"So true, Sophia," Ezekiel said. "Take our friend Andreas here. You'd never know he was made of shadow and smoke."

Andreas scowled. "I'd be careful Zeke, if you don't wish to be turned into smoke by my blade."

"This is not the place to be talking about swords and such. Not in front of such a lady," Edric said.

"Oh, I don't mind. I know my way around a blade."

All three men gaped at her.

"You do?" Andreas asked.

Whoops. "Yes, I uh, have brothers who are both trained. One time, they let me hold a sword." *Gag. If only they knew I could spar with all of them like a warrior. I could give them all a run for their coins.*

Well, maybe not the sorcerer, as she hadn't seen him fight. But she imagined he could wield magic like no one else. Her gaze took in his hands and fingers, and she had a sudden image of those hands on her. Her body flooded with warmth. She really hoped her cheeks weren't flushed.

"Were they trained here?" Edric asked, interrupting Sophia's rather wanton thoughts. "I've not heard of any soldiers named Oxford."

"Oh no, we're from..." *Think girl, think. Remember the books you've read.* "Rheland. My brothers trained in the army there."

Ezekiel perked up. "Rheland is a charming city. I've traveled there extensively, as well as Ondia, and Verheim. You must know the Templetons."

She stared wide-eyed at Ezekiel unsure of what to say. She didn't know anyone named Templeton, and she sure as shit couldn't make something up that would remotely be truthful. He would know instantly that she was lying, then her whole charade would fall apart. Instead, Sophia turned to Andreas. "Are you going to ask me to dance?"

His eyes widened in surprise, but he quickly recovered and offered his hand. "Of course. It would be my pleasure."

The moment she placed her hand in his, a little jolt of electricity zipped through her. He flinched a little, and she wondered if he'd felt the same thing. Sophia let him lead her out to the dance floor where several couples already waltzed. He spun her around, slid his hand down to the small of her back and glided her around the floor like an expert.

She'd never danced with anyone before. She'd studied the steps; Grindel had made sure to teach her proper etiquette although she suspected he'd never thought she would ever be in a need to use it. She knew what hand went where, and when to step to the right or to the left. It was all kinds of different with an actual partner; an attractive male partner, especially one as tall as Andreas.

He towered over her by almost a foot, but as he moved her around the dance floor, he made her feel just as tall. Just as imposing. Others on the floor moved out of their way, until it was like they were the only two dancing.

When the music ended, Andreas walked her back to where Edric and Ezekiel stood waiting. Her head swam with musical notes and the floaty feeling of the dance. She didn't realize something like that could feel so good. She wanted to do it again.

And she did.

This time with Edric.

He was almost as tall as Andreas, but most definitely wider. He held her close as they waltzed, and she felt protected and safe in his arms. Her body thrummed with energy at his nearness. It was as if nothing could touch her on the dance floor. Even if a thousand enemies came after her, she knew they would never be able to get to her, to hurt her. Edric would protect her. It was a strange thing to feel all that during one spin around the floor.

Her next dance was with Ezekiel. He spun her around in circles, making her dizzy with joy. They laughed together, as they danced across the floor. At one point, they were going in the opposite direction as the rest of the couples, but Sophia didn't care. She was having too much fun. By the time the music ended and they came back to the others, she was breathing hard and her heart felt lighter. Her problems didn't seem as daunting as before.

"Thank you for the dance," she said.

Ezekiel bowed deeply. "My pleasure, my lady."

"I'm not a lady, but I appreciate the gesture."

Edric handed her a goblet of mead. She'd mentioned in passing that she preferred mead to wine, but was surprised he'd gotten it for her.

Andreas offered her a plate of her favorite pastries. He must've noticed the ones she'd been eating before when she'd been talking earlier with Claudine.

Their attentiveness was almost too much, but she appreciated the fact that they kept away all the other suitors, including Winston, who stood nearby, glaring over the rim of his wine cup. Other glares were aimed her way as well. By the other young women in the room. They were obviously displeased with her monopoly of the most attractive men at the gala. She had to tamp down the urge to gloat openly especially when she spied the big-nosed girl and the girl with the dark hair glowering in the corner.

As she drank and ate and laughed, Sophia relaxed around the three men. Each regaled her with stories about aspects of their lives, trying to outdo one another. They all boasted of the skills they each possessed, and she wished she could do the same. But alas, she was not Sophia, trained warrior, protector of Nighthelm, she was Sophia Oxford, sought after debutante in a tight dress and uncomfortable shoes. She wondered if anyone would notice if she took hers off and paraded around barefoot.

To her surprise, the duchess appeared next to their group, and interrupted Ezekiel in the middle of his telling about a spell gone bad. Each of the men, bowed a little in respect to the duchess.

"Good evening Lady Tryst," Edric said.

"Evening, Commander Axton," she responded, and then looked at Andreas and Ezekiel. "Andreas, Ezekiel."

"Duchess," both Andreas and Ezekiel said.

Up close, the duchess was stunning. Sophia didn't know her age, but her pale skin was flawless. There was not one imperfection visible. The blue of her eyes was like the ice that sometimes froze on Ghost Light pond in winter. Cold, yet beautiful. Dangerous when prodded too hard.

"I make a point to know all my subjects individually," the duchess smiled at Sophia, "but I have not had the privilege to meet you, my dear."

"I'm Sophia Oxford."

The duchess narrowed her icy blue eyes. "Lord Oxford never said he had such a beautiful niece."

Despite the compliment, Sophia wasn't impressed

with the duchess. She dressed royally with jewels on her ears, and on her fingers, with a large, ruby pendant hanging from a silver chain around her throat, but she was no queen, however much she acted like one.

"I was under the impression, Lady Tryst, that you are the steward of the throne, a ward of the castle, and not its ruler, and therefore have no subjects." Sophia knew she shouldn't say such things, but sometimes her mouth had a mind of its own. Grindel often reminded her of that.

The men were silent; Edric looked like he might react, though both Andreas and Ezekiel smirked with approval behind the duchess's back.

Sophia expected a barbed retort, maybe even a call for the guards to remove her, but instead the duchess nodded her head regally. "I will bid you a good night. Enjoy the rest of the gala."

The duchess moved away from them, addressing others in the ballroom, with a smile and a tilt of her head, seemingly unaffected by what Sophia had uttered.

All three men stared at Sophia.

"Who the heck are you?" Ezekiel laughed. "I have never seen anyone speak to the duchess that way. I'm in awe."

In her periphery, Sophia spotted Grindel speaking with another professor, and she strategically stepped in front of Andreas to stay hidden. If he found her here, Grindel would definitely find some way to make her life even more miserable than it was. It was time to wrap this evening up and return to the woods.

She looked around and saw a set of doors leading out to the garden. It was her escape route.

"I need some air," she said as she started for the doors. She looked over her shoulder at the three men. "Aren't you coming?"

They looked at each other, and then Edric said, "You're quite bossy even for a lady of nobility."

Obviously, none of them ever had a woman tell them what to do. She grinned. *This is going to be fun.*

"I usually get what I want," she said.

Andreas inclined his head, a little flash of humor in his dark eyes. "And what does the lady want?"

She made a point to look at each of them. "You have to follow me to the garden, to find out."

Ezekiel was the first one to eagerly step forward. He wriggled his eyebrows at Andreas and Edric. The other two quickly followed suit, until they were all outside in the garden, where it was quieter and more private.

Once they had all come together, she pointedly asked, "Were you serious about your little wager?"

Edric shook his head. "Of course not. We were only joking."

"As men tend to do around each other," Andreas added.

Ezekiel slapped Andreas on the back. "Exactly, right."

The wraith turned and glared at the sorcerer. It was obvious these men were not the best of friends. They were more like combatants.

Sophia was certain her soul was in one of these men, likely in the two she'd been drawn to for so much of her life. She decided to hold a little contest of her own in an attempt to figure out which of them had her soul. And have some fun while she was at it.

"That's too bad, as I was hoping for a challenge myself."

The three men glanced at one another, and then Edric stepped forward. "What do you propose, my lady?"

"I will refuse all other suitors and allow only the three of you to court me. From the three of you, I will pick one winner. The one who can best sway my heart."

They all perked up, puffing out chests and adjusting confident stances. It was meant to buy her time, and she felt a little bad about pitting them against each other, but by the looks on their faces, they clearly liked the contest. All eager for it, actually. She imagined there was a history of rivalry between them all since birth, according to the various stories they'd told her, which she found fascinating.

"Do you agree?" she asked.

"Agreed," they all said one by one.

"There are rules, of course," she said.

"Name them," Andreas responded, with a confident lift of his chin.

"I will spend one day with each of you, but only after two o'clock each day."

"Why two o'clock?" Ezekiel asked. "Doesn't give us much time to woo you properly."

She couldn't tell them it was because that was when her training with Grindel ended every day. She understood that they wanted to know why, but she needed to keep her cards close and play coy. Besides, as far as she could tell, men loved a woman who played coy. It was all part of the game.

"My reasons are my own. A woman needs her secrets."

"This is true," Ezekiel said, "Makes it more tantalizing to discover those secrets." His playful grin made her belly tighten a little.

"I'll meet with Ezekiel first."

His grin broadened and he looked at the other two men tauntingly.

"Then with Edric, and then Andreas."

Frowning, Edric stepped toward her. "Surely, you wish to start with the best first."

"Are you saying you're a better man than I, Edric?" Ezekiel got in his face. "Do you wish to test that theory?" He flexed his fingers, and his skin started to glow.

Edric's hand went to his waist where his sword would normally be fastened.

As fascinating as it would be to watch the sorcerer and the commander battle for her hand, Sophia didn't have time for their childish posturing.

"Stop," she said, then she looked at Edric. "I'll make you go last if you don't stand down."

He did, and took a step away from Ezekiel. Although Andreas didn't appear too happy to be going last, he held his tongue, which she was grateful for. She didn't have time right now to prevent them from killing each other.

On the other hand, Ezekiel was grinning ear to ear, obviously reveling in the other two men's discomfort at being put in their place. "You've made a wise decision, Sophia."

Edric gave him a lethal stare. "I'd quit while I was ahead, Zeke."

Ezekiel's grin faded, but only a little.

She shook her head, questioning her decision to conduct this contest. Maybe it was not worth the hassle. But as she looked into each of their faces, she saw something in each of them that she desired.

"I'll meet each of you here in the garden at two each day. On Wednesdays, I will take time to reflect and be alone."

"But Sophia," Andreas protested, "would it not be wiser to spend the day off with your current favorite.

Give us more time and opportunity to win your favor."

The other two nodded in agreement.

"I'm the prize, am I not?" She looked at each of them, and they nodded. "Then I'm the one making the rules. If you don't like the rules, you can easily be dismissed from the contest."

Ezekiel pressed his lips together, stopping him from sounding another protest.

Oh, they were adorable looking so admonished and humble in front of her. She could barely contain herself. To have three powerful yet vastly different young men at her fingertips. It was more than she could've ever hoped for. She hoped she could pull the ruse off in time. The oracles' words filled her head again.

In two harvest moons...

As the men bickered among themselves, each trying to convince the other that they were more worthy of her attention, Sophia silently and quickly dissolved into the shadows. When they looked up and noticed that she had disappeared, she smirked from the nearby darkness at the astonished looks upon their handsome faces. Perhaps she would have fun with this whole dating thing after all.

CHAPTER FIFTEEN

SOPHIA

Sophia was actually a bit nervous for her first date. She'd faced grimms and minotaurs, pixies and even the fae, so it was stupid to be so nervous to face one simple man. Despite all that, butterflies had definitely settled in her belly. She took a steadying breath and focused on finding the missing piece of her soul. And to do that, she had to go on the date.

After training, she plucked herself up from the ground and then headed for the meeting point. She made a stop first at the cabin, so she could wash. She would have to change later though, as she couldn't ride Haris and climb through a drainage tunnel in a dress. If she showed up in her usual manner of dress—frayed leather pants, suede jerkin over a not so white shirt—Ezekiel would certainly have a ton of questions she didn't need or want to answer. Once she was through her secret tunnel under the wall, she put on one of the simple yet elegant frocks she'd stolen from the Oxford estate and then stashed her other clothes in a bag, hiding them just inside the tunnel.

When she arrived at the garden, Ezekiel was already there, looking dashing and handsome in his dark green, doublet embroidered vest, and pressed, black trousers. He dressed like nobility, and she wondered if he was from an aristocratic family. He had strong magic, a must in order to be a sorcerer, so she assumed he must be of noble birth. To her surprise, her body ached like it had the night before, though not as powerful, which was odd as she was convinced either Andreas or Edric held a piece of her soul since she'd always been drawn to them over the years. Not Ezekiel. It seemed strange for her body to react this way. Maybe it was just good, ole fashioned attraction and desire. The sorcerer was definitely alluring. Although she had nothing to compare it to, as she was still a maiden.

The moment she stepped onto the cobblestone path, he turned toward her and grinned. That made the ache in her body quicken just a bit more. He had a devastating smile.

He inclined his head. "Good day, my lady."

She nodded. "It is a good day, but you can stop with the 'my lady.' I'm just Sophia."

"All right, Sophia, what would you like to do for our date?" He held out his arm for her to slip a hand through the crook of his elbow.

She gave him a wry smile. "Impress me."

His eyebrows lifted, and then he chuckled. "Challenge accepted."

He led her through the city pointing out various shops, vendors, and establishments that he liked to visit. There was the tailor where he got all his clothes made, and he offered to have any type of dress she wanted made for her. He showed her the inn where he said the best food and brandy was served. Sophia didn't know what brandy was, but she didn't want to appear foolish and ask in case it was something well known to ladies of high society. Then he stopped at a small vendor on Market Street and bought her two honey cakes, much to her delight. He must've noticed she had a sweet tooth by all the pastries she'd eaten at the ball. She was sure it was just a coincidence that he'd chosen honey cakes, which were her absolute favorite. Surely, he couldn't have known that about her.

Eventually, they walked through market square and past all the shops to a lesser attended part of the city, to a secret, locked gate in the wall. To unlock it, Ezekiel held out his hands, spoke quiet words, and magic glowed along his skin. Within seconds the lock disengaged, and the gate swung open. She had to tamp down the urge to ask him to teach her that spell. He couldn't know she possessed magic.

She gaped at him. "Impressive."

"I aim to please." He gestured to the open passage. "Shall we?"

Sophia went through, Ezekiel behind her, and then they were out of the high city walls and walking lazily toward the Witch Woods on the king's road that ran right through the trees, neatly splitting the woods in half. She was a bit hesitant, yet, curious about what he was up to.

He quirked an eyebrow, obviously mistaking her curiosity for fear. "Are you afraid of the forest?"

"Not at all. If anything I'm astonished that you aren't afraid." She walked a little ahead of him, eager to be back among familiar territory.

He had to take longer strides to catch up to her, and then they were side by side strolling through the picturesque pathway through the trees. As they walked, Ezekiel pointed out some interesting flora and fauna of the area, like monkshood and hemlock, both she'd used for herbal medicines. When he pointed to a snapping turtle plant, she had to press her lips together to stop from telling him about the time she nearly lost a finger to the carnivorous plant while saving a sprite from imminent death.

"You seem very familiar with the woods. I can't imagine you get all that from books," she asked.

Ezekiel ran his hand over the fuzzy leaves of a velvet bush. "I come out here as often as I can. There's always been something here that I've been drawn to. Ever since I was a child, I've been sneaking out of the city to walk through the woods. I'm surprised Howard survived my childhood with all my exploits."

She was surprised at his confession. The forest was large, certainly, but Sophia thought for sure she would've run across this handsome, young man in her woods at some point. He was definitely not someone she would've overlooked.

"Who's Howard? Your brother?" she asked.

He shook his head. "My butler. I have no siblings."

His eyes turned sad, and a lump formed in her throat. She hadn't meant to make him melancholy. She squeezed his arm gently to soothe him.

He gave her a soft smile. "Tell me more about you, Sophia. You seem quite at home here in the woods. Most women would be clutching skin off my arm by now," he said.

"I have a feeling that was your plan." She feigned annoyance then quickly added a smile.

He gave her a wicked sly look that made her belly clench. "Maybe."

She chuckled. "I am not most women."

"That's obvious." He touched her hand, and a soft buzz of pleasure vibrated over her skin.

"Do you bring all the ladies you're courting out to the dark and dangerous woods?" she asked.

He rubbed his thumb over her knuckles. "No, I don't bring anyone out here, and for the record, I'm not courting any other ladies."

Coyly, she pulled away and stepped onto a shale rock bed along the edge of the stream. "I love it here as well. My… tutor has made sure I know as much about thc woods as I can possibly know."

"He sounds like a task master."

"Oh he is, most definitely. Sometimes he'll push me so hard that I can't hold my arms up any longer. Sometimes, I'll be sore for days." Off his confused look, she added, "From carrying so many books of course."

Feeling light and free, Sophia spun on her heel, then jumped off the rocks, landing silently on the ground. She remembered herself too late. Without even speaking, she was giving too much of herself away.

Ezekiel watched her with an amused arch of his eyebrow.

"My tutor demanded I had extensive dance lessons as well," she said in way of an explanation of her stealth in the forest. "He insisted I have a graceful and sturdy body as well as a sharp mind."

He gave her a look that told her he appreciated the way she moved and how her dress fit snug across her breasts and hips. "He definitely succeeded in that regard."

She blushed.

He grabbed her hand. "I want to show you something." He pulled her off the path and to a dark stretch of trees. "Watch."

He rubbed the palms of his hands together, and then slowly pulled them apart. A soft blue glow developed between them, enveloping his hands. When he held them up, a gust of wind rushed past. Instantly, thousands of glowing lights spiraled into the air. They were pixies spinning about, leaving trails of glowing dust in their wake. All the colors of a rainbow coiled into the air above Sophia's head.

She held onto Ezekiel's arm and watched the spectacle in awe. She'd never seen anything more beautiful in her life. Not even a glowing hive of fairies could compete. And he'd created it for her.

"This place is so beautiful and shouldn't be feared," he said, then locked eyes with her.

She thought he spoke about her, not just the woods. He could truly see her, and she liked being seen.

Sophia reached up and placed her hand to his cheek. She was drawn to him. As her fingers touched his skin, warmth spread through her, her body brimming with crackling energy that snaked through her very core.

He placed his hand on top of hers, his fingers strong and rough, and he leaned into her. Gently, softly, he brushed his lips against hers. The kiss was feathery light, and she barely felt it on her mouth.

But she felt it everywhere else in her body. Her thighs warmed. Her back arched, her entire essence aching to be closer to him, every ounce of her needing *more.*

He pulled back and then tucked a stray hair of hers back behind her ear. "I have so much more to show you."

She smiled, wrapped a hand around his arm, and let him lead her back through the woods to the city. She was surprised by her reaction to him. She thought dating Ezekiel would be a bit of fun mixed in with her real mission to find the piece of her soul. But the more her body responded to his touches, to his looks, she realized that the game just got way more complicated.

CHAPTER SIXTEEN

EZEKIEL

*L*ater that night, Ezekiel fell back onto his big four-poster bed, shirtless and happy. He had a wonderful day and evening with Sophia. He'd originally joined in on the little wager simply because he liked her feisty personality and because he wanted to irk Andreas and Edric. He would jump on any opportunity to annoy those two.

But she'd surprised him. Impressed him. Enchanted him, even.

When he'd arrived home at the estate, his butler Howard, had even commented on Ezekiel's uncharacteristic smile on his face, and just the fact that he came home and not to the castle to work on one of his spells said something.

From the moment Ezekiel had first touched her, something shifted inside him, and he couldn't get her out of his mind. Where spells and desires to leave Nighthelm normally took residence in his head, now there were images of Sophia. He could still taste her on his lips when he licked them.

Although the kiss had been soft and quick, it had jolted him. He'd kissed other young women over the years—several in fact—but it had never felt like *that*. Like the room wouldn't stop spinning. He wasn't sure he wanted it to.

He stared up at the high, painted ceiling of his bedroom, a goofy grin on his face. He couldn't stop smiling as he thought of the way she'd looked at him when he'd performed magic. Like *he* was the most magical thing she'd ever seen.

After they had returned to the city, Ezekiel took Sophia to another of his favorite places—the Metropolis, which was a museum holding every piece of lore on Nighthelm and the surrounding kingdoms. Over the years, he'd spent a good chunk of his life poring over books about the royal family and all the noble families. His family, Wickham, even had a volume about their lineage. On nights he couldn't sleep at home, that was where he went. It helped him battle the nightmares. Helped keep the images of his family's massacre at bay.

Sophia had seemed honestly interested in everything inside the museum. She'd asked a lot of questions and stayed riveted when he'd answered. Not once did he see boredom in her beautiful eyes. Other women he'd brought to the Metropolis would often start to ask when they could leave within fifteen minutes of getting there. But not Sophia. They had stayed in the building, wandering from floor to floor, looking at artifacts and art, for over an hour.

He'd never met another person who was as thirsty for knowledge as Sophia seemed to be. She almost rivaled him for needing to know more about everything. Every question she asked just enamored him more and more. When she questioned him about Nighthelm history and the oracles and lighting up when he was able to answer a few of them— though, not all, as some of her questions were obscure even for him—he was sure he'd found his intellectual equal. He could imagine many days and nights—oh yes, plenty of long lovely nights—sharing everything he knew.

Ezekiel got off his bed and paced the room. He had too much energy swirling around inside to sleep. He wished their date hadn't ended. He'd asked her if he could see her safely home, but she'd refused, claiming she was perfectly capable of walking alone. He didn't doubt her. Anyone would be a fool to mess with her. She could easily take a man down with just a look from her intense, blue eyes. And those lips... all night, he hadn't been able to stop watching them as she spoke. He couldn't stop thinking about how he wanted to kiss them again, to feel them on his face, his neck. Anywhere. *Everywhere.*

He rubbed his hands over his face. Now, he definitely wouldn't be able to sleep. He changed into more relaxed clothing, something he could move around in easily, and then left his room. He thundered down the stairs and ran into Howard checking on the security of the house before retiring to his own room for the evening.

"Are you heading out again, sir?" Howard asked, his tone even and surprised, as he was no doubt used to Ezekiel's constant comings and goings.

"Yes, I'm going for a run." He spoke without looking at his servant. Howard shifted in his sight, almost like he was jolted. Ezekiel looked at him then.

Howard's eyebrow came up. "A *run*, sir? You've never gone *running* before in your life. Except for that time that spitting hornet chased you across the estate grounds when you were ten."

He shrugged. "Well, then, I guess this is my first day of running."

"As you say, sir." Howard stared at him in baffled confusion, but true to form, didn't add further comment.

Ezekiel left the estate and, once out on the street, started to jog. Over the years he'd seen Edric and Andreas along with other soldiers run through an obstacle course in the warrior commons, and the grim looks of determination on their faces made it look exhilarating. The physical movement, the sheer focus it required, running seemed like a good way to clear the mind.

And that was what he needed right now.

Soon, he'd run through his neighborhood, the market square, and into the central part of the city. He didn't really have a destination in mind, but it didn't surprise him when he turned the corner and ended up in front of the Metropolis again. He shook his head at himself. It was obviously going to be a lot harder to shake Sophia from his mind.

He entered the building with a special key that only three other people in the whole city possessed. When he stepped into the dark, opulent lobby, he paused. The scent of wildflowers drifted to his nose. It was how Sophia had smelled. All earthy and untamed. Frowning, he scanned the area, the feeling of being watched unnerving him.

There should have been no one else in the building, no one lurking in the shadows. He shook his head again. He tensed, wondering if he should call for a guard, and it took him a moment to realize this was all in his head.

There was no one else here—he had simply fallen head over heels for a girl he barely knew. Now he was smelling her long after she was gone, aching for her, thinking of her when he should be asleep.

After only one date, Sophia had firmly settled into his psyche. And he had a feeling it was a permanent arrangement.

Thoughts of just playing along with the contest for a bit of fun vanished. After today, he actually wanted to win their little wager. Not to dominate his lifelong rivals, but because the prize was a wonderful one, indeed, and one most certainly worth fighting for.

~

EDRIC

*I*nside his room within the castle, Edric sat at his small, wooden desk and penned a letter to Sophia's uncle, Lord Oxford. With every dip of his quill into the ink, he felt his confidence rising. He was determined to set himself apart from the other two contestants. He was sure neither Andreas nor Zeke would ever think to do the same.

Andreas would only be thinking about how to physically impress Sophia. His size was imposing, even to Edric. Although Edric had more muscle, Andreas was taller, leaner, and if he was being brutally honest with himself, possibly even stronger. It was his wraith genes that set him apart. And Edric knew Andreas would use that to his advantage.

Zeke, on the other hand, would use his wit and his

magic to impress Sophia. He wasn't a warrior like Edric and Andreas were, but the sorcerer could definitely fight. He had firsthand knowledge of that fact. But Edric would use his other abilities to get a foot ahead in the contest.

For a brief moment, Edric thought about what Zeke had planned for the first date he had with Sophia. He would do something to show off, that was for sure. Probably some magic trick with lots of flash and show.

Edric didn't possess casting magic, his magic involved other abilities, like his heightened senses and his ability to heal, so he planned on getting more information on Sophia. Her likes, her dislikes, anything he could ascertain to get an advantage. He would be fully prepared to woe her properly.

Andreas would likely call him a cheater. But Edric was a commander. He was well versed in war tactics. He knew when to press forward and when to retreat. He knew how to manipulate a playing field and use it to dominate his opponents. He didn't know how to surrender.

And this was a battle with the greatest prize of them all. Sophia.

He had no doubt in his mind that she was a woman worth fighting for. Just from the few hours he had been around her at the ball, he knew she had strength of character and a boldness that called to him in many ways. She was obviously a woman who got her way, and pressed her advantage, and he respected that.

It didn't hurt that she was beautiful. She actually had beauty that transcended physical traits. A light shone from inside her. He'd seen it the moment he'd seen from across the room. In fact, there had been something about her that drew him into that room, and across the floor. It was not a sensation he was used to experiencing.

He'd courted other women. Jasmine, who had been on his arm that night, was one of those women. He'd taken her out a few times and had enjoyed her company for the most part. Her father was a powerful man, a senator in the courts of law, and Edric had thought it would be a good match, an advantageous one as well. But the moment his gaze landed on Sophia's, Jasmine, and every woman he'd ever courted, kissed, talked to, faded from existence. Sophia was who he wanted. No one else could ever compare to her.

He sealed the letter, using melted wax and his family crest stamp, fully willing to use a few of the favors he's amassed over the years to win this contest. It would take some time, but Edric had friends in high places, and he could get even the elusive Lord Oxford to speak with him... eventually.

CHAPTER SEVENTEEN

SOPHIA

The training was running late, and Sophia impatiently watched the sun tick across the sky as Grindel forced her to stand on a board precariously balanced over a wine barrel as he shot arrows at her. She deflected each of them with her magic, almost reflexively.

Another arrow came whizzing toward her head. He was obviously getting impatient with her, and she pushed the arrow away with a small blast of her magic from her hands. Her control was getting to the point where she didn't even need to direct it with her hands, her intention seemed enough for her magic to obey. She hoped that meant she was healing more of her broken soul. She did feel stronger since meeting the three men. The piece of her soul definitely called to her, she just didn't know from which of the men yet.

Finally, after another slew of arrows were batted away, Grindel sighed. "If you're not going to focus, you might as well go off and do whatever is so important that you aren't paying attention to your training."

Relieved she jumped off the board and was about to run off when he fumbled with a small, wrapped package he had tucked in his robe. He shoved it into her hands. "Here. It's for your birthday. Open it later." He cleared his throat, then nodded farewell, and took the path back to the cabin.

She shook her head at his obvious distress with any sign of affection. She unwrapped the scarf the gift was swathed in to reveal a beautiful ornate dagger inside. The intricate gold inlay on the hilt was stunning and wildly expensive. There was ancient writing along the blade, in a lavish style that must've been an enchantment, faintly glowing at her touch. Grindel must have saved his coins for years to afford something like this. Smiling, she slipped it into her belt, undeniably pleased at her teacher's affection for her, whether he'd admit to those feelings or not.

Excited to finally be on her way to her date with Edric, she ran from the training ring deep in Witch Woods to find Haris waiting for her on the outskirts. She jumped on his back, as it would be faster to get to Nighthelm. She was wary, of course, of Grindel following her, but on Haris, not even horses could keep up.

She arrived roughly an hour late. After sneaking in, she found a fountain to quickly wipe down, then changed into her Lady Oxford clothes. Once she arrived at the garden, she was relieved to find Edric still sitting on the edge of the fountain, carving a piece of wood with a knife. As she approached him, he looked up and smiled. "I'm so sorry I'm late. It was impossible to get away," she said.

"I figured you were just trying to test me." He chuckled. "Did I pass your test?"

She gave him a coy look.

He winked at her, and then presented her with the beautiful rose carving. "A beautiful flower for a beautiful woman."

She took the flower between her fingers and said, "Thank you."

As they strolled through the gardens, Edric set his hand on the small of her back, it was a possessive move, and Sophia was surprised she liked it.

"Do you like it here in Nighthelm?" he asked.

She gestured to the scenery. "Oh, yes. It's such a pretty city. I love it most at night, though."

"Really?" His eyes narrowed. "Why?"

She had to watch what she said. She couldn't tell him about sneaking through the shadows in the city, climbing onto roofs and watching people; people whom she protected; people she knew would condemn her if they knew what she was. She couldn't tell Edric how she watched them do mundane things, like have a family dinner, or play a game; things that she'd never done, and would never do. She had to pick her words carefully to protect her true identity.

"Because it's quiet but there is still so much going on that most other people don't see. They're too busy with their lives to fully appreciate what is around them. The flowers, the trees, the buildings. The history of the place."

He smiled. "I completely agree."

The warm buzz of his hand on the small of her back drew her to him. She liked being around Edric. She felt comfortable in his presence.

Through her periphery, Sophia spotted Winston lurking nearby, watching them. It wouldn't have surprised her if he had been following them through the garden. He had that way about him. Jealousy seethed off him like heat waves. When he saw that she'd noticed him, he turned away in disgust and then stormed down another path. She was going to have to watch out for him. She wondered if she should mention his skulking to Edric. They were both elite castle guards—Edric a commander—maybe he could do something about Winston. She'd have to think about whether or not bringing him up was worth the risk.

As Edric escorted her through the grounds, he asked her questions about her interests and her family.

She told him she liked dancing and reading, and had an interest in archery. She left out her love of sword play and hand to hand combat and magic. Answers about her family were even more difficult to answer as she had to trust that Edric didn't know much about her family either.

"My parents weren't involved much in my upbringing. They traveled a lot to other cities on business. I have a good tutor though. He's taught me," *how to fight, how to strike a man down with a sword, how to use a bow and arrow,* "a lot about the realities of life."

Thankfully, after her date with Ezekiel, much later in the night, she snuck into the Metropolis and located a book on the Oxford family. She'd shoved it into her bag, but before she could escape into the night, she spotted Ezekiel entering the building. He'd looked very pleased with himself, and she wondered why he returned to the Metropolis. Was he thinking about her? For a brief moment, she considered staying and watching him, but when he stopped, frowned and looked her way, Sophia decided not to press her luck. It would've been disastrous if he discovered her stealing a book. She wasn't sure she could talk herself out of the situation.

So, she did what any intelligent thief in the night would do, she crept through the shadows and got out of the building before he could find her. She took the book back with her to the cabin where she stashed it under her straw mattress. Grindel would never find it. She'd gone through the latest entries of the tome surrounding "her uncle," Lord Oxford, and found out all she could about his brothers and sisters and their children.

She obviously didn't find a niece named Sophia, but she did find a brother that was estranged who did, in fact, live in Rheland. She'd gotten lucky there. He had two sons and two daughters. One of those daughters was around her age. He and his wife were silk merchants and traveled extensively. So, the lies weren't too far off the mark.

"What about your family?" she asked, best to keep the questions focused on Edric, so she didn't screw up.

"My parents are very supportive of me. My father was a soldier. My grandfather too. So, it was natural that I trained at the academy."

"You're the youngest in Nighthelm history to ever become commander."

He looked surprised but pleased that she knew that. "Has the lady been asking around about me?"

She shrugged, not wanting him to get too full of himself. "Maybe."

He smiled. "I like that."

"What about your mother?" she asked. "What is she like?"

His eyebrows lifted. "My mother is probably fiercer than my father. She keeps everyone in line."

"Like her commander son." Sophia nudged him in the side.

He grinned and it lit up his entire face, and she had to tamp down the urge to sigh at his handsomeness.

"Do you have siblings?" she asked.

"An older sister."

"Is she a soldier too?"

He scoffed. "Absolutely not."

She crossed her arms over her chest. "Why not? You don't think women can be soldiers?"

"No, that's not it at all." He stopped midstride. "I think women would make great and strong soldiers. My sister would not. She's as frail and timid as a mouse. To the chagrin of both my parents."

Sophia put her arm through the crook of his elbow again, satisfied with his answer. "Good. Then we are on the same page."

SOPHIA

Edric led her to the stables near the castle barracks. Other soldiers gave him looks of approval as he urged her down to the last few stalls. A few of the horses whinnied as they passed by them, and Sophia knew from the similarities of Haris's sounds, they were warmly greeting her. She wanted to pet every single one, but didn't want to deny Edric his surprise. Because the look on his face, told her that he was eager to show her something even more magnificent. Inside the last stall, which was larger than the rest, was a great winged horse—a pegasus. Sophia gasped when she saw the magnificent beast. It was powerful and intimidating, absolutely beautiful, not the sort of creature to be tamed.

"They're part of the royal legion," Edric said, puffing out his chest. "Someone has to keep them ridden and strong in the heirs' absence."

While Edric entered the stall, she thought about the heirs and her duty to find them. The oracles had tasked her with this, and she was bound to achieve her quest. Healing her soul was part of that quest, and she would do what she must. Although, spending time with Edric didn't feel at all like hardship. She liked him.

"Did you think you would sweep me off my feet by showing me secrets of the crown that are hidden away from the public eye?"

He patted the pegasus's flank and the beast neighed. "Yes. Is it working?"

"Possibly," she said, as she entered the stall. "I'm definitely not bored."

He laughed. "Well, that's good to hear. I would hate to be boring."

"I suspect, Commander, you could never be boring."

He gave her a sly look that had her belly clenching. Then he grabbed hold of the beast's long white mane and hopped onto its back. The horse snorted in annoyance. He offered Sophia his hand to help her up, but Sophia had been around many wild animals before. She studied their behaviors and how to gauge their thoughts. She first approached the pegasus in the front then bowed in respect. Its movements stilled as if surprised by the gesture. Then it bowed in return.

She patted its face, and it nickered to her playfully and nuzzled her hand.

"How did you know to do that?" Edric asked.

The horse's ears pinned back against its head, obviously not that fond of her date.

Sophia patted its face again and chuckled. "I like to read about the creatures of Nighthelm. I know quite a lot about them all."

Edric offered his hand again, and this time she took it, letting him pull her up to sit in front of him on the pegasus's back. He clicked to it, then they were out of the stable and running across the pasture. After two flaps of its giant, white wings, they were airborne.

Sophia laughed as the beast soared high over the city, higher than she imagined possible. Edric grinned at her obvious joy, pressing his hands tighter around her waist.

"I wanted to share what I love with you." He gestured to the grand city spread beneath them. "Nighthelm. My city."

"It's extraordinary from up here." She lifted her face to the wind as they soared over the city center.

"I love everything about this place. The buildings, the history, the people. It's my purpose to protect it and why I became a soldier. To do my duty. To serve my kingdom," he said.

Sophia was overwhelmed with how stunning everything looked from up above. Her belly did a little flip when the pegasus dove. But it wasn't just the flying that made her body quiver, it was Edric's hands around her, holding her in place, keeping her safe. She moved her hand to cover his at her belly, and felt his warm skin beneath hers. She felt impossibly safe in his arms, grateful for his secure touch. Her body stirred again, as if she'd found a piece of herself in him.

But from the riddle, she assumed there would only be one piece of her soul missing, one piece to find. She couldn't choose both Ezekiel and Edric. Could she?

CHAPTER EIGHTEEN

ANDREAS

On the day of his date with Sophia, Andreas waited for her from the shadows of the surrounding trees in the garden. His gaze stayed firmly on the fountain where they were supposed to meet. His mind raced at the woman who had so quickly captured his thoughts. He was a hopeless romantic at heart, though he hid it well. His wraith brothers would razz him to no end if they knew.

They could be relentless. The one time he mentioned courting a woman, a wraith daughter of one of the blacksmiths, his brothers had pestered him about it every day for months. Snide comments turned into rude ones, until eventually Andreas stopped courting the girl and he had to endure her father's wrath for having rejected the girl. After that, he stopped telling his brothers about women he courted, and then he stopped courting altogether. The whole idea seemed to be more trouble than it was worth.

He was raised a warrior and assumed he would never marry, especially after seeing so many of his brothers in arms die in battle, their widows grieving for years as was the wraith way. Having a wife and family seemed more like a weakness than a benefit, and really he never saw the point.

But Sophia awoke something inside him that made the idea less foreign.

When she arrived, he waited in the shadows, wanting to see what she would do. She sat on the edge of the fountain and looked a little disappointed that he wasn't there yet, and to his surprise, that thought made him happy. To think a woman like her—so beautiful, so fascinating—could miss him, would want to spend time in his company.

He shook his head to make the thought disappear so that he didn't get his hopes up at actually winning the bet and this woman. He went to step out of the shadows but her eyes met his the second he moved. It was as if she could feel him somehow, like she'd known he was there waiting and watching from the shadows. He felt an odd sense of familiarity about her that he couldn't place.

"Sorry, I'm late," he said.

She studied him like she knew he wasn't at all late but wasn't about to embarrass him. "I'm sure I can overlook that."

He smiled and tipped his head. As he sat beside her, Andreas took her all in. From the top of her beautiful blond head to the tips of her brown leather shoes. She was extraordinary. In his mind, he created poetry about the depths of her blue eyes, deep enough he could swim in them; the way her dress, a simple shift, molded to her beautiful form, and made him want to settle his hand at her hips; the way her smile, when bestowed on him, made every muscle in his body clench. But he didn't say these things. His heart just stirred them around.

Sophia glanced up at the sky. "It's a beautiful day."

His gaze never left her face. "It is indeed."

She pressed her lips together, and he thought she was fighting a blush in her cheeks. At least he hoped she was.

"I love the gardens in the city," she said.

"There are many special places in Nighthelm," he said.

"I've seen most of them. I love the busy market streets and the quiet lanes near the large estates."

"I'll take you somewhere you've never been." He stood and offered his arm.

She took it. "Where?"

"The wraith district."

He watched her face, expecting to see fear there. He needed to know now if what he was would be a deal breaker for her, as it was for so many before. The last non-wraith woman he dated had run away screaming after he'd shown her his wraith form. That had been over two years ago. He never dared show anyone again. He didn't want to experience that kind of heartbreak another time. But there was only excitement blooming in Sophia's cheeks and eyes. Yet again, she boggled him. Who was this woman with no fear?

Together they strolled through the streets, the road darkening despite the broad daylight and no clouds overhead. The looming shadow of his kind seeped around them. This was the Shade, where only the bravest of men—and women evident by the woman at his side—dared venture.

Sophia appeared unfazed by the obscuring light. In fact, she still looked excited to explore his part of the city. His guard, which he always kept up, came down a little as this fierce, petite woman surveyed the buildings and people around them with curiosity and glee. Her face actually lit up the moment they became completely entrenched in the district, despite its narrow streets and cramped living quarters. The Shade was exactly the opposite of the spacious, wealthy district she was accustomed to. But she didn't seem to mind one bit. She almost seemed more at ease here among the darkness and the danger.

She gestured to one of the oldest buildings—a gothic place of worship with black stone and red frosted glass. A lot of the wraiths worshipped Britus, the God of War, and Sona, the Goddess of the Underworld. Andreas didn't have time for gods. They asked too much of their worshippers. His mother was a devout woman, but all she did was pray.

"Is that a church? I've never seen a building like it. It's beautiful." She reached out to the touch the smooth black stone.

"It is over a hundred years old. Many of my kind go there to worship."

"But not you?"

He shook his head. "No, not me."

Some of his brothers in arms saw Sophia with him and raised their eyebrows with judgment that he would court a non-wraith, and even bring her here. But he gave them stern glares to back off, which they adhered. As with much of the wraith culture, entire arguments were had without a word. Just with a look or a gesture. They had body language down to a science. And his look said, stay far, far away from his woman.

My woman. Was that how he was already feeling about her? Had he already staked a claim?

He led her to a small, wraith-only garden area surrounded by a six-foot stone wall. It was a safe space for them to train and shift without the scrutiny of outsiders. Unlike the gardens in other parts of the city, where there were cobblestone paths meandering around little manicured plots of pretty flowers and a charming bubbling fountain, this garden was wild and untamed. Flowers grew with abandon, mixed with the climbing weeds and moss that carpeted the walls. There weren't any cute pathways or a pretty siren spouting water.

"Thank you for trusting me enough to bring me here. I'm honored that you would share this with me." She gaped around, obviously realizing how special this place was to him, to his people.

"I've never shared this with anyone before." He brushed his fingers along her jaw, tempted to kiss her right there and then. Her head lifted, her lips parting in anticipation. But he resisted. There was something he wanted her to see before she invested any more of her time in him. And he in her.

He dropped his hand and took a step away from her. "I want to shift. I want to show you what I truly am, and what it means to be wraith."

He worried over this part, but he might as well get it over with. Save them both some time and energy. He was sure she'd be terrified of him, and that he'd be able to let her go without becoming too emotionally invested… though the thought alone tore through him like a blunt dagger.

Preparing himself, he took in a deep breath, letting the cold shadow inside consume him. The shift was neither pleasant nor painful. It just was. As he loomed over her more and more, his form growing in size and shape, he waited for her to recoil in disgust. Then that would be that.

CHAPTER NINETEEN

SOPHIA

*E*nchanted, Sophia couldn't stop gaping at Andreas as he floated in front of her, his cloven feet hovering just inches from the ground. His wraith form was stunning—a creature of power and fear, of death and strength, of wisp and shadow. He was beautiful in a terrifying way, like rolling, black, storm clouds after a drought.

She reached for him, running her fingers along the feathery shadows of his arm. The tips of her fingers tingled from the icy chill of his wraith form. Fast as a blink, he was right in front of her face. It was like looking death in the glowing red eyes, and yet, she knew it was Andreas looking back at her. He had no reason to hurt her. While she'd seen he and his brothers fight in the forest, and knew this terrible power that wraiths held, she also knew in her heart

Andreas would never harm her. At least, not as long as he believed her to be Sophia Oxford.

Lost to his deadly beauty, Sophia leaned into his swirling black form, focused on the inner, red glow that came from his mouth and kissed him. Under her lips, he transformed back into his human self. He lifted his hands and cradled her head, as he accepted her kiss and deepened it. She was just as entranced to him in human form as she had been in his wraith. Her body responded to him on many levels. Her contest had just become infinitely more difficult. Choosing a winner was starting to feel like an impossible feat.

How could she ever choose between three incredible but vastly different men?

They spent the better part of the day touring the district, holding Andreas's hand while he pointed out where the shifter soldiers trained, and the small stone house he lived in with two of his wraith brothers, Mica and Ozul. She couldn't stop herself from popping into the house, wanting to see how Andreas lived, where he slept and dreamed. Mica and Ozul, she assumed, sat at a small table drinking and playing some kind of game with black and white stones and grunted to her in greeting as she did a quick look around. Amused, Andreas put an arm around her and quickly escorted her out again. Another grunt from Mica and Ozul followed them out.

Next, he took her to a small, cramped vending stall

down the street that smelled of boiled cabbage. Outside the stall, as if guarding over it, a little, black goat bleated at everyone who passed by. The moment that they approached, the goat ran at Sophia and butted his little head into her leg.

"He likes you," the portly woman, dressed in colorful scarves, behind the stall said with a chuckle.

Sophia petted the goat's head, and it bleated at her. "I'm not so sure about that."

Andreas leaned on the cart. "Masilda, this is my," he smiled at her and her belly clenched again, "friend, Sophia."

"Blessings on you." Masilda dipped her head.

Sophia returned the little bow. "You as well."

"You must be here for my sarma," Masilda said as she shoveled whatever had been cooking onto a thick slice of bread. She handed it to Andreas. "This boy always come to my cart for sarma. Every day. Sometimes twice."

Sophia smiled, taken with the wraith woman, as Andreas handed her a small dumpling made out of cabbage. The smell made Sophia's stomach grumble. She'd forgotten she hadn't eaten since breakfast, which had been the usual, lumpy bowl of porridge with some pine nuts and dried berries.

Under Masilda's watchful eye, Sophia plopped the whole thing into her mouth and chewed. The tastes exploded in her mouth and her eyes enlarged. It was spicy and rich and delicious.

Masilda chuckled. "I think she likes it, Andreas. You may make a wraith woman out of her, but only with more sarma." She laughed hard, her whole body shaking.

"It was very good, thank you," Sophia said.

"Make sure you eat more. You too skinny." Masilda pursed her lips and frowned.

When they moved on from the cart to see more of the Shade, Andreas took her hand again, and her heart swelled. She loved that he was so open with her, that he trusted her with where he lived, where he trained, the people who mattered to him, and with the most inner part of himself—his wraith.

The rest of the day went by too quickly, and then they were back at the fountain. Sophia wished Andreas a good night.

"I wish you would allow me to walk you home. It's not always safe on the streets for a beautiful woman."

She liked that he called her beautiful, and that he wanted to protect her, but she didn't need it. "I'll be fine. I like to stroll alone at night. It helps me sleep." This wasn't necessarily a lie, even if it wasn't quite the truth.

The sun had already set and the sky darkened. It wouldn't be long before Grindel started to suspect she was up to something. Although she suspected that he knew about her secret trips to the city. She left the garden and headed toward the wall, needing to get through the secret tunnel and change her clothes. She knew Haris would find her the moment she stepped out into the woods eager to go for another run. He would likely try and convince her to play with him in the stream on the way back to the cabin, as he did almost every night.

Just as she rounded a corner, she found Winston leaning against the wall, as if he'd been waiting for her this whole time. He looked a little threatening in the dark, skulking about, and she swished she had her sword with her. The damned thing wouldn't have fit in her dress though. She did have her dagger though, strapped to her thigh. Her fingers twitched with the need to reach for it under her skirt.

"Winston," she said, her voice even, not wanting to give him any satisfaction of startling her.

He pushed off the wall. "Did I scare you?" His eyes sparked at the question, and Sophia realized that he'd wanted her to be afraid.

If she'd been another girl, she might've said yes, and he would've apologized and told her that she shouldn't be afraid and that he'd never hurt her. But she wasn't another girl. She wouldn't even give him that kind of enjoyment as Sophia Oxford.

"No," she said, knowing it would throw him off.

"I've seen you've allowed Zeke Wickham, Edric

Axton, and now with Andreas Hylt to court you." His lips twisted into a sneer.

She leveled her gaze, a hand propped on her hip. "Yes, what of it?"

He met her gaze. "They are not good men."

"How so?" she asked, lifting an eyebrow.

"They are all men of low character. I've seen them all court women until they've grown tired of the chase, if you know what I mean," he said.

She did know what he meant, and she didn't like the insinuation.

"They will flirt with you, string you along you and then break your heart."

Just from spending a day with each man, Sophia knew what he was told her was horse shit. Out of the three of them, Edric had a bit of a reputation with the ladies, but she'd never heard a cruel word said about him around the city. Every person spoke highly of him, including the young women he'd courted in the past. He was a gentleman through and through.

Winston took a step closer to her. "If I were to court you, I would treat you properly. Like the goddess you are."

From another man, she may have felt a slight tingle of pleasure at his words. No one had ever called her a goddess before. But his words weren't authentic. They dripped with condescension and deceit.

"Just give me one chance to show you how a real man treats a lady." He smiled.

She was tempted to tell him to go hump a grimm, but his father was very influential. If she pissed him off enough, it might prompt him to complain to his father, and then to her "uncle," Lord Oxford. It would quickly become evident that she wasn't who she claimed to be. She could likely be arrested for her treachery, and then once they discovered who she truly was—*what* she truly was—she'd be executed.

She had to pick her battles here, and she resisted the urge to tear into him with a barbed tongue. Grindel would be proud of her for keeping her bold opinions to herself. For once.

"Thank you for your concern, Winston." She moved away from him, just a little. Standing so close to him made her skin itch, like she'd been attacked by the stinging hairs of a climbing wood nettle. "I'm flattered by your offer." She wasn't. It actually made her want to puke. "I need some time to consider it."

"I hope you won't take too much time." He smiled again, but it didn't make her feel relaxed. It caused the little hairs on the back of her neck stand on end as a warning. Predator in vicinity.

She gave him a little bow, and then slunk away from him, none too soon. Her skin crawled. There was something about him that raised a lot of warnings in her mind. He wasn't someone she could trust. Yet, he was also someone she shouldn't underestimate either.

As quick as she could, Sophia made it to the wall, found her bag with her clothes, and then changed. She had maybe another hour before she would be missed. She needed to be more conscious of her time if she was going to succeed in her mission. If Grindel ever found out, she'd never fully heal her soul, and she would not be able to see her three suitors again. That was something she was not willing to risk.

A week of affection and stolen kisses from charming men sped by, and before Sophia knew it, she was on her second day off from her dates with her three candidates; three, incredible men she couldn't stop thinking about. It interfered with her training. Enough so that she was practicing her swordplay by herself in a secluded glen not far from the walls instead of hidden in the training field within the woods. The cabin felt too far away from the city, and her body ached to be closer to Nighthelm, to the man who carried a piece of her soul inside him. If only she could just figure out which man it was.

She lunged with her sword. Then passed back with her front foot, swiveled, and lunged again. As she did this routine several more times to the right, then to the left, she wondered what Edric or Andreas would say if she asked either of them to spar with her. Would they find her mad? Most likely. And she knew Ezekiel could teach her a thing or two about her magic, and controlling it. But he too, would certainly be suspicious of her if she asked, especially when she wasn't supposed to possess any magic whatsoever.

She hated that they were slowly revealing themselves to her on their dates, but she had to keep the most important parts of herself secret. What was going to happen when she truly found the other piece of her soul? Would she be able to reveal herself even then? Would her soul be instantly repaired, and she could finally take her place among society? She could find a small apartment above a shop to live in, and a job as a blacksmith or a stable hand, although she didn't think those were occupations for women, and the three men could continue to court her. She shook her head, knowing that wouldn't likely ever happen. She had too many questions still. She wished the oracles had been clearer about her fate.

While she was preparing to do some spinning lunges with her sword, the battle horn of Nighthelm sounded. Its mournful cry reverberated over her, even as she ran toward the city gate. As she crested a turn in the path, she found a full-on battle raging barely two-hundred-feet from the gates. The soldiers from the walls fought a herd of minotaurs. Her blood ran cold. These creatures never came so close to the city and, even on her patrols, she had no indication they were heading this way. Had she been so distracted she missed some sign?

Sophia never made mistakes, especially not mistakes *this* big. Something was wrong here, but she didn't have time to figure out what it was. She had to help the soldiers, but she could already feel her power returning, wild, untamed, getting frighteningly close to the surface. She pushed it down as she was in better control of it than she'd been in years past. She knew she could keep it at bay… for a while.

Too involved in the fight, no one saw her approach the field of battle. As she grabbed a dead soldier's bow and arrows, she prepared to help from afar without tapping her magic too much, preventing anyone from tying her to the magical episode from before. In the fray, she spotted Edric fighting a minotaur entirely on his own, away from the others. The beast had obviously lured him away from his squad.

Her mind blanked. All she could feel was the utter compulsion to protect him. Not the other soldiers, not the city of Nighthelm and its people, but *him*.

Still unseen, she drew her sword and joined his fight. She lunged at the beast, cutting it off from advancing on Edric. It swiped at her, its claws cutting into her shoulder. The pain was instant but didn't slow her down. As she positioned herself to advance again, she was careful not to use her magic. She wouldn't allow an episode so close to someone she was beginning to care so much about.

Edric gaped at her as she sliced at the minotaur's back leg, hoping to fell it, but missed and nearly received a back hoof to the head for her efforts. She was lucky it hadn't turned and tried to gore her with its horns.

"Sophia! What are you doing? You must run and hide! It's too dangerous here!"

She refused to waste words as the beast charged at Edric again, probably thinking he was the biggest threat in the field.

Stupid choice, Sophia thought.

Edric feinted to the right, then brought his sword up to strike, but Sophia saw how the minotaur was going to veer and come along Edric's flank. He would be gored by the beast's horns if she didn't act fast.

She ran to Edric's side and swung at the beast. Her blade slashed across the minotaur's belly, gravely wounding it. This gave Edric time and the opportunity to advance toward its head. With a deft hand, he sliced open a gaping gash into the beast's neck. The minotaur stumbled, listing to the right then falling to its side. Blood pooled around its body, and Sophia knew it wasn't getting up again.

More fighting raged on nearby. The minotaurs were overpowering the soldiers. There were several dead castle guards scattered across the battlefield, their bellies and necks slashed open by claws and teeth. While Edric ran to help his fellow soldiers, Sophia moved to the cover of a few trees. Using her procured bow and arrows, she shot several of the beasts before they could advance to the city gate. With the element of surprise on her side, she took down a couple of minotaurs that had been charging toward the walls without anything in their way, turning the battle into victory.

After Edric took down the last beast, he sheathed his sword then returned to her side, as no one else had yet taken notice of her. But that wouldn't last long. Soon she would be spotted and her presence questioned. Women were not soldiers and were not supposed to be on a field of battle.

"What in seven hells are you doing, Sophia?" He looked her over, his gaze fierce, his frown deep. "This is no place for a woman! You could've been killed."

She bristled at the fury coming off him. She couldn't believe he would admonish her after she just saved his life. "I wasn't killed, and if I'm so bold to say: neither were you, thanks to me."

He huffed in frustration, but she could see his face soften a little. "This makes no sense." Pacing, he shook his head and rubbed a hand over the stubble on his chin. "How did you...?"

"My uncle hired trainers for me when I was young. I'd always been precocious and he liked that about me.

But instead of having me underfoot all the time, he set me out in the training field and put a sword in my hand, hoping I'd expend all my energy whacking at wooden dummies and padded men."

He stopped pacing and his eyes narrowed. "That's surprising considering what I know of Lord Oxford. He's never seemed like a patient man, and definitely not a man who put any value on a warrior's way of life or a woman's."

Bloody hell, she needed to do some fancy word dancing. She didn't like that suspicious look in Edric's eye. "My uncle is an enigma, to be sure. He hides many things from people. He doesn't like how the other noble families scoff at such things. That's why he's kept my training secret."

She took a step toward Edric and placed her hand on his arm. "And I'd appreciate it as well. I wouldn't want others to look down on me for my secret love of swordplay." She gave him a flirty smile. "What would the other young ladies of society say?"

He sighed heavily, and then nodded. "Of course. I'll keep your secret."

"Thank you, Edric." She lowered her head demurely.

His gaze on her was no less intense, but she didn't think it was full of suspicion any longer. She'd placated him. For now.

Then he flinched and his frown deepened. "Your shoulder." He reached for her. "You're hurt."

During the battle, she'd completely forgotten she'd been injured. She looked down at the tear in her shirt and the blood staining the fabric. "Oh, yes. I guess I am."

With gentle fingers, he pulled the hole in her shirt apart to inspect the wound. "It's not bad. Just needs to be cleaned and bandaged."

She was surprised he hadn't commented on her entire state of dress. She wore her training clothes, of leather jerkin, suede pants and tall boots. And everything had dirt and grime on it. Not a very appealing look for a high society lady.

"I'll be fine. I'll take care of it," she said. She rolled her shoulder, not planning on telling him she'd had worse. Way worse.

"You'll do no such thing. After I check on my men, I will come for you and tend to you myself." He gestured to the far side of the wall. "Wait there and I will sneak you into the barracks."

He returned to the field, then as if remembering something important, he came back to her, cupped her cheek with his hand and pressed his lips to hers. Then he was back, jogging toward his wounded men.

The kiss was quick, but no less potent. The feel of his mouth burned on her lips, sizzling of want, desire, and possession. And she liked that a lot.

CHAPTER TWENTY-ONE

SOPHIA

*T*rue to his word, Edric had returned for her after checking on his men. He snuck her through the city and into the barracks through a secret gate in the wall. One that only the leaders of the castle guard knew about. Sophia secured the location in her memory, just in case she ever needed to use it.

Once at the barracks, he quickly escorted her to his room before any of the soldiers could see them. He locked the door, and pointed to his bed for her to sit. Sophia wanted to argue but the stern look in his eyes told her that it wouldn't be a great idea to do so. So, she sat on the edge with a harrumph.

While he went into his storage cupboard to retrieve bandages and an antiseptic, she surveyed his room. He had modest living quarters; she suspected they were a bit bigger than other soldiers, as he was the commander. He had a bed, desk and chair, cupboards, and a small counter with a wash basin and mirror on the wall. He returned to her with cloth bandages, and a small bowl full of tepid water.

His eyes narrowed as he studied her shoulder. "You're going to have to take off your jerkin and shirt so I can properly tend to the wound."

The cut along her shoulder was just a scratch in her opinion. She'd had worse injuries, but it was obvious he wanted to patch her up. So, she indulged him.

"Turn around so I can," she said.

He did, and she untied her leather jerkin, took it off, and then pulled her shirt up over her head. She winced at the sharp pain when she moved her arm. After tossing her clothes to the floor, she pulled at the bed sheet over her and wrapped it around her breasts in her best attempt to be modest, given the circumstances.

"Okay, you can turn back around," she said.

When he did, his lips parted in awe. She wasn't sure if his surprise was at her oozing wound—it did appear to be worse than she had first thought—or because she sat there virtually naked, wrapped in a sheet. His sheet. Covered with his scent.

He crouched next to her then gently wiped the blood away from around the gash. She watched him as he worked, noticing how he swallowed and licked his lips with each tender stroke of the cloth. She liked the way his jaw clenched, and she had an urge to trace her fingertips along the muscles on his chin and jawbone.

Once the gore was wiped away, Edric dabbed the wound with a gel made from the aloe vera plant that grew in various places in the woods. She used the same antiseptic ointment at home when she got injured. Then he slowly and gently wrapped her shoulder with the soft cloth.

With each turn of the cloth, his fingers brushed against the side of her breast, and tender jolts of desire shot through her each time. By the time he was done, Sophia was biting on her bottom lip. It wasn't because she was in pain. Quite the opposite. Ribbons of pleasure seared her with every warm touch of his hand.

After tying off the ends of the cloth, Edric lifted his head and met her gaze. His fingers lingered on her shoulder, the tips brushing lightly on her skin. The muscles along his jawline twitched, and this time she didn't hold back from reaching out and tracing her fingers across his stubble.

His eyes darkened to a stormy blue, as if in that moment, he had lost his final ounce of control He leaned in, brushing his lips against hers. She sighed, her lips opening a little, inviting him in. Edric cupped her cheek with his hand and deepened the kiss.

Her whole body buzzed as he slowly pushed her back onto his bed, crawling on his hands and knees until he was entirely on top of her. Sophia let go of the sheet covering her breasts and reached up to bury her hands in his hair, bringing him closer, kissing him *hard.*

Her very soul ached for him.

She needed him.

Now.

They kissed until they were breathless, then Edric pulled away and looked at her. With her hands on his chest, she felt his pulse thumping hard against her fingertips. She reveled in the fact that she'd made his heart race. Hers was going as fast as a jack rabbit.

"Once we start, I won't be able to stop." His voice was gravely, hoarse with desire.

"Then don't stop," she panted and brazenly pulled the sheet away from her body.

Edric made a low groan in his throat as his gaze traveled over her breasts. Her nipples hardened into tight buds as he shamelessly studied her body, taking in her every curve. He pushed off the bed and tore at his clothes, until he was left in only a pair of cloth breeches that did nothing to hide his erection.

She drank him in. His strong, muscular body, the light sprinkling of hair that lined his sternum. There were scars along his arms—one thick white one stood out—and a couple over his stomach. They held the appearance of knife wounds. He stood like a warrior, battle ready and battle scarred.

Edric was the most powerful man she'd ever seen. And he was all hers.

Not wasting a moment, he returned to her and untied her pants, then yanked them off, until she was naked, trembling with lust and need, her legs parted, waiting for him to take her on his bed. His gaze devoured her whole. Though she ached for him, she still fought off the unconscious impulse to cover herself. She had never been in this position before, never had the chance to give herself to a man before, and trace hints of her nervousness fluttered through her chest.

But there was no room for modesty now.

In seconds, he was beside her again, capturing her mouth with his, kissing her until she was languid, half-drugged with desire and open to his touch.

He moved his hand down her body, softly caressing every crest and valley. He went slowly with his surprisingly gentle touch. Molding a breast with the palm of his hand. Gently rubbing a nipple. Fingertips feathering over her rib cage. A firm palm over her belly as he pressed hot kisses to her chin, and then nuzzled into her neck.

It was a slow, loving preparation of what was to come.

Sophia gasped as his hand pressed between her thighs, opening her up, and his fingers sunk into her sex. He only explored her for a moment but it was enough to set her body aflame. He pulled his hand away, and then was on his arms, hovering over her, as if he was trying to decide which part of her he wanted to taste first.

Impatience won out, and he nudged her legs apart with his knee, then settled between them. She didn't mind. She liked that he hungered for her and wanted to take her quickly. He yanked down his breeches, and guided his cock to her opening. She was hot and wet for him, ready to be filled. She sucked in a breath as he pressed into her.

Being as this her first time, she suspected this would hurt, that the thrust of his cock would bring her pain and blood, but she didn't care. All she wanted was Edric inside her. She burned for him. Inside and out. She never thought she could ever feel this much for one person.

His arms shook with exertion as he slowly sheathed himself inside her. With every inch, she moaned as her body adjusted to him. He filled her completely, stretching her, the two of them connected in the rawest sense of the word.

Reaching up, she pulled his face down to hers and kissed him. She wrapped her arms around him and bowed her back as the first pinch of pain needled her deep between her legs. Then he was fully seated, and hot, pulsing pleasure erupted from within.

His movements were slow at first, and she knew he

restrained himself for her. So he didn't hurt her. But she didn't want slow. She wanted fast. She wanted primal and raw. Giving herself entirely to him, she dug her nails into his back, and wrapped her legs around his waist, urging him with the press of her heels on the backs of his legs.

That was all the encouragement he needed.

He moved faster and harder over her, in her, through her. Sophia dug her fingers into his back and held on as wave after wave of heat and pleasure surged over her. She didn't know that sex could feel this way.

So fevered.

So intense.

So beyond reason.

How could she have known what she was missing, when she'd been a virgin? When she never thought any man would want her enough to try.

Their sweat mingled as their bodies intertwined. The smell of it filled the air. Sophia drew it all in, reveling in it. She gasped as her pussy contracted around Edric's cock. Her orgasm hit suddenly, powerful and hard, and she tightened her thighs around him. She moaned, leaning into him, trying her best not to scream his name.

After all, these walls weren't very thick.

With a long, loud groan, he buried his face into the crook of her neck. His hands sunk into her hair and he pulled on it a little as his body quickened. She felt all his muscles bunch, and then he bit down on her flesh like an animal and then came in a hot, heady rush.

"Sophia," he said with a rasp.

She hugged him tight to her body, loving the feel of their combined muscle spasms and the sound of their twin heartbeats. He shuddered once more, then rolled over onto his back, rolling her with him so she was snuggled on top of his chest.

She could barely catch her breath as she lay across his hard body, listening to his heart hammer inside his chest. His one hand swept into her hair, and the other caressed her arm, careful not to jostle her injured shoulder.

"Did I hurt you?" he asked, his voice low; a loving murmur.

"No." She smiled against his skin.

"Good." He pressed a kiss to her head. "I never wish to hurt you, in any way." He nuzzled her closer to him, as if he couldn't bear to ever lose her.

Sophia drew her fingers up and down the smooth, hard plane of his chest. How could one man be rough and dominating one second, but sweet and endearing the next? It baffled her, but she was slowly coming to realize that was just Edric. Her beautiful contradiction.

"Next time it shouldn't hurt at all," he said, "then you can fully experience all your pleasure."

"It can feel even better than it did?"

He chuckled, sweaty and exhausted. "Just wait, darling. Next time I will make sure that you orgasm harder than me." His hand stroked over her ass, and little flicks of heat ignited deep inside her again.

She pressed a kiss to his chest, astonished at what she'd just done, but not for even one second regretting it. There were plenty of plants in the woods that acted as birth control, and she would brew a tea from one later when she was back home, just to be safe. She'd never thought she would need one.

In truth, she thought she would always be a maiden. She never thought she would ever have an opportunity to explore her sexuality. Especially not with a man such as Edric Axton, Commander of the Nighthelm castle guard. As her eyes drooped, sleep slowly taking her, her skin buzzed while she snuggled with him.

As she drifted asleep, something deep inside of her thumped hard at his nearness. Was this the thunder that the oracles had told her to seek out? Was Edric the one?

She held that thought close as her breathing softened and she drifted into bliss.

EDRIC

*E*dric lay next to Sophia, stroking her arm, until her breathing slowed and became steady, and he knew she was asleep. As gently as he could, without waking her, Edric slipped out from under her and rolled off the bed. She murmured once but didn't open her eyes.

He pulled the blanket over her shoulder and carefully tucked it around her body. He took in the sight of her, memorizing everything about her: the small dimple on the side of her luscious mouth, the way her forehead furrowed as if the worries of the world pressed on her as she slept, the gentle rise and fall of her chest as she slumbered.

The sight of this woman in his bed nearly brought him to his knees. How could he have been this blessed?

He busied himself around the room, cleaning up as she slept. He dumped the water, now cold, out of the window, and tossed away the cloth he used to wipe away the blood from her wound.

Seeing her cut and bleeding like that had torn at his heart. It surprised him to no end how easily she had handled the injury. As if it had been nothing. Or, worse, that she had possibly faced deeper wounds in the past, and this was nothing to concern herself with. The thought of someone cutting her, of something injuring her in any way… it broke him.

Nothing would harm his woman.

While he had been patching her up, he had noticed another scar on her arm, close to her shoulder. It hadn't looked like a knife or sword cut, it wasn't straight and even. It had been ragged and curved, as if something jagged had ripped at her skin. A claw possibly?

She was an enigma, his Sophia. *His.* He paused, hands on the edge of the basin as he lost himself in thought. When had he begun to think of her as his?

Maybe from the start. Maybe from the first moment he spotted her from across the room, laughing with another girl, shoving pastries into her mouth as if she'd never tasted anything so delicious before in her whole life. The pure innocence on her face during that moment had instantly enamored him to her. He didn't think he'd ever seen another woman quite like her. Both innocent and dynamic.

Definitely not one who could fight like she did, not only with a sword but with a bow and arrow. Her precision and accuracy were phenomenal. Edric wasn't sure he'd ever seen anyone shoot like that before. He was good with a bow, had trained for over ten years to be great, but he wasn't sure he could've made those shots from the cover of the trees, and from that distance, amidst all that chaos.

He moved toward the bed again, and stood over her, looking down at her beauty. *Who are you?* he whispered in his mind. Sophia didn't sound or act like a young woman raised in high society. She wasn't as rigid or reserved or composed as most of the young women he'd courted before. She had a wildness about her, that he adored.

He thought about the sex they just had. She'd been a virgin, but she hadn't seemed prim about it, or afraid. She'd let herself go, had opened up to him in a way he hadn't experienced before. She'd given him a gift, and he couldn't have been more beholden for it. He promised himself he would never squander that gift. He would protect and honor her.

Leaning down, he pressed a soft kiss to her cheek. Slowly one eye opened and she smiled. She reached a hand up and cupped his neck.

"Edric," she said, sleepily, her voice barely a whisper against his skin. It sounded like a plea for him.

He pulled the blanket down, and slipped back into bed, nuzzling in beside her warm, pliant body. Without fully waking, she wrapped herself around him. Edric softly kissed her again on the head and then followed her down into sleep.

CHAPTER TWENTY-TWO

SOPHIA

*N*ight had fallen when Edric kissed her awake. Lamplight flickered over the hard planes of his face and body as he looked down at her from the side of the bed. Heat flared inside her again, but she knew there wasn't enough time for them to go another round. Edric had a guard shift on the wall, and Sophia had to return to the woods before Grindel started asking questions.

He kissed her again then nibbled on her chin and ear. "I could say I'm sick. One of my captains could cover my shift."

She nudged him away with a laugh. "You'd be the first commander in history to call in sick to work."

"But it would be for a good reason. I know the other men would completely understand." He reached for her, intending to roll onto her. "Let me show you that thing I mentioned earlier. I promise, you'll be thanking me." But she shuffled off the bed in time and slapped at his bold hands.

"Go and do your duty. We will see each other again soon." She picked up her clothes from the floor and started to put them back on.

Edric watched her dress, licking his lips. "Not soon enough."

She blushed, as she finished pulling on her tunic and lacing up her pants.

Once they were both dressed, Edric pulled her close and kissed her thoroughly, then he opened the door to his quarters, peering out to make sure no one was around to see them sneak out. After he led her from his room, and through the barracks, he left her near the market so she could disappear into the crowd. He turned to look at her once more, a deep longing on his face that make her heart skip a beat, before he rushed toward the wall and his duty.

As Sophia walked through market square, her body hummed with life and energy. It was like she'd been asleep before, but now was very wide awake. She wanted to dance with joy, and she laughed out loud at that notion. A few people nearby glanced her way, frowning at her outburst, and likely at her manner of dress. She looked like a combination of a vagabond and a bandit with her dirty, blood-stained shirt and leather pants. She didn't care, her happiness was too jubilant to contain.

She stared at the night sky as she weaved her way through the streets. The stars shone bright, as if they turned on just for her. So caught up in her joy, she didn't realize she'd stumbled right into the oracle's park. One of the great trees loomed near her, reminding her of her quest.

Her smile faded a little as she thought about the dilemma she had on her hands: how to figure out which of the three men possessed the piece of her soul. Instead of getting easier to decipher, it proved more difficult with each passing day. Bliss or no, she had a mission to complete.

She had hoped that the riddle the oracles bestowed on her would tell her everything she needed to know, but she needed more information on what she was in order to figure it all out. She looked up at the castle at the south end of the city, set in the mountain, and figured the castle library would surely have something about anima contritums. That was where all the very important and secret history of Nighthelm was kept, away from the general public, only available to those who meant to control that history. Over the years, she'd never been able to locate the library within the stone fortress, having only been allowed underneath the castle in the training caverns, but the clock was ticking, and she needed to double her efforts.

She went around the park then ducked down a darkened alleyway out of eyesight of any city folk out on the streets. Thankful that she wore her usual clothes and not one of her dress disguises, Sophia climbed the side of the stone building to the roof top. It would be easier to reach the castle this way, instead of down on street level where the guards were trained to survey.

After leaping from one building to the next, she was able to get on top of the second level of the castle, then using the stones as foot and hand holds, she climbed four stories to the very top. From there, she snuck along the sloping roof in the shadows, careful to make little noise.

Hanging off one parapet, she looked down to see a solider nailing propaganda to a notice board. The large letters pronounced the dangers of the woods were getting worse. That the monsters in the forest were getting more and more dangerous, and staying in Nighthelm was the only choice. There were other warnings of the mountain's magic and the woods beyond. Sophia frowned, wishing the duchess wouldn't make the people live in such fear, but she continued on. There was nothing she could do about it, and her mission was more important than some flyers.

About four feet below her, she spotted an open window. Thankfully, it was dark in the room beyond.

Gripping the edge of the roof with her fingers, Sophia swung down in hopes to easily slide through the opening. Her feet slammed into stone as the window disappeared and morphed into a solid wall. Gasping, she fell.

The ground six stories below came too fast. If she hit, her bones, along with her head, would certainly crack. Reaching out, she grabbed hold of a flag pole protruding from one wall and then swung herself into a dark crevice just under the roof's eaves.

Bells sounded from the tower nearby, nearly splitting her ear drums. There were four tolls indicating an attack on the castle. The window reappeared below, and light filled the room as silhouettes of guards entered. They were obviously looking for her. But how did they know? Did the castle itself actually sound the alarm in its defense?

A guard stuck his head out of the window and surveyed the wall around it. When he turned to the left, she saw Edric's stern face, looking fierce and ready to kill to defend his home. She leaned back into her hiding spot, trying to make her body smaller, but she knew he wouldn't be able to see her. The shadows became her camouflage.

She held her breath, waiting for him to retreat. Her heart raced, hammering hard in her throat. Finally, he withdrew his head, and she relaxed a little. How the hell had the castle changed? She'd heard rumors over the years that the castle had a life of its own, an energy and magic that couldn't be beat, supposedly controlled by the acting ruler. Did the duchess have that kind of power? It didn't seem possible. If only she could ask Grindel about this, and many other things. But she couldn't, unless she wished to tell him what she was truly doing behind his back. She didn't think he would appreciate it, and she didn't think he would allow her to continue. So, no, Grindel wasn't someone she could confide in.

Could she risk asking Edric or Ezekiel about it? Surely, they would know, one being the commander of the guard, the other having access to the castle's secrets and possibly its magic. But what explanation could she use for her interest? It was an impossible problem to have and she didn't know the answer.

She looked at the foreboding fortress as a shiver rushed down her spine. A sensation of being watched feathered over her, like spider legs on her skin. She swallowed the wariness down, and made her way down the castle wall to the ground. Before any of the guards could spill out of the castle to search for intruders, Sophia slipped into the shadows and disappeared.

CHAPTER TWENTY-THREE

SOPHIA

*B*eneath the castle, in the great hall, Sophia ran through her sword handling techniques with Grindel. She'd been surprised that he'd suggested she train in the castle, especially with her magic growing restless inside her again. But he had his reasons, not that he would ever share them with her. And she wouldn't dare ask.

"Ox ward," he called out, his voice echoing through the cavernous room.

She dragged her left foot forward, the bottom of her boot scraping against the rough stone floor, and held her sword close to her face but aimed toward the upper region of her imagined opponent.

"Plow ward," he said next.

Out came her right foot, and she held her sword near the knees, with the blade aimed at her opponent's chest. The sword wobbled a little, her arm getting fatigued, and he frowned. She wouldn't admit that she was a little tired from her nighttime activities in the city. And a whole lot distracted by thoughts of the three men in her life. She couldn't erase Edric and the sex they had from her mind. Sometimes she could still feel his hands on her skin. She definitely could still smell him.

"Oberhau!" he shouted at her.

Sophia brought her sword down on her opponent's head.

"Zornhau!"

This time she struck in a diagonal across the body from above.

"Mittelhau!"

A middle strike, she swung her sword from the right. But the blade tip dropped at the last moment, pulling her off balance.

"No, no, no! You are not focused." Grindel shook his head and slapped his fist into the palm of his other hand. "If you want to learn to control your powers, you must be a creature of habit, of discipline, of—,"

Headmistress Mittle entered the hall, cutting off the rest of Grindel's lecture, and surprising them both. She looked regal in a forest green, brocade dress with gold embroidering. She always seemed to appear more regal than even the duchess.

"My apologies for interrupting." She waved a

bejeweled hand toward Sophia. "I'll be watching during the rest of the training. Please, continue."

Still frowning, Grindel nodded to Sophia. "Do the attack moves again until they are perfect."

Sophia considered complaining. If they had been alone, she might have, but not with the headmistress in attendance. She couldn't appear weak in front of her benefactor.

She worked the four attack moves, one right after the other, until her arms shook with fatigue. She must've done them correctly, because Grindel nodded to her in approval then told her to pick up her bow. He instructed her to shoot the straw-filled dummy positioned on the wall across the room. At 100 feet, it was an easy shot, but Grindel had her running and shooting, shooting from up high and down low, and even after a forward roll on the ground. She hit every mark with precision. Heart and head. Sometimes, the groin when she was feeling cheeky.

She risked a glance at the headmistress and saw an amused look on her face, which Sophia found surprising. She didn't think the woman possessed a sense of humor. At least she'd never seen a whiff of it in all the years she'd known her. Not until now.

After her weapon lessons, she moved on to her balance training. Grindel had set up an obstacle course consisting of a beam of one-inch thick wood resting precariously on stacked crates, and small rocks and crevices in the stone wall she had to climb to, then get back down again without falling. She figured it was better than her usual balance training in the woods, where she had to balance on one foot as Grindel threw rocks at her to try and knock her off. On those days, she usually ended up with bruises on every part of her body. But she never fell, not anymore at least.

As she ran the balance course, Sophia glanced at the headmistress. She'd been pacing the room slowly, watching Sophia train. It was unnerving having her there, just observing without question or comment. What did she want? Sophia didn't think for one minute that Headmistress Mittle came to just observe quietly in the background. There had to be another motive for her presence. The woman had never been this concerned and attentive to her training, not even at the beginning, when she was just a scared little girl.

When Sophia had ran the balance course three times without a wobble in her step, the headmistress stepped forward to talk to Grindel.

"Now I'd like for Sophia to test her magic."

Grindel shook his head. "No. Not beneath the school. It's too dangerous."

"It will be fine," the headmistress said. "You worry needlessly."

"Too much time has passed. Even with her dampening gloves, she's too vulnerable for another episode. I do not think you would want to take that risk with so many lives in the castle."

Sophia bristled at that. Anger surged through her. Anger at herself for not having mastered her magic yet, after all these years. The headmistress was probably close to giving up on her completely. Would she stop funding Grindel's efforts to train her, to control her magic? What would happen then? Would she end up homeless? Not that she couldn't take care of herself. She could easily live off the land; the woods would provide for her even when others wouldn't.

"I'd like to try," Sophia said, her voice a bit strangled by nerves.

Both Grindel and the headmistress twisted around to look at her. The headmistress's eyebrows came up and her lips tilted up in an almost smile. "You see, Grindel, she is ready."

Grindel's frown deepened, the lines on his brow furrowed into trenches. "She's telling you what you want to hear, not what is the truth."

Sophia went to speak again, but Grindel cut her off with a raised hand and a lethal look. She quickly shut her mouth. He had a range of looks that he often shot her, and this one was the most serious.

"You entrusted me to train her, to care for her, and I'm telling you she is not ready for that kind of test in this environment. You risk the safety of everyone in this castle." He lifted his head and regarded the headmistress. "I know as headmistress you wouldn't do anything to jeopardize the academy or the students who train within."

For a long tense moment, the two of them stared at each other. To Sophia, it appeared to be a standoff; a battle of wills.

Eventually, Headmistress Mittle sighed. "Very well." She walked toward Sophia. "Then I believe it's time Sophia and I began private lessons." She reached for Sophia's hand. Wary, Sophia set her hand into the headmistress's. The headmistress pulled off her glove, then rubbed her thumbs over Sophia's knuckles, and then turned Sophia's hand and ran her fingers over her palm. The touch sent cold uneasy ripples up Sophia's arm.

Sophia tried not to flinch away or recoil from the headmistress's touch. But she certainly wanted to. She didn't like the look in the older woman's icy blue eyes. Her gaze seemed greedy. Like she wanted to take something Sophia was not willing to give.

"Since Grindel is not succeeding with helping you, do you not think it would be wise to try something else?"

Sophia swallowed, worried about offending Grindel, but the headmistress concerned her more, so she nodded. "Yes, Headmistress."

"Good." She dropped Sophia's hand and moved across the room to the door she'd come in from.

Grindel watched her leave, his body held upright and stiff. Obviously, something wasn't right with the headmistress's offer, and Grindel knew it. And that made Sophia very nervous. Her teacher wasn't always the kindest man, but she knew he cared for her in his own way.

She grabbed his arm. "What's going on? I know something's not right."

"There's nothing for you to worry about," he said without looking at her.

"I don't believe you."

He pulled his arm away. "Just do as you're told for once. Shut your mouth and don't ask questions." He turned and walked toward the tunnel to leave the hall and return to the woods.

Sophia watched him go, then looked around the room. "What about the weapons and training apparatus?"

"Leave them. We'll be back for training again."

She followed him out of the hall, but didn't rush to catch up with him. Something was wrong. She could feel it all the way to her bones. Grindel wasn't telling her everything, or anything for that matter. He was usually guarded, but this was different. He was afraid.

It was more important than ever that Sophia heal

her shattered soul, and fast. She feared she was quickly running out of time, with the oracles prophecy and with the headmistress's leniency. Something was going to give, and soon.

CHAPTER TWENTY-FOUR

SOPHIA

*T*he next day was her second date with Ezekiel. Sophia was quiet, lost in thought, wondering what the next, best move for her should be as they walked along a quiet trail into the woods. She was surprised that Ezekiel wanted to take her out to the forest again, especially after the recent minotaur attacks.

"You're not worried about the minotaur attacks? I heard they were very close to the gate," she said, careful not to reveal information that would indicate she was in fact there during the attack.

"There's a lot of fear mongering going inside the city," he said, with a shake of his head.

She agreed, but wasn't sure if it was wise to voice that opinion.

"The method is used to keep people controlled and

obedient, dependent on the queen—sorry, *duchess*—and her armies."

She heard the distaste for the duchess and the current situation in his voice. She was surprised, having thought of him as a loyal servant of Nighthelm.

He glanced at her, and then shook his head. "I'm sorry to go on like that. Sorry, if my opinion offends you."

She touched his arm. "It's all right. I feel the same."

"You do?" His eyes widened at that. "I've heard Lord Oxford is a staunch supporter of the duchess."

Sophia shrugged. "Just because he's family doesn't mean I agree with his views."

"I like that you have a mind of your own," he said.

"I like that about you as well." She grinned.

He gave her a sly look that sent a pleasant rush over her body, and then he reached for her hand. His skin was soft against hers, and she liked how touching him filled her with a warm glow. They continued down the path through the trees hand in hand.

"Does your family share your views?" she asked.

Ezekiel turned his head and looked at the water sprites playing in the pond. "I lost my family when I was very young."

"Oh, I'm sorry." She squeezed his hand. "I didn't mean to bring up—"

He shook his head. "Don't be sorry, you didn't know." He gave her a small smile to ease the guilt of having asked. He led her to the stones on the edge of the pond just inside the woods and sat, pulling her down with him. The rocks made a great sitting spot as they were flat, and Sophia had sat here a time or two to think or to pass an hour in leisure by watching the water sprites hop on top of the water during the rare chance she had to get away from her training.

As they sat watching the sprites, Ezekiel used his magic to make tiny spouts of water that danced across the surface of the pond. Sophia laughed as two of the spouts seemed to waltz on the surface of the water. It reminded her of the night at the ball when he had swept her around the dance floor with delightful abandon.

"I've never seen anyone use magic like you do," she said. "It's beautiful."

He ducked his head a little as his cheeks flushed. "I got my magic from my father. He was the greatest sorcerer in Nighthelm." He did some more fancy hand movements then the water spouts spun in a figure eight. "He did some work for the royal family."

"Did you know the royals?" Maybe Ezekiel had the information she needed right there in his brilliant mind. Or, at least, he would know where to find it.

He shook his head. "No, but my family were loyalists to the crown. I guess that's why I'm still a little bitter that the heirs are still missing, and no one seems to be doing anything about it. Least of all the duchess.

My family died serving the crown." His voice was hard.

His pain wafted off him in waves. She'd never experienced something so raw before, especially from another person. Sophia caressed his face. He leaned into her touch. Soon, she leaned into him, and lightly brushed her lips over his. He sighed, and it was as if the weight of the world had lifted from his shoulders.

She wrapped her hands around his arm, settling her head on his shoulder. Sitting with Ezekiel, passing the time, filled her heart with joy. A lightness she hadn't felt before enveloped her. Surely, this was what it felt like to be whole. Was Ezekiel the one who the oracles promised? Did he have a piece of her soul inside him?

She couldn't be sure. She needed more information about the oracles and about being an anima contritum. Since she couldn't get into the castle, which was evident the other night, she hoped Ezekiel would help her. Although she couldn't tell him outright why she needed the books.

"I was reading a couple of interesting books the other day. On the oracles. Fascinating stuff." She picked up a small rock and tossed it into the pond. The ripples made the water spouts list sideways. "One of the books mentioned something called anima contritum."

He nodded. "Yes, those with broken souls."

"I found it interesting, and was wondering since you study at the academy, if you had access to the castle archives."

"I do."

She squeezed his arm and looked up at him. "I would love it if you could bring me some books on that, and the oracles. I find it all so fascinating and would love to learn more."

His eyes narrowed. "Doesn't seem like a topic you'd be interested in."

"Why not?"

"I don't know, not a lot of young women are interested in studying the old ways."

"Well, I'm sure, by now, you know I'm not like other young women." She batted her eyelashes.

He grinned. "I'm fully aware of that fact."

"Good."

"I'll see what I can find for you."

"Thank you, Ezekiel." She leaned over and kissed him again. This time he cupped her face with his hand and deepened it. Her entire body flushed and her toes curled. Great oracle, the man could kiss.

"What the hell are you doing?"

They broke apart and turned to see Edric marching toward them, in full commander uniform, his eyebrows knitted in anger, his fists clenched.

Sophia jumped to her feet, as did Ezekiel. Her heart sped up and her belly clenched a little at the sight of Edric. An image of his powerful body hovering over her filled her mind. But that didn't deter her from the anger that bubbled up from his interruption of her date with Ezekiel. A date she was very much enjoying.

"What the hell are *you* doing?" she threw back at him.

He ignored her and got into Ezekiel's face. "How dare you put Sophia's life in danger for your cheap thrills."

"She's not in any danger," Ezekiel said.

"Did you forget about the minotaur attack?" Edric demanded.

"I didn't," Ezekiel said, "But there is a lot of fear mongering in the city. The woods are no more dangerous than before."

"My last patrol encountered grimms. I heard that a wraith party, Andreas's squad in fact, was attacked by canids. You're delusional if you think that isn't more dangerous." Edric's face was getting redder by the second.

"Don't involve me in your squabble," Andreas said as he silently appeared and slid in beside Sophia.

"What are you doing here?" she asked him.

"I saw you and Zeke heading into the woods, and then I saw Edric follow you. I didn't want to miss out if there was some secret meeting no one told me about."

"There isn't a secret meeting. Just Edric being rude and interrupting our date," she said, loudly enough that Edric could plainly hear, but he was too busy arguing with Ezekiel to notice anything but the sorcerer, with flashing green eyes, in front of him.

"These woods aren't safe for anyone, you have deliberately put Sophia in danger." Edric poked his finger into Ezekiel's chest.

"You sound like the fake queen with her propaganda to keep the citizens of Nighthelm in control." Green and blue sparks sizzled at the tips of Ezekiel's fingers.

Sophia couldn't let these two kill each other. She moved in between them, making them both back up. "You are both being ridiculous."

"Me?" Ezekiel put his hand up to this chest. "I'm not the one making stupid statements about the woods like a political puppet for the duchess."

"You are making things worse," she said to him.

Edric made a noise in his throat. She whirled on him. "And you ruined my date."

"I just wanted to make sure—,"

She cut him off with a look. There was something not right nearby. An ominous hush fell over the woods. Even the chattering sparrows and chirping leafhoppers had gone silent. She scanned the surrounding trees, then turned and locked gazes with

Andreas. He sensed it too, his hand already going for the hilt of his sword.

"Back to the city! Now!" she shouted, as she broke into a run.

The men followed her, but just as they reached the worn path, a grimm floated out of the shadows and into the sun, blocking their way. It growled at them even as smoke curled up from its burning, black skin. It was even more grotesque in the glaring daylight. Sophia saw the pock marks in its face, as if acid had burned its flesh away. She wondered if that was from previous forays into the sun. Grimms were creatures of darkness, not light.

The grimm glared at Sophia, its purple eyes glowing with hate. She knew it wasn't alone. Grimms always traveled in packs. It was here for her. She felt it all the way to her bones. The grimms she'd encounter before had promised to avenge the creatures she'd murdered. She knew that they would carry a grudge against her for life. Either she killed them, or they killed her. There was no third option. There would be no truce. That was the way a grimm's grudge worked. Although she didn't want her men to be caught up in the crossfire, it was too late. This battle was going to happen whether she wanted it to or not.

Without a word, Edric tossed her his second sword and took up a defensive stance with his blade raised. She took a position beside him. Both Andreas and

Ezekiel frowned at Edric and looked like they were about to say something, but they both knew it was too late for questions. Andreas positioned himself next to her with his sword out, and Ezekiel on his other side, his hands sparking with magic. She barely took in a breath to steady herself as the rest of the grimm pack rushed out of the woods and attacked.

Both Edric and Andreas rushed forward, swinging their swords. Edric found his mark, wounding the grimm that attacked him but Andreas swung wide as his grimm moved like the wind and bore down on him. Ezekiel blasted the grimm with a bolt of magic that knocked it to the ground, enabling Andreas to slide his sword into the back of its head, killing it instantly.

Sophia lashed at the wounded grimm before it could swing around and attack Edric again. Her blade sunk deep into its gut, and it fell to the ground. It bled out in seconds. She rushed over to Ezekiel and Andreas as two more grimms charged at them. She slashed one grimm across the back as it swiped at Ezekiel's face with distended, hooked claws. He ducked just in time, then came up with his hands pulsing with magic, and blasted the creature backward with a powerful bolt. The smell of burnt skin filled her nose.

She turned toward Andreas and Edric fighting a grimm together, coordinating their blows for the best effect. Her heart swelled at the sight of her three men working together to battle the grimms. She lowered her sword for a moment to take in the scene, when her body turned to ice. Another grimm loomed over her, inches from her head, its long razor teeth dripping with saliva and other, more caustic, fluids.

"Your bodyguards can't help you," it said, its voice a rasping hiss of spite.

She was thankful the creature couldn't sense her affection for the men. It thought them only to be her guards, not her companions, her friends... maybe even more.

It lifted its head then inhaled the air. "You smell like dinner. The master won't know if I take a bite." The grimm reached out with its talons intending to skewer Sophia through the chest, but she was quicker, and she lunged up with her sword, nearly slicing the creature in half. It dropped to the ground, ink like blood seeping into the dirt.

Master? The grimms were being controlled, that much was obvious now. The question was, by who, how and to what extent? And what did they want with her?

Sophia looked up, finding only one grimm left. Ezekiel blasted it back before it could advance on Edric, then she and her men ran out of the woods toward the castle guards' secret gate in the wall. When they reached it, Edric opened it for them, and they entered the city. Edric slammed it shut then leaned against it, breathing heavily from the fight. They all were.

Andreas wiped the black blood of a grimm off his cheek while looking at Sophia with a furrowed brow. "How do you know how to fight? I've never seen a woman move like you did."

Ezekiel nodded. "I was just going to ask the same thing."

With a slight blush and a quick look at Edric, she told them the same lies she'd told Edric about her uncle getting her training as a child. She wasn't sure either of them bought it completely, but they didn't press the issue.

"Impressive," Andreas said, then bowed to her. "You fight like a wraith."

She smiled, the compliment filling her with elation. To be compared to a wraith warrior was some endorsement. "Thank you. That is high praise, indeed."

"She did fight well," Edric added, "As did you, Andreas. I thought that grimm was going to gut me."

Andreas laughed. "It would have if Zeke, here, hadn't blasted the one aiming for my head." Andreas slapped the sorcerer on his back which sent him stumbling forward.

Sophia watched the men laugh and begrudgingly thank each other for saving one another's lives. They had certainly saved hers.

"Maybe you were right after all, Edric," Ezekiel said begrudgingly, "The woods are getting dangerous."

Edric nodded. "Something is stirring up the creatures. I don't know what it is, but we need to find out."

Sophia didn't respond as she knew he was right. Evil was growing in Witch Woods. She felt it more every day that she walked through her home. Something stirred the creatures that lived in the darkness, and she feared the truth was worse than they could ever imagine.

CHAPTER TWENTY-FIVE

SOPHIA

*I*n the late morning, Sophia trudged through the secret tunnel that led to the training room beneath the castle. Grindel had left before her and she planned on asking him why, but when stepping into the great room she saw, with surprise, he wasn't there. Nervousness rippled through her. She'd never been alone with the head-mistress before for her training.

Headmistress Mittle stood in the middle of the room beside a six-foot tall glass cube. Inside the struc-ture was a chair and next to it was a wooden box with two metal rods sticking out of it, wires connecting it all, and a bunch of other weird moving gears and parts. Sophia had never seen anything like it. Out in the woods, there was never need for any machinery. The only two machines she'd ever seen in Nighthelm was one that helped a person stitch clothing, and the other was a printing press. Neither of these looked like the contraption sitting inside the glass structure.

"Please, step inside, Sophia," the headmistress said as she gestured to the glass box.

"What is it?"

"It's something that can heal you."

Wary, Sophia curiously eyed the strange cube. She didn't like the look of the machine on the floor next to the chair, but if the headmistress said it could heal her, she had to try it out. She stepped inside then sat in the wooden chair. The headmistress knelt before her and took Sophia's hand in hers.

"I understand your pain, my dear. I wish I could simply wave my hand and mend your soul." She sighed and squeezed Sophia's hand tighter. "I've tried to distance myself over the years as I hate to see you in so much pain, but I can't. I care too much about you, Sophia. I want to see you master your magic and heal yourself."

Sophia glanced at the odd machine beside her, unsure of how it could help her. It looked like something that made lightning in a bottle. She'd read about such machines in a book that she'd stolen from Grindel's personal library. They were popular in other parts of the world.

"This machine was designed by the greatest alchemists of the age," Headmistress Mittle said, "On the cutting edge of contritum research, to understand and help broken souls heal. It will contain your power if you have an episode, but it is also designed to help seal the cracks in your soul."

"Will it hurt?" Sophia asked, it wasn't that she was afraid of the pain—she'd experienced her fair share over the years—she just wanted to prepare for it.

The headmistress nodded, and her eyes looked sad. "But, I will work with you through the pain. I will always be here for you. We will conquer this together." She gave Sophia a reassuring smile. "I know Grindel has gotten you this far, and I'm grateful to him, but I don't think he's equipped to take you all the way. I'm not sure he even wants you to be whole again." Her eyes turned sad again.

"Grindel's been a good teacher," Sophia said.

"Oh, yes. I don't doubt that." She patted Sophia's hand. "He's put his whole life into training you, so I worry that he's afraid of seeing you whole and healed. What would he do then? He'd be just a history professor, and nothing more."

Was what she saying true? Grindel had always pushed her to be better, be faster, be a great swordsman and bowman. To exert herself to the extreme. But when it came to her magic, he'd always warned her to be cautious. Not to press forward, to hold back. He always said it was to protect those around her, the creatures in the woods, the people in

Nighthelm. What if he wasn't concerned with protecting others, but with hampering her progress?

Gritting her teeth, Sophia nodded to the headmistress, accepting the fact that maybe she didn't really have a choice. "Let's try it."

The headmistress gave her hand one last squeeze then stood and stepped out of the glass box. She swung shut the last glass panel then secured it with a brass hinge. She took a few steps back to watch.

At first, Sophia didn't think anything was happening. Then the machine started to make clicking and whirring noises, the little gears starting to spin. Within seconds, heat swelled inside her body. Not the pleasant sensation that rose being near her men gave her, but a fire. A burning, searing, hungry fire that ate at her insides. It was similar to the magical attack she suffered before in her room in the cabin from who she assumed had been some sorcerer trying to unlock her identity.

She gripped the sides of the chair and clenched her teeth together as the fire surged. Her skin began to glow a radiant, blue-white, like the hottest part of a flame. The light swelled so bright she could only catch glimpses of the world outside the cube through the blinding light. She turned her head—it was hard to do as it was like her body was glued to the chair—and sought out the headmistress.

Headmistress Mittle's face contorted with worry,

her hands wringing together, and Sophia wondered if she was going to open the box and stop the machine. Beyond the headmistress, she spied a darkened shadow filling the doorway at the far end of the room. Was someone else there to watch? Was it Grindel finally arriving? She hoped so. Even though he angered her with his aloof nature and disciplinary attitude, she needed him. She needed him to get through this. Why was he not here?

Sophia's grip on the chair hardened until her fingers formed grooves in the wood. Her magic rippled inside her, swelling. It boiled and churned like a tide pool. Shaking her head, she tried to reach for her magic inside, to catch it before it could destroy, but it slipped through her fingers like sand. There was no way she could clasp it. Her magic had a mind of its own.

It spun inside her body, like a burning top, spiraling up and up, reaching a crescendo that she could no longer restrain. Wild, chaotic magic exploded out of her, shattering the glass of the cube. As glass shards and fragments flew across the room, the very ground beneath her feet shook. A stone tile near her boot heel cracked in half.

Clamping her eyes shut and clenching every muscle in her body, Sophia refused to let her magic destroy everything in the room and to vaporize the headmistress. Concentrating, she imagined sucking her magic back inside her. Drawing every thin tendril of it back through the pores of her skin. Within seconds, she felt her magic lessen, just enough that it didn't completely demolish the room and the castle above.

Spent, Sophia collapsed onto the floor, naked and shaking. As usual her clothes had burned off during the episode, but at least she hadn't seared everything else around her. Although weak and exhausted, she fought off the blackout. She rapidly blinked to stay awake. She felt stronger this time, better than past episodes.

Perhaps it was the machine that aided her, but she doubted it since it was in a hundred pieces on the floor beside her, some metal pieces stuck into the far wall, another casualty of her episode. Perhaps, it was finding the other piece of her soul and spending time near it, even though she didn't know which man held it for her, which one was making her stronger. Though she was sure it was most likely Edric, as she'd spent the most time with him, and had been intimate with him.

Putting her hands on the ground, Sophia pushed up, battling a wave of nausea as she did. She scrambled to her feet, wobbling a little but able to stand on her own mere seconds after an episode for the first time in her life. A sense of pride rose within her. Maybe she could really be a whole person soon, and finally walk through this world without hiding in the shadows. For twelve years it had seemed like an impossible dream, the thought that it might become real nearly made her knees buckle again.

Stepping over glass pieces, Headmistress Mittle came to Sophia and draped a heavy, fur robe over her body to cover her up and keep her warm. Sophia looked up as she did, in time to see the shadow she saw earlier dart out of the doorframe and into the hallway beyond. She supposed it wasn't Grindel, after all, and she bristled. He hadn't come, although she was certain he knew what the headmistress was going to put her through. She didn't care that he didn't necessarily agree with Headmistress Mittle's methods; he should've been here for her. He should've pushed aside his pride and been by her during what he would've known to be an immensely painful process.

The headmistress smoothed a hand down her back. "You did well, my dear. Very well."

Sophia looked around the room, taking in the shattered glass cube and the ruined machine, and smiled, happy she didn't destroy everything within a fifty-foot radius like before. To some, it may not have seemed like a victory, but to Sophia, it was a miracle.

"Are you sure? I did break the machine," Sophia said.

"It's nothing that matters," the headmistress said,

"you're what matters. Healing you is the most important thing in this world."

Sophia asked something she'd always wondered about. "Why?"

Headmistress Mittle met her gaze, looking right into her eyes. "Because you are important, Sophia. You have no idea how much."

Sophia wanted to ask more questions, but the headmistress was leading her over to the tunnel, which meant it was her clue to leave.

"Who else was here?" Sophia asked before she could be ushered away. "There was someone in the doorway. I thought maybe it was Grindel finally showing up."

"Grindel had an errand to do for me, that's why he wasn't here." The headmistress glanced briefly toward the door, then back at Sophia. "As to that, no one else was here, my dear. It was just you and me."

"Are you sure?"

"Oh, yes." Her voice went up an octave. "Quite sure. No one else knows about our work. Just you, me, and Grindel," the headmistress said, as she rubbed Sophia on the back again. "Now, go home and get some rest. You earned it."

After Sophia pulled the robe tighter around herself, and tied it closed with the belt, she shuffled into the tunnel. She glanced over her shoulder one last time at the headmistress, who was standing there, twisting the big emerald ring around her finger, watching her leave.

Headmistress Mittle was hiding something, that much was obvious. She'd been nervous when Sophia had asked about someone else being in the room. The twisting of her ring on her finger was a huge tell. It was a sign of nervousness. And hadn't her voice gone up a little when she'd talking? Sophia had definitely saw something hovering in the doorway, if not another person, then what? And why was the head-mistress lying to her about it?

CHAPTER TWENTY-SIX

SOPHIA

*D*espite still being exhausted from her episode earlier in the day, Sophia was early for her date with Edric, even after bathing at the cottage. Grindel hadn't been there either. When she arrived at the garden fountain, she found a wrapped package with her name on it. She looked around, but she was alone. She opened it to find a stack of books that she'd asked Ezekiel for, and a little note in elegant writing. *A curious mind is a beautiful thing.* She smiled, impressed with him, falling for him just a little.

Before she could open one of the books, Winston stepped onto the cobblestone patio near the fountain. "Hello, Sophia."

She bristled at the sight of him, but remained polite. "Hello, Winston. What are you doing here?"

He sat on the edge of the fountain next to her then reached out a hand to toy with the end of one of the ribbons on her dress. She had to suppress the urge to pull away from him and slap at his brazen hand.

"There was an unexpected change in the shift rotations, so Edric won't be able to make it. He sent me instead to check on you."

She knew it was horseshit. Edric would never send this man to do anything for him. There was no way that Winston was any kind of friend to Edric. She bet that Edric's shift had been changed on purpose, as well.

"What do you want?" She got to her feet, not wanting to be next to him.

"You look tired," he said, frowning. "I hope your... suitors haven't been running you ragged."

She heard the innuendo in his voice and she twisted her hands at her waist to stop one of them from slapping the condescending smirk off his stupid face.

"What do you want, Winston?" she asked again, her voice clipped.

"I want that date you promised."

"I never promised you a date."

His jaw clenched, and she thought she should placate him at least, in case he got angry. She couldn't afford a scene. She couldn't afford having him as an enemy, not while she was so close to fixing her soul. He could make a lot of unnecessary trouble for her. And for her men.

She'd done a little bit of research on Winston and discovered the Kent family were staunch supporters of the duchess. His father, Walter Kent, was a general in the castle guard and not the most gracious of men. General Kent had been a vocal dissenter when the royal family had granted the wraith community access to the city and had given them homes inside the walls. So, Winston's obvious prejudices and such didn't surprise Sophia one bit. He'd been raised to be an ignorant cad. And he was living up to that standard without fail.

"But, I will think about it," she said.

He smiled, then tugged at the skirt of her dress arrogantly. "Did you think about it?"

She tried not to glare at him. She had enough of him, and wanted desperately to put him in his place or to smack him across the head—whichever worked best—but she needed more time to figure out which of her men had the piece of her soul. She couldn't afford to piss him off, not quite yet.

He stood to get closer to her, and she took a step back. He sighed and gave a little shake to his head. "Eventually, you'll realize I'm the one for you. That we're perfect for each other."

"You know nothing about me to make that claim."

"Oh, I beg to differ, sweet Sophia." He lifted an eyebrow. "As I saw you with the oracles. I heard what they said."

Her hackles rose and she frowned, wondering how much of the clues of her identity were revealed in that prophecy. Did he discern that she was an anima contritum? She didn't think so or they wouldn't be having this conversation; there would be city guards here instead, coming to arrest her and take her to the castle cells to await her execution.

He chuckled at her obvious distress. "I know you're a special woman, and special women deserve the very best man." He took another step toward her. "I'm that man, Sophia. I'm from a prominent family. I can get you anything you want. Anything at all. Just name it and it's yours." He glanced down at the books on the fountain. "I'll get you your own library, if that is your wish. I have access to more books than even Ezekiel, the castle's pet sorcerer."

"Winston, you are—"

"I will treat you like a goddess." He reached out and wrapped his fingers around one of her braids.

She gritted her teeth against the onslaught of revulsion that surged over her. She could hurt him just a little, couldn't she? A man could still live a long happy life without a few fingers on his hand. She'd even take them from his left hand, so that he could still wield a sword for the castle guard.

"I heard the oracles say you need to be healed. I don't know what was done to you, but I can heal you, absolutely. I can hire all the best healers from not just Nighthelm, but other kingdoms. Money is no object. Just give me a chance to show you what I can, and will, do for you."

To another woman, his words might have been sweet nectar, but to Sophia, who knew better, they were rotten and stunk to the high heavens. He just wanted to be special through her, to show her off like a trophy, to his bawdy friends, to his haughty family. That's all wealthy men like Winston understood. Possessions. To have. To own. She would never be anyone's possession.

"I appreciate your offer, Winston, but I have a lot going on, and—"

"Yes, I heard you were having sex with Edric, the wraith, and the sorcerer."

She stiffened at his brazen statement. No man had ever talked to her in that way. She gave him a withering look.

"I knew it." He laughed. "You'll realize how wrong you are the moment they break your heart, and they will break it. All three of them have a string of lovers left broken in the streets. They use women for their own depraved ways, then toss them aside. Especially that wraith. His kind are naturally immoral."

She knew he was talking horseshit again. Anything to rile her up.

He jerked on her braid. It wasn't a playful little tug but a warning. "I won't wait around forever, Sophia." He let his hand drop, then he walked away.

She really wanted to shout after him, "Promise?" but she didn't. She was just relieved that he'd finally left her alone. In case Edric was able to get off his shift that Winston no doubt orchestrated to get him on, Sophia sat at the fountain and read through some of the notes Ezekiel prepared in order to answer some of her questions. She ran her hand over the pages and the ink, pushing away the uneasy feelings Winston had given her. Ezekiel's gesture was so sweet, she found herself smiling as she skimmed the sections he marked for her.

Reading through a ton of notes and scribbles, she finally found the pieces that mattered to her. The oracles had, a few times before, instructed the honored—or those who they spoke to—to bring certain people before them. If those chosen people were not worthy, they were killed by the trees' roots, and the wish of the honored ones granted in exchange.

Sophia realized she ran the very real risk of a deadly choice: sacrifice one of the men she was begin-ning to love, or live forever broken? This was the decision that the oracles had forced upon her. If she wanted to be whole again, she had to make a sacrifice. How could she do that and live with herself?

She continued flipping through the pages and the other notes Ezekiel made until she came upon some information about contritums. As she read the words, her hands shook. Contrary to what the headmistress had explained to her in the past, anima contritums weren't born… they were made purposely. Frowning, she continued reading, heart slamming in her chest. A contritum was broken through witnessing a truly horrific event. She'd seen this event when she was little.

Someone had broken her on purpose.

After shutting the book, she picked them up and placed them under her arm. She left the garden to return to the wall and the exit to the woods. Haris found her the moment she crossed through the tunnel, and she jumped on his back, urging him home to the cabin as quick as he could.

When she arrived at the cabin, she stormed inside, intent on demanding answers from Grindel about all the lies she'd been fed over the years. But the cottage was quiet and empty. Anger fueled her, and she swiped her hand at the clay cups, knocking them off the kitchen counter. They broke on the wood floor. She wanted to break more, but she reined the urge in, knowing it would do no good. Besides that, she would have to clean it all up since he was absent. Her anger was at Grindel, not at the things in the cottage.

She would find out the truth. She would demand to know what the hell was done to her and why. Whoever did this to her would pay.

CHAPTER TWENTY-SEVEN

SOPHIA

*T*he night and day sped by in a bit of a blur, and as Sophia walked with Andreas to the wraith district near the far wall, she was quiet and lost in her thoughts just as she had been with Ezekiel the other day. She couldn't help it. Her mind buzzed, and for the life of her, she couldn't silence the noise.

Andreas didn't seem to mind, as he held her hand and looked at her every now and then to make sure she was content. She enjoyed the silence. She liked that he didn't feel the need to fill up the space with words. His presence alone gave her comfort, made her feel strong, powerful, and capable.

And right now, the silence was soothing as she contemplated the last few days.

The experience in the great hall with the head-mistress and what she learned from the books that

Ezekiel had given to her swirled around in her head. She tried to make sense of it all, to form a plan to move forward, but it seemed so damned complicated.

Deep down, she didn't *want* to do this alone. She wished she could tell Andreas everything. She knew he would be able to help her sort it all out. Keeping it all inside was torture.

Maybe out of all of her men, Andreas would be the most understanding, since he was a wraith and considered an outsider, unfairly, by many of the people in Nighthelm. What Winston had said about him still made her shake with anger.

She looked up at him, intent on saying something about what she was going through, when they heard a cry from beyond the wall.

It was faint but discernible. High pitched. Terrified.

A child. Beyond the wall. Hurt, by the sound of it.

Without a word, Andreas grabbed her hand and they ran together to the wall, then onto the rampart, where very few guards patrolled. Sophia spotted a little girl in the grass not far off, a commoner by the look of her simple frock and lack of shoes. The girl lay on the ground not far from the wall, maybe half-way to the edge of the woods, crawling through the grass. From the tilt of her ankle, it looked as though she had a broken foot.

How and why she had gotten out there concerned Sophia deeply, but her protective instincts kicked in.

This was a child of Nighthelm, and it was Sophia's duty to protect her at all costs.

"We have to save her," Sophia said, her voice tense and urgent.

Andrea nodded. "I agree, though this reeks of a trap. It's a classic strategy, although I don't know who would be laying a trap out here or for whom."

She hesitated only for a moment before she said, "Grimms."

He frowned. "Why would grimms be laying a trap, and for who? It's not how they usually behave."

"There's no time to discuss it." She implored him with her eyes. "We can't let her die out there."

"We won't." He gave her a soft look. "I suppose it's pointless asking you to stay put and allowing me to go get her?"

"Yes, it is."

"That's what I thought." He unsheathed the two blades strapped to his back and handed her the smaller of them. "Let's go."

They left the city through the secret gate that Edric had shown her after the minotaur attack. It certainly seemed like her dates were getting more dangerous by the day, but such was Sophia's life. Never a dull moment.

Silent and swift as ghosts, they hurried across the grass to the girl. When they reached her, the child immediately reached for Sophia to pick her up and soothe her. There wasn't time for that. They needed to get her to safety, and immediately. Sophia's skin crawled, and she could feel beady eyes watching them from the woods. Without a doubt in her mind, she knew she sensed the ominous presence of grimms nearby.

She looked to the woods. "Haris," she called softly, knowing full well her friend would be able to hear her even if he was miles off. Such was their connection—neither was far from the other. When she was in the city, he stayed close by in the event he needed her, like now.

Within moments, Haris sprinted out of the woods, a green swirling blur of light and magic. Andreas flinched at the sight of the creature, freezing in awe as he watched it near.

"A forest spirit?" he asked, surprise raising the tone of his voice.

Sophia didn't answer him. She didn't have time. Quickly, she put the little girl on Haris's back. "Hold tightly to the fur at his neck, little one," Sophia said, trying her best to be soothing even though her body tensed, waiting for the fight she knew would come.

The girl obeyed, whimpering and sniffling as she held on tight. Streaks of tears lined her face, and Sophia's gaze quickly drifted to the girl's twisted ankle. It jutted off to the side, the unnatural angle unquestionably broken. Sophia gritted her teeth in anger, disgusted that the grimms would stoop so low.

Andreas eyed her with a frown. "A forest spirit doesn't bond with just *anyone*, Sophia. And this one *clearly* obeys you."

"You need to take her to safety," she said to Haris, ignoring the way Andreas was looking at her. They didn't have time to play around and ask a whole lot of questions. The grimms would be upon them in any moment.

"Who are you?" Andreas asked, his voice commanding and dark. "Tell me, Sophia. The truth. *Now*."

"Andreas, hear me out."

"I'm listening."

"I—look out!" From the depths of the forest, five grimms bolted toward them in a flash of shadow and darkness. Haris darted around one hovering form that reached out with its hooked claws. Thankfully, her pet listened, bolting toward the city fast enough that he managed to get himself and the child out of the fray. Before disappearing into the trees with the girl on his back, Haris looked over his shoulder, clearly worried for her safety.

Sophia knew that expression: *I'm coming back.*

Once Haris had vanished around a bend in the city's defenses, Sophia lashed at the nearest grimm. Her blade cut across its chest. It shrieked as tar-like blood spewed from the wound. It didn't slow it down, instead, advancing on her, forcing her to duck under the swipe of its talons. Beside her, Andreas took a grimm down, just as another launched at him from the side.

"They are becoming more brutal, more desperate," he said as he took a step back toward her. "I've never seen them act this way."

Sophia hesitated a second as her body convulsed. All her muscles seemed to twist at once. She knew that sensation. Her magic swirled inside her, ready to burst. Heat built in her center. Soon, she wouldn't be able to control it. She couldn't believe she was going to have another episode so soon. It must've been the stress of the situation pressing down on her.

Shaking off the feeling, Sophia ran toward the grimm with her sword raised. As she rushed toward the creature, it turned and glared at her, its violet eyes glowing with hate. Before she could cut it, it hissed at her.

"You will pay for what you've done," it said, saliva spitting out from between its sharp rows of teeth.

Andreas looked at her with a mix of curiosity and suspicion, even as he dodged out of the way of another grimm. He pressed his back against Sophia's as the grimms paused, circling them, waiting for an opening to attack.

His jaw tensing, Andreas snuck a glare at her.

"What is it talking about, Sophia? Grimms only hold grudges against those who have severely harmed them."

Sophia shook her head, trying to think beyond the heat swelling inside her body. Her magic bubbled too close to the surface, and with her exhaustion, her recent discoveries, and her anger at having been lied to and used for years, she knew she couldn't hold it back. It was too much to contain.

He must've noticed her distress as he asked, "What's wrong?"

"Run!" she shouted at Andreas. Her throat tightened, the emotion overwhelming as she tried to make him leave.

He frowned. "What are you talking about?"

"Run! Before I hurt you!" She dropped to her knees, as her hands began to glow blue-white.

His eyes grew wide at the magic in her hands, but he didn't back away. "I won't leave you to die." He reached for her, but she slapped his hand away.

"Go. Now. I can't… hold… it…"

She clamped her eyes shut and curled into a ball as the swirling, chaotic energy exploded out of her. It burned. It consumed her. It fried everything nearby, reducing the world around her to ash.

Exhausted, her body spent, she slowly blinked open her eyes. She lay on her side on the ground. Had she passed out? If she had, for how long? Everything around her was scorched, including the grimms. Naked, she pushed to her feet. She wobbled once, then stood firm. Her body was weak, but not immobile, as she feared the worst.

Where was Andreas?

Frantic, she searched the area for him, shouting his name, afraid he'd burned up like everything else that mattered. "Andreas?"

A groan came from the nearby trees. She rushed over to find Andreas on the ground, his clothes burnt off like her own. He looked up at her, but she didn't see fear and hatred like she expected.

Instead awe and wonder filled his eyes.

Sophia helped him to his feet, sure he was going to push her away in disgust. "Are you hurt?"

"You're an anima contritum." His wide eyes moved over her, from her face down her body.

She sighed and pressed her lips together, waiting with bated breath for his condemnation; his hatred. She didn't know what she would do if he rejected her. It would break her heart, for sure. Instead, he grabbed her around the waist, pulling her to him. Leaning down, he kissed her. It was so deep her whole body flushed with pleasure and she became fully aware that they were both naked and pressed together intimately.

Before she could take another ragged breath, he shifted into his wraith form and whisked her up into the air. It was an odd sensation, floating above the trees, wrapped in shadow and smoke. She could still feel Andreas's arms around her, feel the solidness of him, even if she couldn't actually see his form.

They sailed over the big oaks, across the stream and settled down in the relative safety of a nearby knoll. Rays of sunshine bathed the soft, green grass with warm, yellow light. As Andreas shifted back into human form, Sophia ran her hands over her arms. Her body quivered, her limbs loose and weak, but she knew it wasn't from the slight chill. It was being here with Andreas, completely vulnerable and naked in every way.

"You're not disgusted with what I am?" she asked when he moved toward her.

He didn't speak, he just pulled her to him again and kissed her as an answer. She liked his answer, it made her head swim and her heart thunder against her rib cage. And there was no mistaking his interest in her, as she could feel the hard length of him pressed against her belly.

"You're the most extraordinary woman I've ever met." He peppered her face with kisses, and then nibbled on her bottom lip and along her chin. Her belly clenched with raw desire from his touch.

While they kissed, his hands explored her body. A little gasp escaped her lips as he caressed her breasts, lightly pinching her nipples. His hand moved down lower and a swell of pleasure rushed over her when he cupped her between her thighs.

She shivered, and he wrapped his arms around her and gently lowered her into a warm pool of sunlight on the carpet of soft green. He covered her with his powerful form. She should've felt small and fragile beneath his large hard body, but instead she felt invincible. He did that to her, made her feel like she could do anything, like she could conquer the world if she wanted, with him at her side.

Burying her hands in the silkiness of his dark hair, Sophia rolled him over, until she was on top, straddling his body. His already dark eyes darkened further, becoming dark as the blackest night as he gazed up at her. He groaned low in his throat as she stroked her hands down his torso, feathering fingers over his rippled stomach, and lightly tracing the dark hair that lined his pelvis. She made him gasp when she boldly wrapped a hand around the hard length of his cock.

He had discovered the truth. He knew what she was, and yet he accepted her. Loved her as she was, for all her flaws and fractures.

This man was a treasure, and she was entirely lost in him. She couldn't wait even one more minute.

She needed him. Now.

Lifting up on her knees, she positioned herself over him. As she slowly lowered herself onto his shaft, Andreas gripped her hips in strong hands, guiding her, supporting her. When she was fully seated, licks of pleasure fluttered over her body. There was no sharp sting of pain as there had been with Edric, but only the euphoria of being intimate with a man she adored.

Andreas bit down on his lip as she started to move, undulating her hips. She saw how he struggled to let her lead, to hold back. But she loved him for his restraint. Heat swelled inside her with every stroke, until she thought she would burn up from the inside out.

"You are a fierce warrior, Sophia," he said, his voice low and raspy. "My warrior."

His words spurred her on, until she panted and gasped, every muscle in her body on fire and quivering like the string on her bow when she shot an arrow. Unable to hold herself up any longer, Sophia fell over Andreas's chest, burying her face in the curve of his neck.

He cupped her face with his hands and brought her mouth to his. He kissed her hard, tasting her and teasing with his tongue and teeth. She was languid and liquid, fever and fire from the top of her head to the tips of her toes. Right before she could handle no more pleasure, Andreas grabbed her ass and flipped her over, rutting hard between her legs.

She dug her nails into his back as he buried himself deep inside her and groaned out her name. She bowed her back as a wave of heat and light slammed into her, forcing a grunt between her lips. It was a powerful orgasm, strong and overwhelming, beautiful and fierce. Closing her eyes, she let the wave carry her away until they were panting hard, bodies shaking from the passion that had consumed them.

When she was able to move again, Sophia opened her eyes to see Andreas next to her, looking at her, smoothing a hand over her hair. She smiled at him, feeling love blossom in her heart, grateful that he'd accepted her. Grateful for his understanding.

"You're not Sophia Oxford, are you? Lord Oxford's niece?" he asked.

She shook her head. "Sophia, yes, but not the Oxford part."

"And the training? Where did you learn to fight so well? It was obviously not from your non-uncle."

"From Matthew Grindel," she said.

His eyes widened. "Professor Matthew Grindel? Who teaches history at the academy?"

"Yes. There's a lot more to him than just boring history."

He laughed. "Obviously."

She laughed with him, relief flowing out of her at finally being able to share her secret with someone.

"Do Edric and Zeke know?" he asked.

She shook her head. "No, and you won't tell them, will you?" Her voice was low, pleading.

"Never," he said.

"Thank you." She sighed.

He pressed a kiss to her shoulder, as if he sensed her unspoken concerns. "You are so beautiful and perfect to me. I could never betray you."

She wanted to cry with joy, the emotions welling up to the surface. She realized that she had fallen in love with him, with Edric, *and* with Ezekiel. All in different ways. She wondered what on earth she was going to do, and what the bloody hell she was going to tell the oracles.

CHAPTER TWENTY-EIGHT

The next day, Sophia returned to the training hall under the castle to find Head-mistress Mittle waiting for her with another device similar to the last one. Surprisingly, Grindel was also present, looking on from afar, without comment. She glared at him, not yet having a chance to interrogate him about the lies and omissions he'd been feeding her over the years. He hadn't even been back to the cabin to sleep or anything. He'd obviously been avoiding her, like a coward.

She took a step toward him. "I need to speak with you."

He looked like was going to say something to her, but the headmistress blocked Sophia from going to Grindel by stepping between the two of them. "I'm sure whatever it is you need to say to Grindel, you can do later. Now, is about healing you. That's more important, don't you think?"

Sophia nodded.

"Since you had an episode yesterday in the forest." The headmistress looked at Sophia with a pointed expression. How had she known about that? She didn't think it had been witnessed by anyone. Someone was spying on her and reporting it to the headmistress. "Today, we can begin to explore the cracks without fear of destroying the castle above us and hurting innocents within a fifty-foot radius."

Her comment about innocents rattled Sophia. It plainly said to her, that Sophia didn't belong in that group. She probably didn't, but in her mind, neither did the headmistress or Grindel, for that matter. As far as she was concerned, they were both culpable in what had happened to her in the past, and what was happening to her now.

Headmistress Mittle gestured with a hand to the simple, wooden chair next to the machine inside another glass box. Sophia suspected the glass helped the machine direct its power or energy toward Sophia by keeping it contained. Although the last one didn't do its job whatsoever. Sophia had nearly blasted it back into sand.

Sophia sat in the chair while the headmistress adjusted some dials and switches on the machine. Those were definitely new additions. Then she picked up a leather strap with wires connected to it and then secured it around Sophia's head. Also, something new.

"What is this?" Sophia asked. Bile in her throat starting to rise.

"I know it's uncomfortable, but it needs to be done," the headmistress said as Sophia fussed in the chair, not wanting to be bound to the machine. "After the last time, we need to focus your magic even more. The alchemists assured me this would help."

Once the head strap was secure, the headmistress stepped out of the glass box. For a moment, Sophia thought that maybe the machine wasn't going to work, that the headmistress hadn't hooked it up properly. Then a bolt of pain speared her in the right temple, and she screamed. Out of the corner of her eye, she saw Grindel flinch. It was the first honest emotion she'd seen from him in years.

She pitched forward as another bolt jabbed her in the left temple. The skin on her hands lit up like a shooting star as her magic came to the surface. She reached up to tear the strap from her head, when Headmistress Mittle shouted.

"Stop! I know it's painful, but it's necessary to heal you."

She looked to Grindel, the man she trusted her whole life, as he watched stonily from nearby. Obviously he'd gained his composure. But she knew him. His body was rigid. She saw the pain etched on his face, and in the way he regarded her. She could see how much her torture hurt him too. She knew he cared.

And yet he did nothing to stop it.

She wanted to scream at him, "Help me!"

But as always, Sophia had to save herself.

Sophia gritted her teeth as surges of electricity bombarded her body. Pain zipped from her head down to her toes and then back again. Blood filled her mouth as she bit her tongue to stop another scream from ripping from her throat. She was locked in, forced to endure the worst.

To protect herself, she willed her magic forward to create a shield against the pain. Once that was in place, she concentrated on the machine picturing it in her mind, dissecting all its parts to find its weaknesses. She tried to overwhelm it, to break it and make the torture stop. Little sparks jumped out of one of the wires and shorted out the machine. The headmistress rushed into the box to turn off the machine before it broke into a hundred pieces like the last one.

"We'll take a break," Headmistress Mittle said as she unstrapped Sophia. "Come back to it in a little bit. Go get some air."

Sophia nodded, but she knew this was it, the moment she was going to quit. The moment she realized that these two would never help her. Maybe they could never do it, or maybe they never wanted to.

They had been lying to her about many things, she suspected.

When the head gear was removed, Sophia collapsed onto the ground. Grindel was there at her side, lifting her up, but she smacked him away. She didn't want or need his sympathy now. She stood on her own, limped out of the box and across the room, the final betrayal too much to bear.

These two knew more than they were letting on, and she couldn't tolerate the lies any longer. She couldn't trust them. She wouldn't. She would heal herself with the help of one of her men, restore the heirs to the throne, and get the bloody hell out of the city forever. She was tired of being broken, of being pried apart and studied, to be put back together only to be torn apart again, too tired of being a freak.

On the way out through the tunnel, Grindel came up behind her. "Stop, Sophia. Where are you going? We're not done."

She whirled on him. "We *are* done. You and me, and the headmistress. You've been lying to me from the beginning. Both of you." She poked him in his bony chest. "It was no accident that I was broken, was it? This was done to me. Someone did this to me!"

He sighed, his whole body sagging into itself. After a glance over his shoulder, he grabbed her arm, pulled her close and whispered, "One day, you'll understand. You must trust me."

She wasn't having it. She pulled away from his grip and turned to continue the walk through the tunnel back to the woods and eventually the cottage, alone. That was all it seemed that she would ever be, was alone. Alone in her fight to fix her soul, alone in her mission to find the heirs.

She stepped out of the tunnel and instantly found Haris waiting for her. He must've sensed that she needed him. Without a word, she climbed onto his back and he took off at a gallop, knowing she needed to go, and fast.

CHAPTER TWENTY-NINE

EDRIC

*E*dric sat in the back of the Black Horse Pub, among the shadows, with three pints of ale in front of him on the long, worn, wooden table, waiting on his guests. He'd chosen the pub because it was off the main roads, in a working-class district in Nighthelm and not frequented often by castle guards. It was quiet, except for the table of smiths and cattlemen nearby who were very loudly celebrating the impending marriage of one of their young members, and not too many people would recognize him to interrupt his plans. He didn't wear his uniform, opting to dress in simple trousers, shirt and leather overcoat. He forwent his sword as well, but still had two daggers strapped to each ankle under his boots. He never went anywhere unarmed. And in this neighborhood where bar brawls were frequent, he liked to be prepared.

The buxom barmaid sashayed up to the table again. He swore there was one less button done up on the bodice of her dress. "Are you sure I can't get ye something to eat? The lamb pie is quite good."

He shook his head. "No food, thank you."

She leaned forward, giving him a full view of her ample cleavage. "Can I interest you in anything else?"

Three weeks ago, Edric might have taken the girl up on her brazen offer. She wouldn't have been the first barmaid he'd bedded. But now he only had eyes and feelings for one woman. Sophia. She was the reason he'd invited Andreas and Ezekiel to meet him in this pub for a drink. She was quickly becoming the reason for many things.

He sat back farther into his seat, placing as much distance between him and the offering as he could. "I appreciate the offer, but I'm well spoken for."

She pursed her lips and pouted. "That's too bad. You're the best-looking man to ever walk into this pub in years." She sashayed away, giving her wide hips an exaggerated swing for his benefit.

Moments later, Andreas walked in, looked around, spotted Edric, and then joined him at the table. He eyed the beer warily.

Edric laughed. "If I wanted to kill a wraith, I

wouldn't be lame enough to do it with poison. It would be with my blade and nothing more."

"You wish." Picking up the mug, Andreas sat on the sagging bench and took a sip. "Thank you for the drink." He took another hearty drink, and then wiped the froth from his mouth with the back of his hand. "Why did you ask for a meeting?"

Before Edric could answer, Ezekiel swept into the pub, sat, and chugged the ale down. "Thanks, I needed that. All the sorcerers and alchemists have been working overtime at the castle trying to figure out where these tremors are coming from." He shook his head. "I swear its some kind of magic, but I can't discern what kind and from whom."

Andreas visibly tensed and dropped his gaze to this beer. To Edric, it appeared that he might know something about the disturbances. Edric made a mental note to ask him for more information later. For now, they had other matters to discuss. Except Ezekiel kept talking.

"Did you feel that last tremor?" He shook his head. "It really shook the castle. I couldn't get much work done after that."

Edric gave Andreas a look, but the wraith just shrugged and continued to drink his ale.

"Oh, and don't even get me started on all the fear mongering going on in the city by the duchess and her cronies. Yes, there was a minotaur attack, but that is so rare, you can't base new laws around that. It's not right." He shook his head, and then looked at Edric.

He gave Ezekiel a look. "Are you quite finishing complaining?"

Ezekiel shrugged. "Maybe. Depends on why you've summoned us here." Then took another sip of his drink.

"Yes, why are we here?" Andreas asked again, now that Ezekiel had shut his mouth.

"It's about Sophia." Edric sighed.

The other two tensed, anticipating what he was going to say.

"I'm in love with her," Edric said. "Really and truly. For me, this isn't a contest anymore. I want nothing more than to win her heart." He looked at Andreas and then at Ezekiel. "If either of you are in this just for the contest, to win, then I ask you to stop. Please."

They looked at each other then back at Edric.

"I will give both of you whatever you want to end the contest, to bow out. Gold, steel, jewels, a command post in the guard, doesn't matter."

They all sat silently at first. Andreas finished his ale, and crossed his arms. Ezekiel spun his mug on the table. It made a hollow, ringing sound.

Then Andreas said, "I'm in love with her too."

Ezekiel nodded. "I confess I am as well."

"Well, shit." Edric finished his ale, slammed down

the mug, then signaled for the barmaid to bring them three more.

When the barmaid arrived with the tray of drinks, each man took one. She batted her eyelashes at them, but Edric was happy to see that neither Andreas nor Ezekiel gave her a second look. It confirmed in him that they were being true to their word. That they only had eyes for Sophia, as did he.

Andreas finished his drink in two gulps, and signaled for another, while Ezekiel barely sipped his. He looked as miserable and forlorn as Edric did at the prospect of all three of them being in love with the same woman, and not being able to do a damn thing about it except wait for her to make her decision.

Edric looked at his companions and wondered what he could share with them. He and Andreas were seasoned warriors, fighting for their city and the people in it. He supposed Ezekiel did as well, just in a different way. Edric knew the sorcerer was a devout loyalist to the realm. And they all obviously loved Sophia, so they had that in common. They'd known each other all their lives, always battling, always competing to see who was better. Maybe the three men could be more than just competitors.

He cleared his throat, realizing that if there was going to be change, he was going to have to be the first one to open up. "She makes me feel worthy of something great," Edric said.

Andreas unfolded his arms, and leaned on the table, nodding. "I feel that too. She gives me purpose. Real purpose."

Ezekiel traced a finger in the spilled beer on the table and didn't look at either of them as he spoke. "For the first time in a very long time, I feel happy when I'm with her."

"I'm not sure I could imagine a life without her in it." Edric looked at each man. He did it as a challenge. Daring each of them to back away. What he didn't expect was to see the same sentiment in their eyes. Edric sighed. With a woman like Sophia, he really shouldn't have expected anything less. He lifted his drink. "May the best man win."

Andreas and Ezekiel lifted their beers and toasted.

EDRIC

Several ales later, Ezekiel was standing on top of the bar singing a rousing rendition of a drinking ballad he had learned during one of his travels to another kingdom. Edric and Andreas stood off to the side cheering him on.

I'll drink from dusk till dawn
I'll drink a toast to day's end.

Yes, I'll drink from dusk till dawn
And I'll drink to the health of me friends.

He swung his mug toward Edric and Andreas, sloshing ale over the rim, then spun on his boot heel on the last note, holding it until he ran out of breath.

Though he'd never admit as much, Edric thought it was pretty impressive. The sorcerer had a decent singing voice, much to Edric's surprise.

During the night, he'd learned a lot of things about Ezekiel and Andreas. They'd known each other their whole lives, but hadn't really known anything of real importance. Until now. Sophia had brought them together.

When he was done spinning, Ezekiel flung out his arms and let himself fall backwards off the bar.

Luckily Edric and Andreas were there to catch him, or else he would've landed on a burly farmer who had scowled through Ezekiel's entire ten-verse song.

The beefy barkeep glared at them, his little, beady, black eyes narrowing into tiny points. "Better carry him out of here. He's done drinking."

Edric nodded, tossing a few gold coins onto the counter top. "For your trouble."

As they half-carried, half-dragged Ezekiel out of the pub, the sorcerer was still singing his song about "me friends." When they got outside, he perked right up and started to dance a little jig. Despite being completely sloshed, Ezekiel was quick and light on his feet. Edric had been sure he was going to fall flat on his face the moment he'd stood without their help.

"Let's go to another pub," the sorcerer said, with a lopsided grin. "I have a lot of coins to spend."

Edric shook his head. "You've had enough."

"But he hasn't." Ezekiel pointed his finger at Andreas.

Andreas shrugged. "I can't get drunk. Alcohol doesn't impair wraiths. I could drink ten more ales and be completely sober."

Ezekiel made a face. "That's interesting. They don't teach you that in the academy."

"I think they miss a lot of things at the academy," Edric said. After all that he'd seen and was startling to learn, he realized that the academy wasn't doing the best job.

"Look at what I can do." The sorcerer rubbed his hands together and produced a small ball of blue light between them.

"That's impressive," Edric said. "However, I don't like the idea of drunk magic. Seems like an easy way to lose a leg."

"Psh, you old hen." Ezekiel scrunched up his nose in drunken disappointment.

Edric chuckled. "Now, let's get you back to the castle." He glanced at Andreas. "Let's flip a coin to see who carries him."

While they were busy figuring out the coin flip, Ezekiel precariously bounced his ball of light from hand to hand. "The color's the same as Sophia's eyes, don't you think?"

Then it got away from him, and landed on the bench nearby. It burned a hole right through the wood.

"Whoops," he said.

"Let's both carry him," Edric said, "it'll be faster."

Andreas nodded. "Agreed."

They picked him up and started the walk back up to the castle.

Ezekiel closed his eyes and started to hum. "You know, if Sophia had to end up with someone, and not me, I suppose the two of you are the better choices than anyone else in the city," Ezekiel said, with a bit of a slur.

Andreas laughed. "That's mighty big of you to admit there, Zeke."

Ezekiel lifted his head and smiled. "My pleasure."

During the long walk to the castle, and as Ezekiel regaled them with a story about the time he played chess with a giant in the kingdom of Verheim, Edric thought about Sophia and the contest. The same question was likely running through their minds, *who was Sophia going to pick and when?* Edric didn't have the answer. Neither of them did, but what he did know was that regardless of the outcome, he had gained two brothers. Men he'd fight for, and defend to the end. Hopefully, it would never come to that.

A small thread of dread weaved through his mind. The attacks of the minotaurs and the grimms on the city seemed like a harbinger of things to come. Something was brewing in Witch Woods. And Edric had a feeling that it revolved around Sophia.

CHAPTER THIRTY

*S*ophia was having a really shitty day. She wasn't feeling all that well either. Her head ached, as did the muscles in her arms. The machine had done some damage the other day, and she was still feeling the after effects despite the long, hot bath she'd taken and the eucalyptus ointment she had slathered all over her body to ease the pain.

She sat at the fountain, which had become a place for her to think in relative solace and feel connected to her men, even though her date with Ezekiel wasn't for several hours. She couldn't be at the cabin. Not after yelling at Grindel back in the tunnel. And with the grimms hunting her, the woods were no longer safe for her, so she was here.

She made Haris promise he would find a safe place and that he wouldn't wait around for her on the edge of the woods where the last grimm attack had occurred. She didn't know what she would do, if her best friend got hurt because of her. She'd never forgive herself. If only he could be in the city with her.

She lifted her face to the sun and closed her eyes, enjoying how it warmed her skin. Living in the Witch Woods and training every day, didn't often give Sophia an opportunity to bask in the sunlight as she was surrounded by shadow and darkness. It was such a simple thing that most people took for granted. She reveled in it now, soaking it up. Then there was a subtle shift in the air next to her and she opened her eyes.

Winston sat next to her without an invitation, and she repressed an impulsive groan of disgust. Her aversion to him had to have been written all over her face, but the man just couldn't take a hint.

"I can tell you're not feeling great," he said matter-of-fact, as if they were best friends. "Did one of those bastards hurt you?"

She flinched. "No, of course none of them hurt me. It's unrelated."

He gave her a knowing smile. "It's okay, I won't say I told you so or make you feel dumb about dating them. I just want to help."

No, she thought, *you just want to parade me around the town like a sex trophy you won.*

Winston leaned close to her. "You know I'll always love you, Sophia, no matter what you are."

Sophia stared at him in surprise, and he simply nodded with that ever present condescending smirk on his face.

"I've seen a few of your meetings with Headmistress Mittle." He titled his head to regard her. "Terrible secret, that. It would be a shame for anyone to learn about it." He gave her an unwelcome wide smile, that made her jaw clench. "Thankfully I'm very loyal and honest. I just want to make you happy. Can't be too sure what Edric, Andreas, and Ezekiel would do if they knew. I would think they wouldn't be as forgiving as I am."

She didn't say anything. She didn't want to confirm or deny what he was saying in case he was bluffing. She couldn't be too sure, as she was certain someone had watched the last time she'd been in the glass box, despite Headmistress Mittle's assurances that they'd been alone. Someone had been spying on her for a long time.

He leaned in again, and she had to fight the urge to pull away. "My loyalty does come with a price though." His voice was like the slithering of a snake over her skin.

Instead of leaning away, Sophia got right into his face. "The last few monsters who threatened me screamed as I slowly slit their throats."

His eyes widened, and he stumbled back a step. She grinned in satisfaction, but it was short lived, because he straightened his shoulders and grinned back at her, and some of her bravado vanished at the absolute vileness of that smile. "You're the mistress of the wild and I'm the master of Nighthelm."

He set his hand on her arm. Her skin crawled at the contact.

"But as long as you're in my realm, the one I control, I'll give you one last chance to make the smart choice." He rubbed his thumb along her wrist as her pulse jumped. His grin widened, as he likely thought her heart rate had picked up in response to his touch. It was not the reason that he was expecting.

She was tired of people in high places trying to make her dance like a puppet on strings. She was tired of being controlled, of being tortured and abused in the name of people who swore they actually cared about her. No more. Never again.

She yanked her arm away from him and sneered. "Go fuck yourself, Winston."

Furious, he stood, blustering like a child. "You'll regret this." He pointed a finger at her.

She wanted to reach out and snap it right off like a twig from a branch.

"And not just because I'm such a great guy, but because I can make things difficult and, well, you should just use your imagination." He turned on his boot heels then stomped away, muttering under his breath about how she could sleep with the entire castle guard and their horses for all he cared. Two other people who were in the garden had to leap out of his way or be knocked over. They looked over at her, giving her a disparaging look, as if it was her fault Winston had a temper tantrum. She hated that his outburst had drawn attention to her.

Tense, angry, and fueled with rage, Sophia jumped to her feet and paced the garden. She'd lost her temper on Winston and was sure she was going to pay for it in some way. She was running out of time. The full moon was coming. She didn't have much time before she had to present her men to the oracles and hope that she made the right choice.

CHAPTER THIRTY-ONE

EZEKIEL

For the past week, Ezekiel had been perfecting his spell, the one that failed to show him what tied him to Nighthelm and kept him coming back. He stared at the circle drawn out on the gray stone floor, and then sighed deeply, wondering if he should bother to use it. Over all, he'd spent years on the spell, but now he had Sophia. He found a reason to stay, finally, that didn't include whatever black magic kept drawing him back home. She was his reason.

He stared at his lifetime of work around the dark hall, etched on walls and floors, on papers spread across tables, and wondered if he really had Sophia. He hoped that she would choose him, but after meeting with Edric and Andreas and seeing that they too had fallen for her, he wasn't so confident.

If she didn't choose him, he would want to leave and never return. If she rejected him, it would be the final, devastating blow from a city he could no longer live in. If she rejected him, he would want to leave immediately, and to do that, he had to be free of whatever kept drawing him back.

It's settled, then, he said to himself. *I need to do this. I need to make this work.*

Just in case.

After walking around the circle on the floor, inspecting the extra symbols he'd added one last time, Ezekiel decided to use the spell. This time it wouldn't just show him the source of the magic... it would summon the user and bind her within the circle, so Ezekiel could interrogate her and finally deal with her in whatever way he saw fit.

He checked his belt to make sure he'd sheathed one of his daggers, in case he needed it. He was certain whoever had trapped him to Nighthelm wasn't going to be happy to have been summoned with a binding magic spell, so Ezekiel was just taking precautions.

He clapped his hands twice, and then rubbed them together in a circular pattern to energize his magic and bring it to the surface. Lifting his hands over the circle, he pushed all his intentions into his power as the skin on his hands began to glow.

At first, there was some push back from somewhere. He wondered if it was the source combating his magic. Frowning, he concentrated all his thoughts into one thread of power. He would literally reach through space and time, lasso the source of the black magic, and pull it through the ether and into the protected circle.

In his mind, he envisioned his magic like rope. It wrapped around a form, and Ezekiel pulled back with his hands as if he tugged on a thick, braided cord. With an audible pop, and a blinding flash of light, a form appeared within his magical circle.

Finally.

Victorious, Ezekiel grinned in triumph. Blinking away the black spots in his vision from the white burst of light, he looked at the person curled up on the floor. His heart leapt into his throat, as he couldn't believe what he saw.

Sophia lifted her head, rubbing at her temples as she met Ezekiel's gaze. Licking her lips as if they were dry, she got to her feet. She wobbled, clearly exhausted from his spell, and fell back down to her knees. The trip through the ether wouldn't have been a pleasant one, but that was by design. His spell was supposed to strip the source of the black magic, making it weak, trapping it in his circle so that he could finally destroy it.

But this... Ezekiel didn't know what to make of *this*.

"Sophia? How can this be?" He frowned, not believing his eyes.

She rubbed at her forehead again. "So, you're the one who's been poking and jabbing at me. I should've guessed. Your magic is very strong."

He shook his head. No, this wasn't possible. But then again, maybe that was the reason he'd been so drawn to her. Maybe it wasn't love that connected them.

Maybe it was black magic drawing him to this woman. A curse.

Ezekiel summoned a powerful spell—one that could kill—and aimed it at her. His body rippled and buzzed with the magic as he held it at bay, waiting for the right moment to strike even while he doubted he could bring himself to do so. His anger boiled within him, a lifetime trapped in this damned place of nightmares and bad memories eating away at his resilience.

She lifted her chin and stared him down defiantly, although she was clearly weakened. Her skin was pale, slick with sweat, and she kept rubbing at her head as though it were throbbing. Something had happened to her. It wasn't just his spell, and for this one moment, she was completely at his mercy.

"You're not a sorcerer," he said through gritted teeth. "I would know. There hasn't been a sorceress in centuries."

She continued to stare at him, never saying a word.

She simply waited, and that infuriated him even more. Despite the surprise of seeing her under the circumstances, he respected her defiance. He'd known from their first meeting that she was a woman not to be messed with. He just didn't realize how much that was true.

"But you do have magic," he finished.

"Yes," she said, a bit breathless. "But it's not what you think."

His spell shouldn't have disabled her. It wasn't designed that way, just to summon, so someone else had done damage to her. He swallowed his anger as she briefly closed her eyes and sighed heavily, clearly weary, clearly exhausted, clearly pushed to her limits. He didn't like seeing her so weak.

His anger cracked, if only a little.

He loomed over her, looking her straight in the eyes. "Tell me the truth," he said. "All of it."

She sighed again. "When I was little, my family was killed and something horrible was done to me. My memories are gone, but I must have seen something that traumatized me in ways you'd never understand. It broke me." Her gaze never faltered from his. "It broke my magic. It broke my soul."

"You're an anima contritum."

The realization jolted him. In the silence that followed, he had no idea what to say.

She raised her head and, after a few more moments of silence, nodded. "I am."

He was astonished, but as the truth began to sink in, it all made sense. The contest. The books she had asked him for. Her lack of fear of the woods. Her skills as a warrior. He fought with himself, furious about being lied to but understanding why. Being an anima contritum meant instant death in Nighthelm, and she had been forced to hide, forced to lie, never knowing who she could trust. He would've hidden himself in similar circumstances.

Per the law he was bound to uphold, he was supposed to fire his spell. He was supposed to notify the guard and carry out an instant death sentence. She had admitted what she was, confessed, and it was his duty to the crown to destroy anything that would harm the city.

But he wouldn't. Despite all that, despite the lies, despite what she was... he was too in love to care.

He lowered the spell and broke the circle, freeing her. Stepping into the chalked lines, he helped her to her feet. She wobbled again, and fell into his arms. He held her close, running a hand through her hair as he tried to fully comprehend what had just happened.

"I'm sorry for summoning you," he said softly. "I was trying to find the dark magic that has been tying me to this place, never allowing me to leave. But to realize... to find out it's you..."

"I'm glad you did it." She met his gaze. "I'm glad you know what I am. I can quit hiding from you. I've wanted to tell you for so long, but I never knew how."

"Did I hurt you? I was sure the summoning wasn't designed to injure, just to capture."

She frowned and shook her head. "I don't think it was your magic. I've been in pain for some time now."

He stroked her hair again. "Is there anything—"

"No," she interrupted with a weary chuckle. "I've tried everything I know."

He sighed and tenderly held her chin, brushing his thumb across her lip as the realization of what she was fully sank in. "We're the same, you and I," he said. "My family was killed when I was a boy. They were murdered by grimms during a diplomatic mission for the crown. My parents were loyalists, supporters of the royals, and they opposed the duchess taking over as steward. Their massacre allowed her to ascend without opposition. I know she didn't have a hand in wild animals killing my family, but I've still always hated her for that."

She placed her hand on his cheek. "I'm so sorry for your loss, Ezekiel."

He put his hand on top of hers. "I've wanted nothing more than to leave this city and the cursed memories of my family's murder. I've been trying for years to escape. But now that I've met you, I don't want to go anywhere but here."

A thin smile broke across her face. Without another word, she pulled his face down and pressed her lips to his. Heat instantly swelled inside him at the touch. He cupped her cheek and deepened the kiss, tasting her with his tongue. The kiss was hot, wet and made his groin clench.

"Oh Gods, Sophia, I want you." He nuzzled his face into her neck, tracing the tip of his tongue along her jawline.

"Then have me."

Ezekiel ran his hands down her back and grabbed her around the ass. He lifted her up, carried her across the room and set her down on his desk. All the papers of spells he'd written and agonized over for years scattered everywhere, but he didn't care.

He had what he wanted right here in front of him.

He kissed her again, as his fingers worked the ties on the bodice of her dress. Soon, he was able to pull down the fabric to expose her beautiful breasts. Peppering kisses down her neck, he nibbled on her skin, lathing his tongue over her rigid nipples. She gasped and buried her hands in his hair as he suckled on one and then the other. He reveled in the way she quivered under his touch. He was quivering too, unsure if he could trust himself not to lose control and take her hard and fast.

When he came back up to her face and kissed her again, her hands streaked under the hem of his shirt and ran up to caress his chest. He pulled the shirt off so she could touch whatever she wanted of him.

He was hers, body and soul. Whatever she wanted, whatever she needed, he would provide.

She leaned forward and kissed his chest, her soft lips sending jolts of pleasure straight down to his groin. He groaned as his pants became a bit too tight and uncomfortable.

She must've noticed, because she reached for the ties on his slacks. "Let me help you there," she said with a mischievous little wink.

While she tore at his pants, he pushed up on her skirt. More papers fell from the desk, and the desk moved and banged against the wall. The sound echoed around them, and soon Sophia was giggling. Her joy was contagious and he started to laugh as well as they decimated the workspace he had spent so many nights at, where so much of his time had slipped away from him. Then they were tearing at each other's clothes, eager to feel everything at once. Until finally, he was freed from the constriction of his trousers and was positioned between her legs.

Unwilling to wait a moment longer, he placed his hands on her silky, soft thighs and thrust his cock inside her.

She moaned. Her hands dug into his back, and he hissed as he lost himself in the blurred line between pleasure and pain.

She was so hot and wet that he had to bite down on his lip to stop from crying out with pleasure. He couldn't remember a time he'd been so overwhelmed with desire. With lust. With need.

Sophia made him feel whole.

Being inside her, touching her, kissing her, thrusting into this woman... it was all he could think of. It was all he'd ever wanted. It consumed him.

She consumed him.

She wrapped her arms around him and held on as he lost himself in her. Her little gasps of pleasure spurred him on, until he was sweating and panting as he bucked into her as hard as he could. She took it all, spread her legs wider so that she could ride him to the hilt, and the way she couldn't seem to get enough of him just made him harder.

He was so close to the edge, so near release. Every ounce of him ached to pour into her, but he refused to come before his woman.

As he thrust into her, her beautiful eyes fluttered. Her mouth formed a delicious "O" as she moaned, riding him, a loose curl sticking to her face and framing it perfectly.

She was close.

As her back arched, her sex tightening around his cock with orgasm, he buried his face into the side of her neck and came deep inside of her. Her happy little moans followed close behind, and she arched her back, grabbing his hair and moaning long and low until they were both spent.

He wasn't sure if he could move, so he just leaned against Sophia and hoped his legs didn't give way. She pressed kisses along his cheek and forehead.

"However much I don't want you to move, I think I really need to stretch out my legs," she said.

He backed up. "Oh right, sorry. Did I hurt you?"

She chuckled. "No, just I think my muscles are cramping."

Clumsily tucking himself back into his pants, Ezekiel scrambled around the room, found a blanket and laid it on the floor. "Don't move."

"I don't think I can," she said, wincing.

When he came back, he swept her into his arms and carried her over to the blanket. After gently setting her down, he helped her button up her dress, and then settled in beside her, holding her close. She sighed into him, and he never thought he'd feel as content as he did right then.

For the moment, all his cares and troubles had vanished. There was only Sophia.

"I think we made a lot of noise," she said with an apologetic smile.

He chuckled. "We did. I hope a night guard doesn't rush in thinking something nefarious is going on."

She laughed, and he pulled her tighter to his chest.

Too in love with this moment—with *her*—he never wanted to let go.

Deep down, he wanted to ask her who she would choose in the end, but part of him didn't want to know the answer. He just wanted to freeze this moment, and live in it for as long as she let him.

CHAPTER THIRTY-TWO

SOPHIA

When Sophia woke after a few hours of sleep on the floor with Ezekiel, she realized she'd missed her training with Grindel, but she didn't care. Not even a little. She was so done with all that. No more training with him, no more torture with the headmistress. She was healing all on her own. She wasn't even certain she was going to return to the cabin. Maybe to retrieve her important things, like her weapons, but there was nothing else there that mattered to her.

Ezekiel roused from sleep a few seconds later and smiled at her.

"I could get used to waking up to your pretty face," he said. A light she hadn't seen before danced in his eyes and she smiled in return.

"You wouldn't say that if you truly saw what I

looked like after a long, fitful sleep." She sat up and stretched. Ezekiel put his hand on her back and gently rubbed his thumb back and forth. His touch was comforting and she leaned into him. She needed it more than she realized.

"Who else knows?" He didn't need to elaborate, she knew what he was talking about.

"Andreas does, he found out when we were attacked by grimms in the woods…"

He gave her a look. "Again?"

She shrugged. "But Edric doesn't know."

"You have to tell him," he said.

"I know." She sighed, not looking forward to the conversation. Out of all three men, she knew Edric would have the hardest time accepting the truth of who and what she was. As the sworn commander of the elite castle guard, it would be his duty to arrest her.

"I'll send notes to them both and tell them to come here as soon as possible." He sat up and pressed a kiss to her cheek. "It'll be easier to tell Edric with support from me and Andreas."

She eyed him curiously. "When did you all become so chummy?"

"It's a long story." He turned away from her, but she caught the sly grin on his face. She hoped he would one day share that story. She had a feeling it would be very entertaining.

When Ezekiel finished writing notes to Edric and Andreas and had sent them off by his personal courier so there would be no chance of them getting intercepted, he brought Sophia some food from the kitchens, and together they sat at his table eating hearty stew in a bread bowl with some wine. She didn't particularly like the taste but figured she needed the liquid courage to face Edric.

No more than thirty minutes later, Edric pounded at the door, nearly kicking it in. Ezekiel opened it, and Edric stormed in, his face stony, and his brow furrowed. When his gaze flitted over the blanket on the floor where she and Ezekiel had slept, his face hardened even more.

Sophia jumped to her feet as he stomped over to her, a piece of paper clenched in his hand. She wondered if Ezekiel had told him in the note he had sent, although he promised he wouldn't, or maybe Andreas had beat her to it. Either way he was furious.

She put her hand up in defense. "I can explain."

He lifted the paper. "I heard back from the Duke of Oxford."

Oh crap. She lowered her hand. That she hadn't expected.

"As it so happens, he doesn't have a niece named Sophia and wondered what in hell I was talking about when I asked about you and what you liked to eat for supper." His voice was low and gruff. She wondered if this was the voice he used on his soldiers to get them in line or to discipline them.

Sophia sighed. "I'm sorry. If you will let me, and if you will listen, I can explain everything." She looked at Ezekiel for guidance.

He nodded. "I'll give you two some time alone." He picked up the food tray and then left the room.

Edric gave her a look that said "Go ahead."

She didn't know what to do with her hands, so she played with the ties on her dress as she paced in front of him. "I'm not Sophia Oxford, obviously. I'm not a noble woman. I don't live in Nighthelm. I live in a cottage in Witch Woods with a man named Grindel."

"Professor Matthew Grindel? Who teaches at the academy?" he asked.

"Yes. He trains me in the woods and sometimes in a hall under the castle," she said.

"Train you for what?" His frown deepened.

"To be a warrior, to heal myself." She stopped pacing and really looked at him. "I'm broken, Edric. My soul is broken."

His eyes narrowed, and she saw the second he realized what she was telling him. "You're an anima contritum."

She nodded, wary of what he was going to do. But she wouldn't back down. Not from him, not from anyone. Not anymore. She was tired of hiding.

"I lost my family when I was young, my parents

and my sister. They were murdered in front of me, and I witnessed it. Someone forced me to watch it." She shook her head. "Someone did this to me on purpose. But I don't know why."

His eyes softened a little as he searched her face. She didn't know what he was looking for. Maybe trying to decide if she was telling him the truth or not.

After some thorough scrutiny that made her nerves fizzle, he asked, "And the contest?"

"A way to find the piece of my soul I need to heal. The oracles told me that it lies in someone in Nighthelm, and that night at the ball I felt it in that room, near the three of you." She sighed. "I'm sorry for deceiving you. Can you forgive me?"

He looked her up and down, and she had the smallest thought that he was going to push her away in disgust, and she could feel the tears building, but he didn't. His anger dissolved right before her eyes. "You're forgiven."

She started to smile, but he wasn't having it. Not yet. Obviously, he wasn't done with her. He backed her up against the wall and leaned into her. She could feel his breath on her face, see the small specks of gold and green in his eyes. Her heart slammed against her chest.

"But never lie to me again." He set a hand at her waist, drawing closer. Possessing her.

"I won't." She swallowed.

His gaze went to her mouth. He licked his lips and she nearly let out a small groan. *Kiss me*, she wanted to moan, *please Gods kiss me*.

The moment was shattered as Andreas, followed by Ezekiel, bounded into the room. "Ah, good we're all here, I see," Andreas said as he pulled out a chair and sat at the table.

Edric pushed away from the wall releasing Sophia. She walked to the table and gestured for Edric and Ezekiel to sit. "Now that you are all here, and you all know what I am, I need to discuss this contest with you."

After they all sat, she slid into the empty chair and looked at her men, who once had been enemies but now acted like brothers. She didn't know when it happened, the bond they produced, but it filled her with joy to see it.

"On my eighteenth birthday I went in front of the oracles, they told me I could heal my soul by finding the missing piece of it. That it hadn't been destroyed. When I met the three of you that night at the ball, I knew it was inside one of you. I could feel it. I started the contest to help me find the piece by spending time with all of you. Hoping that somehow the piece would stand out above the others and aid my choice." She looked at Edric, then Andreas and, finally, Ezekiel. "But the thing is, I can't choose between you. I choose you all. When I'm with you three, like now, I feel so much stronger, like my soul is already healed and whole."

"How many oracles spoke to you?" Edric asked.

"All of them," she said.

All their faces lit up at her words. Some with surprise, but Andreas was nodding like he somehow knew it all along. He had been pressing her about the fact that Haris had bonded with her, and forest spirits only bonded with special people. She hadn't wanted to discuss it, but maybe it was almost time to.

Edric also nodded, as if confirming something to himself. "I've learned I could never live without you, so if I have to share with these men," he looked at Andreas and Ezekiel, "who I have come to see as brothers, then I am fine with your decision."

"I accept your decision as well," Andreas said. "I couldn't imagine my life without you in it. And Edric and Zeke have always been part of my life anyway."

Ezekiel screwed up his face like he was going to refuse, but he smiled. "Well, I'm not going to be the odd one out. I'm in. You make me feel like I'm finally home, in a safe place, Sophia. And, these guys, they're all right. I'd definitely go drinking with them again, oh and we're all pretty good in a fight together."

Edric joined in the camaraderie. "I won't go drinking with you again, Zeke, but I do agree about being good in a fight."

Laughing, Sophia got to her feet. She leaned down

to Edric and kissed him. Then she moved in front of Andreas and kissed him. Finally, she leaned down to Ezekiel and kissed him as well. Her men. Her beautiful, strong, passionate men. She'd fight to keep them all. And she had a feeling that was going to become the case. She was so thankful that they had bonded. It would make everything so much easier.

For the first time since she was young, she had a family. She had a sense of unconditional love that she'd always craved, and she would do everything in her power to protect it. But her victory wasn't here yet. She still had to talk to the oracles and convince them that all three of her men were important to her healing, to her being whole. She just hoped that they agreed and didn't kill any one of them.

She also had to stop Headmistress Mittle, as Sophia was convinced the woman was going to be the death of her. Intentionally.

CHAPTER THIRTY-THREE

SOPHIA

*I*n the dead of night, knowing her three men were asleep in their own quarters, Sophia decided to seek out the oracles alone. Andreas had returned to his house in the Shade; Edric retired to his room in the castle instead of in the barracks, and Ezekiel had allowed her to sleep in one of his rooms in the castle, as she had no intention of returning to the cabin. When she was certain they all had gone to sleep and weren't going to bust back into her room with the excuse of just making sure she was comfortable, she climbed out the window and shimmied down the wall to the ground. She snuck through the city, as she always had, silent as the dead, to declare her decision to the oracles and hope they accepted it. She wasn't sure what she was going to do if they didn't.

When she neared the park, she noticed how quiet the area was. Not even the chirps of cicadas filled the air. It was the witching hour, so the shops and taverns were long closed but where were the guards? Two of them usually took up positions by the main gate, but they weren't there now. Had she arrived during a shift change? She waited a few more moments in the shadows then crept across the court-yard to the fence, too eager to talk to the oracles to allow over caution to impede on what she came here to do.

As she neared the fence surrounding the sacred park and started to climb over the iron spokes, some-thing snapped like fire between her shoulder blades. She fell to the ground in agony, trained not to scream in pain, but hurting nonetheless. On hands and knees, she sucked in air through her nose and blew it out as she'd been trained to do.

Recovered from the unexpected blow, Sophia climbed to her feet and stepped back to find Head-mistress Mittle and Grindel standing in the dark, empty street. In the headmistress's hand was a hilt charged with a magical whip on the end of it, and Sophia figured that's what she'd been burned with. She looked at Grindel, the man she once thought of as a father, and tried her best to swallow her rage and sense of betrayal. He stared at her stonily, ever emotionless.

"What's going on?" Sophia asked. "Why are you doing this, Grindel?"

His face didn't change, but she did see his fingers twist a little harder on his staff. Did that mean something? She couldn't be sure. Maybe he was just getting ready to attack her because if he had ever really truly cared for her, he would stop whatever this was before it escalated, which Sophia knew was inevitable. First blood had been spilled. She rolled her shoulders as the pain of the strike still rippled over her flesh.

"Be a good girl, Sophia, and come with us," the headmistress said.

"Not bloody likely." Sophia took a step back with her left foot preparing for what she knew was coming. The headmistress had come here for a fight, and that's what she was going to get.

Headmistress Mittle raised her arm to strike again with the burning whip, but Sophia jumped out of the way as she shot a beam of magic at the woman. Grindel stepped in front of the attack, creating a magical shield, something he'd taught Sophia to do, to deflect the beam. It impacted the cobblestone nearby, scorching one of the rocks.

Obviously, her teacher had chosen a side, and was now the enemy.

Twisting her hands around each other, Sophia built a fiery ball of magic between them, and then threw it as hard as she could at the headmistress. It sailed toward her, but the headmistress was quicker than she looked, and whipped the fireball in half with her weapon, scattering the magic. Some of it hit a nearby wooden bench, searing a hole right through the plank.

Grindel hurled a beam of magic toward Sophia. Despite his age, he was still quick. She created a shield before the beam knocked her on her ass. The headmistress's whip came at her from the side. Sophia lowered the shield to roll out of the way of the sizzling tip, and then was back on her feet. She fired magic back at the headmistress. Grindel blocked that again, but barely. It zipped close to Headmistress Mittle's head. The stench of burnt hair filled the crisp night air.

Aware of how painfully close to the most powerful artifacts in the kingdom they were battling, Sophia moved a few paces before firing off another jolt of magic. Grindel met her magic with his own, and the two beams collided midair and fizzled out. Bright sparks lit up the street a moment before disappearing.

Where were the guards? Surely, they should've been aware by now that there was a battle of some sort on the street near the sacred park. It was obvious that the headmistress had paid them off. But how? The city guards were under the purview of the ruling government, not by the academy. She must've possessed more power and influence than Sophia ever imagined.

"You're not going to win, my dear," the headmistress called out.

"Neither are you." Sophia sent another fireball of magic toward the headmistress. If she'd had her sword with her, the fight would've been over by now. But her sword was back at the cabin. She should've pilfered one from Edric before venturing out into the night.

Grindel blocked it again, and then retaliated. Sophia easily stopped it and wondered whether he'd tempered his power. She was sure he could overpower her if he truly wished to. His magic was stronger and controlled. Either way, the fight was going nowhere. They were evenly matched.

Headmistress Mittle smiled as she lowered her weapon. "Regardless, this was a mere distraction, my dear."

A shiver rushed over Sophia's back. Gasping, she turned, sensing someone behind her, but it was too late. Winston brought the hilt of his dagger down on her head. Darkness swallowed her whole.

CHAPTER THIRTY-FOUR

SOPHIA

Sophia didn't know how long she'd been unconscious, but when she woke, she was groggy and disoriented and inside the glass box, her arms, legs and chest strapped tightly to the chair, and hooked up to the strange machine. Instinctively, she struggled against the binds, but stopped when she spotted Edric, Andreas, and Ezekiel locked in chains, attached to the wall across from her. They must've been taken in the middle of the night as they were all in varying degrees of undress. They were all shirtless; Ezekiel was in a pair of cotton underclothes as it was likely what he usually slept in, both Edric and Andreas wore proper trousers as they were both accustomed to being pulled from their beds at a moment's notice for the call of duty. It must've been some powerful magic to have taken them from their beds, as Sophia knew all three of them wouldn't have gone without a fight.

Her blood went cold at the sight of them, vulnerable and bound, and she bit down on her bottom lip to stop from shouting in outrage. All three of her men pulled at their chains when they noticed she was awake. It was pointless, as they were all bound securely to the wall, and she knew none of them could break steal with their bare hands.

Nearby on the platform, Headmistress Mittle stood with Grindel, Winston, and a strange figure in a shapeless, long, dark blue robe and veil that obscured all facial features. She couldn't distinguish much, not even if the figure was male or female.

A pang of dread hit Sophia as she realized this must be the Nameless Master, who the headmistress was getting orders from. Was this also who had been hovering in the doorway the other day during her magic training? She couldn't be sure as she'd caught a shapeless form out of her periphery. It had been there and gone like a shadow.

"Good, she's awake. We can get started," the headmistress said, as she turned to the unknown figure. "We're going to try something different, Previous attempts were unsuccessful, so this time, we're going to break her further. Doing so will make her obedient."

Sophia rocked in the chair, trying to loosen her restraints. "I will never be obedient to you!"

Ignoring her outburst, Headmistress Mittle continued to talk to the nameless one. "Thanks to our good friend Winston here," she gestured to Winston, who had the gall to grin, "we've discovered that one of these men has a piece of Sophia's soul."

Edric, Andreas, and Ezekiel yanked on the chains around their wrists and ankles again, the rattling echoed throughout the great hall. Sophia saw Ezekiel was trying to get his hands together so he could summon his magic, but they'd positioned his arms a little wider and a little higher, so it would've been impossible for him to do so. They took no chances with such a powerful sorcerer.

"You are all going to die for this," Edric said, his voice low and dark, his eyes like a storm.

Sophia wanted to hug him for his fierceness. He was defiant as ever and she loved that about him. Down the line, she spotted Andreas wincing, and she wondered what they had done to him. They'd probably taken precautions with him so he couldn't shift into his wraith form. Looking him over, she spied a few drops of blood on his arm, but she couldn't tell where it came from, or how they had injured him. Fury surged through her. They were going to pay for that, and more.

The headmistress rolled her eyes at Edric's bravado

and continued speaking. "Killing them in the proper magical ritual will seal the piece of soul in an artifact, making Sophia utterly obedient, with no free will at all. She will be the perfect assassin."

The perfect assassin. So, was this what it had always been about? Making her into a trained killer? Why? For what purpose?

She looked over at Grindel again. He stood stoic, his gaze not on anything particular. He wasn't looking at her, but he wasn't looking at the headmistress or the Nameless Master either. The expression on his face was unreadable. She couldn't believe he'd been okay with all of this from the beginning. Despite his betrayal now, Sophia knew he'd felt something for her. Maybe not friendship, but definitely something akin to paternal concern. He'd been there for her through so many things.

He held her through her worst nightmares when she first went to live with him in the woods. He taught her how to wield a sword and bow, and even healed her after her first wound, telling her next time she'd do better, be better. When she got her first blood at thirteen, he even helped her through it, awkwardly, but he made sure she understood the biology of it all, and gave her a book on the best ways to deal with it.

Grindel wasn't indifferent to her, she knew he had feelings for her. But obviously they weren't enough to stop what was happening now. Like a coward, he stood by and let this woman and some unknown entity torture her, and the men she'd fallen in love with. For what? Power, and nothing more.

"Will they all die?" The Nameless Master asked in a terrifying, grating voice that reminded Sophia of the grimms beyond the walls. A crawling sensation rippled over her skin, as if one thousand baby spiders had burst from an egg burrowed inside her flesh.

"Yes, of course," The headmistress said.

The nameless one nodded. "Good."

Sophia wanted to scream, wanted to beg them to stop, to do anything at all to make this end and save the men she loved. But she knew better than that. She knew Headmistress Mittle. She knew Grindel would do nothing to save her or her men. She knew Winston's petty need for revenge. And based on what had happened to her over the years, Sophia knew the Nameless Master would want to cause her as much pain as possible.

~

ANDREAS

*A*ndreas winced again as liquid fire rushed through his body. He'd never experienced this kind of pain before. When it had first surged through him shortly after waking up shackled to the wall, he'd been surprised and unsure of the source of the pain. But, after he'd inspected his body, and saw the blood spots and a tiny, needle pinprick in the crook of his arm, he knew they had injected him with hemlock. It was the only way they could stop him from shifting into his wraith form and killing them all.

But he would find a way to do just that.

He looked over at Ezekiel and Edric and saw the same looks of cold fury on their faces. They too were trying to figure out how to escape their binds. Ezekiel kept trying to pull his hands closer together, probably so he could conjure his magic. Blood trickled down his arms from his wrists as the metal cut into his flesh. Edric was really strong, Andreas had seen him snap a large tree branch in half with his hands, but even he couldn't break the steal, although he kept trying. Each of them hungered to rip apart the people who had done this to them; the people who were hurting Sophia.

Watching as she struggled in the chair she was bound to, tore at his heart. The wires that came out of the straps and hooked up to the strange, wooden box on the floor next to her vibrated as she moved but never, unfortunately, broke. He wondered how the contraption worked, how it must be dampening her magic, how it was hurting her. The sallow look on her face told him she was definitely in pain. In all his years, he'd never seen such a machine before. Had never heard of it either. It had to have been something powerful to be able to control someone like Sophia.

He'd read about anima contritums during his studies at the academy. They were supposed to be uncontrollable people, unhinged by their broken magic, unfit to be around others in society. Dangerous. A threat to the wellbeing of every person in Nighthelm. He now understood Ezekiel's claims that fear was cultivated in the city at all levels by the reining powers. Before wraiths were allowed in Nighthelm, they were the object of fear mongering. He pulled on his restraints again. If—no, when—he finally got out of the shackles, he was going to show these people exactly what fear meant.

Winston glanced at Andreas as he jerked on the metal chains. "There's no point, wraith. You're not getting out of those chains alive."

Andreas pulled harder on the chains, inching himself a little bit closer to Winston, who instantly backed up. "You're not getting out of this room alive."

Andreas glared at him, invoking as much of his wraith abilities as he could. Winston stiffened and licked his lips. His eyes widened, and Andreas saw him swallow hard. He may not have been able to shift—not yet, anyway—but conjuring fear in the coward was easy.

Grindel, who had been watching this exchange, tapped his staff against Winston's back. "I'd be careful who you taunt. Even with hemlock, I've heard wraiths can still shift."

Winston took another step back, moving closer to the strange, robed figure.

Andreas glowered at Grindel. "You'll be next, old man. You're going to die for betraying Sophia."

The professor turned away from Andreas's gaze, seemingly unaffected, but Andreas swore he muttered under his breath, "I know."

Frowning, Winston waved his hands at the three men chained to the wall. "Let's get on with this. We're wasting time."

The headmistress leveled Winston with an icy glare. "You are not in charge here. You are here as a courtesy."

"A courtesy?" Winston sniffed. "You wouldn't have known about them," he waved his hand at Andreas and the others, "if I hadn't told you. I expect to be rewarded enormously."

Headmistress Mittle pursed her lips, then asked, "And what reward do you want?"

He gestured toward Sophia, who was still struggled against the straps across her body. "Her. I want Sophia. After you've used her, or whatever you need from her, I want what's left."

All three men lurched forward, trying desperately to break their chains. The plate on the wall holding

Edric's cracked under the pressure, and he was able to move his right arm a little more.

"I'm going to rip your throat out, you fucking bastard," Edric said, his voice a low growl.

The headmistress chuckled. "I suppose we should get on with it, the natives are getting restless." She glanced at the veiled figure. "Shall we start the ritual?"

The veiled figure nodded.

CHAPTER THIRTY-FIVE

SOPHIA

*T*he Nameless Master lifted one frail, gloved hand, and the headmistress placed a glowing, red knife, with intricate symbols carved into the gold hilt and along the six-inch blade, into the palm. Eyes wide with fear, Winston moved away from the Nameless Master as it walked slowly toward Sophia's men—Edric in particular—knife at the ready.

Ezekiel and Andreas shouted at the Nameless Master, both yanking hard on their chains. But it was fruitless; they were never going to break them.

Sophia pulled and wriggled against the restraints, frantically dipping into the reserve of her magic to summon everything she had. She would destroy Nighthelm, including the oracles, if it meant saving the men she loved from death. But every attempt was blocked by the machine. She could feel the hum of energy emanating from the wooden box, bouncing off the glass walls to smother her, to inhibit her. The power of her magic was there, just hovering below the surface; just out of reach.

The robed creature swiped the blade across Edric's bare torso, slow and deep, until he cried out in pain. Blood ran in rivulets over his pale skin, soaking his pants crimson. Her heart leapt into her throat and she pulled on her restraints again.

"Stop!" Sophia yelled. "Don't hurt him!"

The Nameless Master did stop, but only long enough to move over to Ezekiel and perform the same act. Ezekiel tried to move away but the blade still found his flesh, slicing him deep. This wasn't just a ritual. This was torture. They wanted to break not just her body and soul, but also her mind. This monster wanted to carve up her men in front of her until she watched them die slowly and in extreme pain.

It was so much like last time. She remembered clearly now. In a tunnel under the mountain. She was there with her older sister, and they had been running from something. The urgency to get away filled the void. Her parents weren't there, they had died sometime before that. Tears leaked from Sophia's eyes as she remembered her sister, Madison. They'd been together, she had held her sister's hand. Then the grimms had come in a whirling, vicious black cloud.

They had descended on her sister, ripping her

from Sophia's hand. Her screams as she was consumed by gnashing teeth and hooked talons still echoed in Sophia's mind. She remembered cowering on the ground, her hands over her head, waiting for her death. Wishing for it, in a way, so the echoes of screams would stop. But it never came.

The grimms had stopped their ravenous feeding frenzy and just left her alone, sobbing. The next thing she remembered was seeing another, dark form hovering near her. She'd thought a lone grimm had come back to kill her, but it wasn't a grimm. She now knew it was the Nameless Master who had come for her.

Sophia pulled harder on her binds. Her wrists were rubbed raw from where the leather cut in. She refused to let this happen. She refused to watch the people she loved most die in front of her. Her men made her feel sane, kept her untamed magic at bay, and made her feel almost normal. She needed to draw on the control over her magic they helped her have in order to do the opposite. She needed to bring about her magic the way she wanted to, to finally command of it in all its untapped power.

Reaching deep inside, she summoned her magic. All of it. Every wild, chaotic part of it, and directed it at the machine she was tethered to. It burned through her like wildfire. Within seconds, the machine stopped buzzing and the wood cracked down the middle. The wires melted, dripping copper onto the floor. She then directed her magic toward everything at once, flinging it all around her. The glass cube shattered into thousands of pieces. The sound of it nearly deafened her.

Headmistress Mittle, the Nameless Master, and Winston were thrown back by the frenzied wave of energy, glass shards nicking faces and hands, but Grindel had been prepared for her explosion and had made a protective bubble around himself and her three men. Pieces of glass bounced off the invisible field, and fell to the ground like frozen raindrops.

With little effort, Sophia snapped the leather straps off her wrists, ankles, and chest and then bolted out of the chair. She shot magic at the chains on Edric, Andreas, and Ezekiel, freeing them even as she ran toward them. When she reached Edric, she tore at the sleeve of her shirt and then held it against his wound. There was a lot of blood, but the cut didn't look as deep as she'd expected. The way the Nameless Master had swiped the blade, Sophia thought it had hit bone.

He grabbed her hands, stilling them. "I'm all right. It's not as bad as it looks."

His touch calmed her a little and she was able to take in a few deep breaths. "I'm sorry."

"You have nothing to be sorry about." He brought a hand up to his mouth and kissed it. "Are you okay?"

She nodded. "Surprisingly, I feel strong."

When he released her, she moved over to Ezekiel

to check on his injuries, but he had already placed one of his hands over his chest and the cut knitted together from his magic. She glanced at Andreas, who had been spared from the torture. But something was wrong, as he was doubled over breathing hard.

He glanced up at her, a pained look on his face. "Hemlock in my blood. It's stopping me from shifting."

Ezekiel put a hand on Andreas's shoulder. "I got you, brother." He then put both hands onto Andreas's chest, his hands instantly glowing blue.

Andreas sucked in a breath, and winced.

"Aw, don't be a baby," Ezekiel said.

After another few seconds, Ezekiel dropped his hands and took a step back. "Better?" he asked.

Andreas coughed hard, expelling a chunk of dark sludge, then nodded, rolled his shoulders and neck, then came to stand beside Sophia. Edric and Ezekiel joined her as well.

As one entity, they turned to face their enemies. It was time to finish this once and for all.

CHAPTER THIRTY-SIX

SOPHIA

*W*inston was the first one on his feet after the magical blast, and running like a coward across the great hall to the door. He bolted the door behind him as he escaped. Fine. Sophia didn't care about him right now. He was irrelevant. She would make sure he'd get his comeuppance, eventually. The Nameless Master and Headmistress Mittle were the ones she would see punished immediately.

The Nameless Master stood and aimed to throw the knife at Sophia, but Grindel reached for the blade, turning it, and stabbed the creature in the side. Sophia gasped at the sudden betrayal. The creature screamed in agony, and Grindel grabbed the hilt, pulled it out and tried to stab the Nameless Master once again. But the headmistress was there in a flash, and with a blade

Sophia hadn't seen before, slashed open Grindel's gut with one lethal swipe. Sophia raced forward as he fell, casting a shield of protection as the Nameless Master and Headmistress Mittle tried to attack him again.

A blast of magic from Ezekiel pushed the Nameless Master back just as Edric and Andreas rushed into the fray. Edric spun a bo staff he must've found discarded in the room, a weapon she'd trained with before, and Andreas twirled a short dagger in his hand. She recognized it from the last training session she'd had with Grindel in the hall. When they'd been leaving, he'd told her to leave it, that they would have use for it again when they returned. Had Grindel known then what was going to transpire?

As her men fought the headmistress and the Nameless Master, pushing them back, Sophia cradled Grindel on the floor with her arms, holding him close as he bled out. She had tried to stem the flow of blood by balling up his robe and pressing it against his stomach, but it was too late, the wound was too big and too deep. There was nothing more to do than just hold him.

He lifted a bloody hand to her cheek. "I'm so sorry it all turned out like this."

"Don't talk, save her strength."

"For what, my child? I'm dying."

She shook her head, but it was in vain, she knew his death was imminent. She could smell it on him.

"I'm proud of you, Sophia. Proud of the woman you grew to be." He coughed, blood bubbling up between his lips.

She wiped it away with her remaining sleeve. "I thought you had betrayed me."

He shook his head. "When I realized the headmistress was actively trying to delay your healing, I ingratiated myself with her over many years until she trusted me. I needed to find the identity of the Nameless Master, the power behind the orders that had corrupted the woman I had once admired and respected." He coughed again, wracking his body from the force of it. "All I got was this." He shoved a bloodstained envelope into her hand.

She blinked back tears as he winced at the pain of his death. While Edric and Andreas continued the fight with the Nameless Master and the headmistress, Ezekiel crouched next to them and examined the wound. He glanced up at Sophia and gave a small shake of his head.

"It's beyond what sorcerers can heal." Ezekiel squeezed her hand. "I'm sorry, there's nothing I can do."

"You can't die," she said to her teacher. "Not when I know the truth." Tears rolled down her cheeks and dripped onto Grindel's robe, staining it a dark green.

"You are the daughter I never had. A daughter I couldn't be more proud of." He moved his hand to lay it over hers. "I'm glad to see you finally healed." He nodded toward Ezekiel who stood nearby ready to defend her, and Edric and Andreas who fought hard to protect her in this moment.

She pressed a kiss to his forehead as his body went stiff, then suddenly lax. His head slumped to the side, and she stared into his steel gray eyes, but she knew he was beyond seeing her. He was beyond everything now. She slowly drew her fingers over his face and closed his eyes.

"Rest now, Father." She settled his body gently onto the floor.

Boiling with rage, Sophia turned to glare at Headmistress Mittle, wondering who she hated more: the headmistress who killed Grindel, or the Nameless Master who nearly killed her men. She jumped to her feet and raced toward Headmistress Mittle, magic already forming in her hands.

She sent a beam of fiery light flying just as Edric joined her. Together, they attacked Headmistress Mittle; Sophia with magic, Edric with the skill of the bo staff. The headmistress blocked the magic with a shield she must've learned to make from Grindel, but Edric's staff hit her in the flank with a sharp snap. She let out only a tiny grunt of pain, but it filled Sophia with pleasure to hear it. To know the headmistress was fallible. That Sophia, with the power of her men beside her, had the strength to hurt her. Hopefully even kill her.

She and Edric kept attacking in unison as the woman slowly lost ground, backing up farther on the platform, precariously close to the edge. Sophia was filled full of fire and fury so powerful that her very veins burned with rage. Her focus was so precise on the headmistress that she almost missed it when the nameless creature screamed with hate, its voice nearly piercing her eardrums, and turned into smoke, effectively deflecting a magical attack by Ezekiel. The shadowy form looked so much like a grimm that Sophia wondered if this was whom they were being controlled by.

Instantly, Andreas shifted into his wraith form, following the smoke through the room. The two shadow creatures battled in the air, black streaks intersecting and colliding. At one point, they spiraled around each other, tendrils of darkness intertwining. Sophia could hardly distinguish the two, the only difference was the red glow of Andreas's eyes. Along the ceiling smoke and shadow twisted and coiled, until there was an ear-piercing shriek, then Andreas was slammed into the ground, He shifted back to human on impact. The Nameless Master escaped through the crack in the door.

CHAPTER THIRTY-SEVEN

SOPHIA

*A*fter determining that Andreas was uninjured, Sophia charged toward Headmistress Mittle and then kicked her in the stomach, knocking her off the platform and onto the stone floor. Seething with fury, she jumped down to follow and then loomed over her sniveling form. Edric, Andreas, and Ezekiel watched from behind on the platform, giving her room for her revenge.

The headmistress swiped at Sophia's legs with a small knife in a last ditch effort to injure. Sophia evaded the attack, and then kicked the blade out of her wrinkled hand. Looking down at the woman cowering on the floor, Sophia couldn't believe she'd ever been frightened of her. Gone was the perfectly put together woman, with the fancy clothes and jewelry, with every silver hair in place and impeccable.

She looked like an old, frail hag now without any power.

"You didn't find me in the mountain tunnel by accident, did you? You didn't take me in by the kindness of your heart to help me, to heal me. It wasn't an accident. You were the one who broke me." Sophia clenched her hands into fists, tamping down the urge to use them on the old woman.

"Yes," the headmistress hissed, "you were broken on purpose. And I was the one who was commanded to do it."

"My family was slaughtered. My parents, my sister... she was only three years older than me. She was all I had left." Her voice nearly broke.

Headmistress Mittle just stared at Sophia without comment, her bottom lip quivering a little. Was that remorse? Or was it just self-preservation? Did she fear what Sophia was going to do with her? She hoped so.

"You could've refused. I was just a helpless little girl," Sophia said, her voice even although it so wanted to break.

The headmistress shook her head. "The Nameless Master controls people everywhere in and beyond Nighthelm. There is no escaping its commands."

"It doesn't control *me*." Sophia lifted her chin up in defiance.

The headmistress laughed, the very sound of it dripped with venom. "Don't you understand girl? You have a singular purpose that you will never escape: to serve the darkness." She lashed out with her magic as she jumped to her feet. The woman was quicker than Sophia gave her credit for.

But Sophia was prepared for the attack, and she easily batted the beam of magic aside with a wave of her hand. Her true power had been unleashed thanks to the torture she'd endured. The headmistress's attempt at real magic was laughable. She'd had enough. She was done playing around. Too much had been lost.

Digging deep inside, she summoned her magic, the very last fiery coil of it. Unafraid of the woman's feeble attempts to harm her, Sophia grabbed the headmistress by the arms. The woman opened her mouth to scream as Sophia's magic poured into her, but no sound came out. Her entire body turned to ash, burned away in an instant. A resounding whoosh echoed through the room. Sophia was left with nothing but gray embers in her hands. She wiped them absently on her pants.

The castle trembled in Sophia's wake. Cracks fractured the walls; the chains which had been attached to her men dropped to the ground with a metallic clunk. The obstacle course Grindel had designed for her weeks ago collapsed and crumbled into piles of wood and rubble. The floor beneath their feet lurched back and forth. Stumbling slightly from the movement, all three of her men stared at the stone in equal measures of surprise and awe, then back at her. Sophia didn't even flinch.

After climbing back onto the platform, she knelt at Grindel's body, exhausted, relieved, and sad all at once. She gathered him in her arms, grieving, wishing they'd been closer, knowing he'd kept her at a distance all these years to protect her. She looked into his graying face and let forgiveness swell over her for his icy demeanor and standoffish behavior because she finally understood why he acted that way. He'd sacrificed everything for her. He'd done it out of love.

Edric, Andreas, and Ezekiel came to her side.

"We need to leave," Edric said gently, looking warily at the door. "The castle guards will be here any minute. They'll suspect the disturbances are coming from this room and they won't listen to explanations. Not even from me. We'll all end up in the cells."

Andreas crouched next to her. "Let me take him."

Nodding, she stood, and allowed Andreas to lift Grindel's lifeless body into his arms.

Ezekiel grabbed her hand and pressed a kiss to the back of it. "We're with you, Sophia. Now and forever. Wherever you go, we go."

Edric and Andreas nodded in agreement.

Together, she led them out through the secret tunnel and into the woods, escaping into the night like fugitives. In fact, they were all now fugitives. They had killed the headmistress of Nighthelm academy. There would be consequences. Edric wouldn't be able to return to his post with the elite guard. Andreas wouldn't be able to return to the Shade and the wraith army. Ezekiel would have to forgo all his work and training in the castle. But Sophia looked at the men she loved, and thought, she'd suffer through those consequences and worse, every single one of them, gladly.

CHAPTER THIRTY-EIGHT

SOPHIA

*T*he heat from the flames singed Sophia's face, but she didn't move away from the massive fire. She stood with her three men around her burning cabin, a funeral pyre for Grindel, and let the fire cleanse her emotions. After they'd ran through the woods and arrived at the cottage, Sophia had instructed Andreas to lay her teacher in his bed, but there was too much blood to ever let herself think for even a moment he was just sleeping. However much she wanted to.

She'd put his gnarled, wooden staff in his hand, and set a few of his favorite books around his body then, with Ezekiel's help and his magic, set it aflame. Edric had to pull her out of the bedroom before the whole place was on fire and her with it. After collecting a few of her things, her bow, sword and scabbard, and a few other weapons Grindel had taught her to use, Sophia stepped out of the cabin she'd spent the past twelve years in, and let it burn.

The light from the fire flickered over the faces of her three men and a few of Andreas's loyal wraith brothers, who he had called in to surround the area. They had come to make sure it was secure and safe from grimms, at least for one night. One night she could properly grieve the loss of her teacher, her friend, her Father. She knew Andreas would have to repay the favor for years, but he told her he was happy to do it for her.

The haunting cry of the chickcharney carried over the crackling of the flames. Sophia glanced at the nearest oak and saw the bird sitting in one of the branches, watching the fire. She wondered if it was the same bird that always dropped fruit onto her head during her nightly patrols through the woods. Maybe he came to pay his respects.

Now that she was looking around at the surrounding trees and bushes, she noticed several of the woods' creatures gathered nearby. A bright, yellow glow grew near one of the bushes, and Sophia saw the flutter of fairy wings. On the ground, she spotted several nippers, small rodents, scurrying about, every once in a while standing on their hind legs to watch the flames. Grindel would've shaken his head to see them here, as he always complained about them and the noise they made.

When she turned her head to look on the other side, she swore she spied a minotaur pacing behind the trees. She was wary for a moment, until she realized it was the minotaur chieftain that sparred with Grindel years ago. She recognized its brown fur and two white stripes across its flank. It locked gazes with her, slowly lowered its head, then turned and bounded back into the shadows of the woods.

Hobs, and wood sprites, and even a few large gargoyle bats gathered around the bonfire. These were creatures that Grindel had taught her to identify, fear, respect, and, in his own way, love. For over twelve years they had shared their forest with Grindel, and with her. She wasn't sure if she could ever repay them for their generosity. She didn't know how.

Numb, she turned back to the bonfire and watched her past burn, knowing she could never live there again. Not with what she knew about her past and the headmistress, and definitely not without Grindel. She looked at each of her men, filled with joy that they stood there with her, beside her, together as one unit. She wouldn't be able to get through this without them, either.

The roof on the cabin finally collapsed into the rest of the burnt timber, sparks and ash exploding outward.

She looked to the rest of the woods, making sure no other trees or bush caught fire. It seemed like the other creatures had vanished from the area. Haris crept into the clearing, cautious and glancing warily at the burning building. Her forest spirit friend didn't like fire.

"Haris," she called.

He turned toward the cabin, kneeled on one leg, extended the other leg in front of him, and then lowered his head to the ground. It was a bow of respect. After he straightened, he came to her side, nuzzling his head against her shoulder. She kissed his nose.

"Thank you, sweet one," she murmured to him, thankful that he came to pay his respects to Grindel, although they had never formally met. But she was sure that Grindel knew about her special friend. She'd caught him a time or two setting out sweet grass onto the porch. He'd said it was for birds, but sweet grass was also a favorite snack of Haris's.

Both Edric and Ezekiel startled at the sight of him. Andreas smiled, as he already knew of Haris's existence.

"Edric, Ezekiel, this is Haris. He's already met Andreas." She patted Haris's muzzle, and he nickered at her. "My sweet beast."

Andreas tipped his head to the creature.

Haris returned the polite greeting.

Eyes wide, Edric approached Haris. "I've never seen a forest spirit before."

"Neither have I," Ezekiel said. "I've read about them plenty though."

As Edric reached out to touch Haris, Haris snorted, and stamped his front foot. Sophia stroked his flank. "It's all right. These men are my..." Frowning, she looked at each of them. "I don't know what to call you."

Ezekiel said, "We're your companions."

"Your paramours," Andreas added, with a quick smile.

"We're yours. It does not matter what you call us." Edric put his hand on Haris's side. "He's as big as a horse. Do you ride him?"

Sophia nodded, and kissed Haris on the nose again. "Yes, when he lets me."

Haris whinnied and snorted into her hair. It was his version of a laugh.

"Forest spirits only protect special souls," Andreas pointed out again.

"I don't want to discuss it," Sophia said with a finality that made Andreas nod to her in acknowledgement. She sighed and shook her head, she wasn't angry with him for bringing it up again. Her heart just wasn't into exploring the notion further, not now anyway, not when it was so damaged.

With all her most trusted and loving companions

surrounding her, she turned back to the burning cottage. It was mostly embers now, the structure no longer recognizable. She was deadened as she watched the last of her past be incinerated into ashes. She held the dagger Grindel had given her for her birthday against her chest, and promised to never let him down, to continue what he'd started with her training.

In her mind, she whispered a prayer for him to finally find peace in the next realm. A peace she knew she'd never find in this realm while the Nameless Master lived.

Reaching into the pocket of her trousers, she pulled out the envelope Grindel had given her with his last, dying breath. She tore it open and unfolded the paper he'd written on. *The child of Ripthorn.*

She showed it to Edric. "What do you think this means?"

Andreas and Ezekiel read it over his shoulder.

"Doesn't make any sense," Ezekiel said. "Do you know what's it in reference to?"

"He said it had something to do with the identity of the Nameless Master," she said.

Ezekiel shook his head. "No way that thing is from Ripthorn."

"Could be about the heirs to the throne," Andreas said. "We have been waiting for so many years, maybe we have been told lies about their existence or their return."

"We shouldn't jump to conclusions," Edric said. "It could mean many things."

Sophia agreed, but she had a feeling they would all find out soon enough.

After folding the note and tucking it back into her trousers, she looked around at her three men. "I'm sorry for dragging you all into this."

"You didn't drag us into anything," Edric said. "We all came willingly."

Andreas and Ezekiel nodded.

"We would do anything for you," Ezekiel said.

Smiling, she grabbed Ezekiel's hand, and Andreas's. With Edric standing right behind her, her back pressed into him, his hand on her waist, they all watched the last of the flames. An overwhelming sense of peace washed over her, and she knew she would be all right without Grindel to watch over her. She had her men. They would help her find her way.

CHAPTER THIRTY-NINE

*G*etting back into the city proved a bit difficult. Because of the incident in the hall under the castle, and the death of Head-mistress Mittle, the guard was on high alert, obviously looking for the murderers. They were probably wondering where their commander was as well. Sophia was heartbroken to know that Edric may have given that all up to protect her.

Andreas's wraith brothers helped them sneak back into Nighthelm through a secret tunnel that went directly into the Shade. Once inside, they had to creep through the streets to one of the oldest parts of the city, to where Ezekiel's family estate was located. Thankfully, there weren't too many occupied houses in the district, most families preferring to move to newer more prestigious areas. This was good for them. It would be easier for them to hide out here.

After her men were settled, well as much as they could be considering the circumstances, Sophia returned to the sacred park to try again to speak with the oracles. They had all protested about her going alone. Not surprisingly, considering what happened last time she went alone. Edric insisted that he, at least, accompany her to the park, but she insisted that she had to do this by herself. They relented, but she suspected that Andreas had shifted into his wraith form and had watched her from above. She couldn't say for sure, as she never saw him, but she had a feeling, and that filled her heart regardless.

Although the streets were deserted of residents due to the new curfew according to a poster nailed to a wall outside of a shop Sophia had read, she kept to the shadows like she was trained to do. Despite there being an increase of guards throughout the city of Nighthelm because of the incident at the castle, she was used to evading them and had done so with ease.

She used extreme caution as she approached the fence around the park. She wasn't afraid of getting ambushed like before, but she absolutely *was* wary of more patrols through the park.

Once she was sure she was completely alone, she climbed over the fence. As Sophia walked through the park to get to the center and the elder oaks, she ran her hand along the trunks of the other trees. She enjoyed the feel of the rough bark on her palm, reminding her of the woods that had been her home for so long. The Witch Woods were tainted now, though, stained with memories of Grindel's death, and she couldn't live there. Not anymore.

But the woods were still Haris's home, and she would never abandon her friend. She wished he could come into the city and live with them. One way or another, she would find out how to make it work. The forest was part of the forest spirit, and living in a house would depress him. The trees were an extension of Haris. He couldn't take him out of it and expect him to survive, but she couldn't leave her friend behind.

For now, just until the rawness faded and the chaos settled, Sophia hoped she would be able to survive without her woods.

Stepping into the center, she approached the oracles cautiously then knelt before the elder trees, alone and covered in blood and ash from the battle. She hadn't bothered to change at the estate. Seeing the oracles was more important than the state of her dress. Besides that, it felt like a dishonor to Grindel if she washed off too soon. In a way, he was here with her.

She clasped her gloved hands together and bowed

her head low, nearly touching her forehead to the ground. "Great oracles, I have failed you."

The great trees groaned, the leaves on their branches rattling like chains. She couldn't be sure if it was in response to what she'd just said or if it was just the night wind blowing through the park. Summer was drawing to a close, and the air was becoming crisper.

"You tasked me with finding the other piece of my soul, but I couldn't do that. You see, I met three wonderful men that complete me so powerfully that I can never imagine being without any one of them."

She lifted her head, risking a look at the trees. Every single one had their eyes open and was watching her. She could feel their power surging over her. The hairs on her arms and on the back of her neck rose with the charged air.

"Leaving even one of them would break my heart. I don't know what to do. I can't make the choice you want me to. I won't give any one of them up. Not even to mend my soul."

She didn't mention her fear for their safety bringing them before the oracles, but if she had to choose between the elder trees' approval and the loves of her life, the choice was easy. She'd find another way to restore the heirs to the throne.

As one they spoke, their voices a symphony of earthy baritones. "Love."

The word reverberated through the air. It hummed over her skin. Tears welled in her eyes from the potency of it.

"Love is worth all. Love is worth everything," the oracles said in unison. "Stand, Sophia of the mountain."

She climbed to her feet. Her head felt a bit woozy from the level of power that filled the park, from the majesty of the oracles who spoke to her.

"You have made the right choice," they said.

She swallowed the anxiety she had been carrying with her, and her heart swelled with glory.

The oracles eyes closed one by one, then they started to hum. At first it was a pleasant vibration, like a buzzing of an insect, and then the tempo and volume increased. The hum was so loud and so throbbing that Sophia clamped her hands over her ears. She wouldn't have been surprised if blood leaked out between her fingers, as surely her ear drums had burst.

A light formed in the center of the trees' circle, about five feet away from where she stood. At first, the white light hovered above the ground, bouncing almost like one of the fairies in the forest. Then the resonance increased until Sophia could no longer look upon it without going blind.

The hum increased at the center of the light, pulsating, undulating, and the power of it pushing against her body. She thought she couldn't handle any more when there was a definitive popping sound, and the light vanished, as did the noise.

Stuck in the ground, shining with its own inner light was a long broad sword.

The oracles opened their eyes. "This is the King's Sword. It is what you will need to return the lost heir from the mountain to the castle. It is now yours to wield."

Sophia couldn't believe what she was seeing. The King's Sword was thought to have been destroyed in the massacre in Ripthorn Mountain which killed the king and the queen and all their royal guard. Only the heirs were thought to have survived. Survived but taken and hidden away, or so the rumors stated.

Swallowing hard, she reached for the leather wrapped hilt. There were symbols and other marks of royalty burned in it, as well as etched along the curved, golden cross bar and down the silver blade. The pommel had a silver ball on top that seemed to gleam and glow from within. She wrapped her hand around the grip and pulled it from the ground. She lifted it into the air, the steel glinting in the moonlight as if it was made of starlight and blue fire.

She was amazed and baffled how this was supposed to restore the heir, but she suspected, like the message on Grindel's note, everything would be clear in time. She laughed, giddy with new found excitement. She swung the sword around, reveling in the feel of it in her hand. It was both heavy and light. Heavy from the sheer length of it, but light as the metal seemed to have no weight. How was she ever going to explain the sword to her men when she returned to the estate?

She didn't linger long in the park as she knew the guards would've been alerted by now to the noise and light. Sheathing the new sword in her scabbard, and carrying her other in her hand, she slunk back into the shadows and made her way back to her new home, with her new family.

~

ANDREAS

He watched from up above the tree tops as Sophia jumped back over the park fence, carrying her sword, and disappeared into the surrounding shadows just as three city guards came running from the other direction. They stopped near the fence, and whirled around, with their swords out, looking for the intruder. An intruder they would never find. Andreas smiled to himself as he floated away, making his way back to the Wickham estate.

Once Sophia had left the estate after telling them

she was going back to see the oracles alone and had insisted that she be able to go alone, Andreas had instantly shifted into his wraith form to follow her. Edric had stepped in his way and he thought the commander was going to command him to stay, but instead he had told Andreas to keep out of sight. That Sophia wouldn't be too happy if she knew they had gone against her wishes, however foolish Edric thought those wishes were.

He'd followed her through the city, always careful to stay high and hidden in the darkness. But he suspected after a few blocks into the market square, she knew he'd been following her. At one point, she had stopped, frowned and eyed the sky curiously. Then he saw a small twitch at her mouth, and she continued on.

When she reached the sacred park, Andreas remained outside. He didn't want to intrude on something so personal and hallowed. He knew she had to face the oracles alone, just as they all had to do. During his eighteenth year ritual, two oracles had woken and told him that he would do something meaningful and significant. He'd always thought that had been serving in the wraith guard, to serve and protect the people of Nighthelm, but now he knew it was to serve and protect Sophia. She was more special than, he suspected, she even knew.

He flew over the tops of shops and taverns,

hurrying to get back before she did. When he came around the corner and over another clumping of three-story buildings, he nearly ran right into Sophia, who was standing on the roof, as if waiting for him. Quickly, he sunk back into the night.

"I know you're there, Andreas." She shook her head. "I should've suspected you would follow me."

He debated on whether or not to keep up the charade, but then he floated down to the rooftop and shifted back into his human form.

"Busted," she said, quirking up her eyebrow.

He gave her a little bow. "You can't blame a man for protecting what's his."

"I'm surprised Edric didn't stop you," she said.

"Whose idea do you think this was?" He smiled.

She rolled her eyes, but there was a smile on her lips.

"You must know we would never allow anything bad to happen to you again," he said.

She lifted a hand to his cheek. "I know."

Andreas leaned down and covered her lips with his. It was a slow, gentle kiss that spoke of love and caring. He wished he could deepen it, make love to her right here on the rooftop, but he knew it wasn't the right time or place.

"Did it go well?" he asked as he looked her over from head to toe.

"Yes." She handed him the sword she carried, then

unsheathed the one in her scabbard, and held it up for him to see. It was a huge sword, over half the size of Sophia herself. He'd seen pictures of it in the books he'd read about the royal family.

"The King's Sword," he said, his voice low in reverence.

She nodded. "I can't believe the oracles gave it to me."

"Why?"

"I'm supposed to help restore the heirs to the throne." She swung the sword. Moonlight glinted off it like fairy flashes. She stopped, and brought the blade up. "Do you think Ezekiel can read these symbols?"

"I'm sure he can. He's read enough books," he said.

Sophia sheathed the sword, and he handed her other one back to her.

"You should get back before Edric marches through the streets to retrieve you."

"He wouldn't dare," she said.

Andreas gave her a look. "On top of that, he and Zeke are conspiring to design a magical tracking device, so they'll always know where you are."

She laughed. "Okay, I'm going." She walked across the roof to the edge to climb down, then looked back at him. "Race you home."

Home. He liked the sound of that. He wasn't sure that the four of them could comfortably live together, but he sure wanted to try.

"You're on." Making a dramatic spin, Andreas shifted back into his wraith and pushed off into the air.

CHAPTER FORTY

EZEKIEL

*E*zekiel was outside the estate on the west side, casting a protection shield when Sophia finally returned home and went inside the house. Andreas, in wraith form, arrived a few minutes later, landed on the front yard and shifted back to human. He had a smile on his face as he looked up at the house, and Ezekiel assumed that the wraith had been caught in the act, which didn't surprise Ezekiel. Sophia wasn't stupid. She would've known that at least one of them would have followed her. She was too important to allow anything else to happen to her.

After she had left to see the oracles, and Andreas followed, he and Edric discussed the best ways to keep Sophia safe, and the rest of them for that matter, now that they all fugitives. Hopefully, they had enough time to put measures in place before the whole city was after them. It would take a few days before the city guard missed their commander, the wraith squad from missing their best warrior, and the castle sorcerers and professors from missing their most knowledgeable pupil. That was unless Winston decided to do a preemptive strike on them and fabricate a bunch of lies in order to make them out to be traitors and murderers.

He'd shown Edric around the estate, pointing out all the security he had, and the places they could increase it.

"I can make protection wards over the house and the lot, so that if anyone but us and Howard, of course, breeches it, an alarm will sound. No will be able to get close without us knowing it."

"Is there other ways out of here besides the front and back doors?" Edric asked.

"Oh, yes," he said, as he unlocked a door under the staircase.

He gestured for Edric to go inside. He did, and Ezekiel followed. They went down another set of stairs into the dark cellar. Ezekiel casted a ball of light in his hand and they moved through the cellar to another door. He opened it and showed Edric that it was a tunnel that went under the house and led to another, small, stone cottage in a copse of trees near the castle.

"My father did a lot of work for the king. This was

how he got to the castle unseen. And how the king came to him."

Edric gave him a look. "You knew the king?"

"No. My father would never let me near the royal family. He said it was too dangerous." Ezekiel rubbed at his chin. "Turned out he was right, and got killed for it."

"I'm sorry for your loss, Zeke." Edric put a hand on Ezekiel's shoulder. "I want you to know that."

"Thanks."

"I'm glad Sophia chose you," Edric said as he dropped his hand.

"She chose us all." Ezekiel gave him a funny look. "Besides that, I never thought you liked me much."

"I didn't." Edric grinned. "But you've grown on me."

Once they were back up on the main floor of the estate, Ezekiel showed Edric the room he wanted Sophia to stay in. It had been his parents' room, and was the biggest, most lavishly decorated room in the house. After all she had been through, Ezekiel wanted her to feel safe and comforted. Honestly, he wanted to spoil her with luxurious gifts, but he knew Edric and Andreas would think he was trying to win her favor. It would've been the truth.

He lit the fire in the hearth, so the room would be warm when she returned. As he stoked it, he looked at Edric. "You should stay with her tonight."

Edric frowned. "I'm pretty sure she'll pick who she wants to warm her bed."

"I know, but I'll be busy placing protections on the house, and Andreas will be patrolling the neighborhood until morning. She needs to feel safe tonight. You're the one who can do that for her."

After a few moments, Edric nodded, and Ezekiel left him in the room to return to his workshop. He needed to prepare to set up the wards. It wasn't that he didn't want to be with Sophia, he did, desperately but he knew she would need the strongest of them tonight to hold her, to support her.

She would need all them in the days to come.

SOPHIA

After a few hours of sleep, Sophia woke, blinking sleepily up at the high painted ceiling of the elegant bedroom Ezekiel had appointed to be her private sanctum. The heavy brocade gold drapes were pulled around the large bed to keep the light out, but she knew it was still full dark. She could feel it in her bones.

She yawned, rolled over and snuggled back into the crook of Edric's arm, inhaling his woodsy scent. He pressed a kiss to the top of her head.

"Are you comfortable?" he asked, as he pulled her even closer to his bare chest.

"Very." She stretched out her legs, all the way to her toes. "This bed is extraordinary." The mattress they were on was down filled. She'd never slept on anything but a straw stuffed, lumpy sack. This was like laying on fluffy white clouds.

Edric chuckled. "Yeah, I'm pretty sure Zeke gave you the luxury suite. I know my room isn't this nice."

"As it should be," she teased.

He pressed a finger to her chin and tilted her head up to his, so he could kiss her. "Yes, as it should be."

After a thorough, toe-curling kiss, Edric rolled her over onto her back, and peppered more kisses to her face and down her neck. He slid his hands over her body. He caressed her breasts, then down to her belly, where one hand slid in between her legs. They'd already made love once, and she was a little sore, but she couldn't deny that his touch sent a rush of pleasure over her entire body again. She couldn't get enough of him.

She opened for him, and he stroked a hand over her most sensitive flesh. As he slipped fingers into her, she bowed her back, panting. He was gentle as he massaged her sex, not going too fast or too slow, just enough to send pleasing jolts through her body.

He licked and sucked on her nipples while he rubbed her pussy. It didn't take too much before she was gasping and panting, her muscles clenching hard. After one, final, firm stroke of his fingers, she bucked hard and came. It was as if the world was a kaleidoscope of color and sound behind her eyes.

When she could function again, she opened her eyes to see Edric smiling down at her. He kissed her again, then collapsed onto his side with a contented sigh.

"I could lie in this bed forever," he said. "Making love to you."

She nodded. "Me too."

Sophia stretched and sat up. Her muscles were going to be sore for the next few days from the battle, and from sex, but she'd face that fact later. Right now, she just wanted to be able to relax and recharge. They still had a long fight ahead of them. They would all need to be at their best for what was to come.

Edric tied to pull her back down. "You should sleep longer."

"I know, and I will, but not right now."

"Are you worried they'll find us?" he asked.

She shook her head. "I trust Ezekiel's cloaking spells."

"Yeah, the sorcerer does know his magic."

She rolled to the edge of the bed and stood. She grabbed the elegant silk robe from the peg on the wall that Ezekiel had gifted to her and slipped it on. The feel of it on her skin was magical, and she couldn't help the smile on her face as she crossed the room to look out the big bedroom window. She spotted Ezekiel outside at the east corner of the grounds casting new wards over the entire estate.

Ezekiel's mansion, now their temporary home, had over ten bedrooms, and he'd appointed each of them one, or tried to. Both Edric and Andreas had other ideas. Edric's room was the corner room on the lower floor that had windows facing both north and west. He'd insisted on it, despite the fact that it had been one of the servant's rooms and wasn't as well furnished. Andreas had taken the room on the opposite side of the estate, so he could watch the areas that Edric couldn't. Ezekiel's room was on the main floor at the bottom of the curved staircase. It was more of a workshop really then a bedroom, with three walls of bookshelves that had made Sophia nearly weep as they reminded her so much of Grindel. She'd wanted to touch all of them at once.

She watched as he constructed some kind of spell that would not only protect them from outsiders, but would help contain any outbursts of magic she might have. She told him she felt more in control than she ever had in her life but he explained it was for just in case. He wanted to protect her, and she loved him for it. She couldn't wait to be able to practice and hone her magic with him.

Edric joined her at the window just as Andreas

floated past in his wraith form. He'd been patrolling the estate from above and from the shadows, watching for Winston and the Nameless Master. Eventually, they would have to face them. Sophia wanted her revenge for Grindel. Although the headmistress had wielded the knife that had gutted her teacher, both Winston and the Nameless Master were responsible.

After wrapping an arm around her, Edric pulled her close and kissed the top of her head again. She leaned into him, comforted, secure and full of joy. She never thought she could feel like this in her entire life. Happy. Loved. Vengeance would have to wait.

For now, though, for now she would revel in her happiness. She had a victory to celebrate, grateful to have found her men, her home, and to have begun the long journey to not only healing her soul, but mastering the well of magic she had inside. She would need it to fulfill her purpose: to return the lost heirs to the throne and heal not only just herself but the kingdom she had always dreamt of belonging to.

YOU'RE MISSING OUT...

Olivia Ash occasionally takes over the Wispvine Publishing social media channels on Facebook, Instagram, and Twitter.

Olivia also likes to hang out with Lila Jean in their Facebook group specifically for readers like you to come together and share their lives and interests, especially regarding the hot guys from their reverse harem novels. Please check it out and join in whenever you get the chance! Everyone in there is amazing, and you'll fit right in.

https://www.facebook.com/groups/LilaJeanO-liviaAsh/

Sign up for email alerts of new releases AND exclusive access to bonus content, book recommendations, and more!

https://wispvine.com/newsletter/nighthelm-academy-email-signup/

Enjoying the series? Awesome! Help others discover the Nighthelm Academy by leaving a review at Amazon.

http://mybook.to/Nighthelm1

ABOUT THE AUTHOR

OLIVIA ASH

Olivia Ash spends her time dreaming up the perfect men to challenge, love, and protect her strong heroines (who actually don't need protecting at all). Her stories are meant to take you on a journey into the world of the characters and make you want to stay there.

Reviews are the best way to show Olivia that you care about her stories and want other people discover them. If you enjoyed this novel, please consider leaving a review at Amazon. Every review helps the author and she appreciates the time you take to write them.